Witness Protection 4
O-Dark-Hundred

Holly Copella

In loving memory of
Emry Hill

ACKNOWLEDGMENTS

Copella Books: First Paperback Edition 2017
Printed by CreateSpace, An Amazon.com Company
Cover Artist: Daniela Owergoor
Dani-owergoor.deviantart.com
Model by Grafvision
Model by Pindyurin Vasily

PUBLISHER'S NOTE

Chapter One

The old stone sawmill had seen better days, although its stone and wood exterior was still structurally sound. At first glance, it could be mistaken for an old, two-story barn. Built partially in the river, the large water turbine remained motionless for decades or longer. The log carriage track, which once carried logs from the river into the sawmill, was deteriorating faster than the rest of the building. It was late afternoon, and the vast, secluded countryside surrounding the lonely sawmill was peaceful. There didn't appear to be a soul around. The building interior contained various sized rollers for moving the logs into the cutting path of now rusted saws. Despite the seclusion of the mill, male voices echoed through the sturdy building.

Two men stood in a faceoff of sorts. By the looks on their faces, Monroe and Holden seemed unhappy with each other. Monroe Dallas was a tall, lanky man in his mid-thirties, who sought a stylish flair to his wardrobe. Despite not being overly muscular, he was more powerful than most suspected. Monroe's light brown hair was neatly trimmed, although not nearly short enough to constitute a buzz cut. Holden Falcone was a ruggedly handsome man in his mid-thirties. He wasn't built excessively muscular, but he had broad shoulders and a toned chest. His neatly trimmed, nearly black hair gave him a professional appearance. Both men were overdressed and looked out of place in the abandoned sawmill.

"What is your problem?" Monroe demanded. "You already said there was nothing that could legally be done."

"Yeah, legally," Holden snarled, "but that doesn't translate into 'going rogue'."

Monroe stared at Holden with disbelief while touching his temple several times then gestured wildly. "Going rogue is *what* we do!"

A third man leaned against one of the large rusted saws. Zack Kinsley was shorter than average, being lucky if he stood 5'8". Non-impressive by most standards, he appeared almost innocent at first glance. He wore black combat attire covering his surprisingly athletic build, which would easily go unnoticed beneath his clothes. His brown hair was kept short and neat, although moderately spiky on top. It was uncertain if the hairstyle made him look slightly intimidating or more like a child's plaything. Zack barely acknowledged either man, although he appeared to be listening to their bantering while cleaning dirt out from under his fingernails with a Bowie knife.

"How am I supposed to justify what you're doing?" Holden demanded.

"Justify it?" Monroe suddenly lashed out. "The guy abducted his niece out from under her mother. You've got a deadbeat dad on the lamb who'd do anything to get his daughter back." He shook his head vigorously. "We're talking about a five-year-old girl here. If they're holding her in the brother's mansion, we're the only ones not sitting on our thumbs waiting for proof."

"So I'm supposed to just sit by and let you and the littlest ninja there," he announced while indicating Zack, "storm this guy's mansion looking for this little girl who may or may not be there?" His look turned demanding. "What's the plan? Kill anyone who prevents you from searching the place? That mansion is like a fortress. You're going to end up killing innocent security guards who may not have done anything wrong."

"This is exactly why you don't belong on the team," Monroe launched back. "You don't know how to take orders, and you question everything. You're not a team player."

The sound of the old, rusted saw grinding stopped the two men mid-argument. Both looked at Zack near the saw. He grinned almost mockingly and hit the power switch. The grinding ceased, and the saw came to a gradual stop.

"If you ladies are finished doing each other's hair, can we get on with this?" Zack announced with bored disinterest. "I'm sure our guest would like to use the outhouse in the near future."

Both men looked from Zack to the man tied to the old log partially cut by the rusted saw. The man was lying on his back with his wrists tied to his side around the log and his ankles bound on either side, keeping his legs spread apart. The saw was uncomfortably close to his crotch, and the fear showed on the man's face. Holden shook his head then glared at Monroe.

"I didn't sign up for this," Holden snapped.

"You didn't sign up at all," Monroe remarked with little interest. "You're only here because you don't trust your wife."

Holden glared at Monroe with hostility. "Keep it up, Monroe. One of these days, saying things like that will get you punched in the mouth."

"Give it your best shot," Monroe snarled and took a step closer, placing him directly in front of Holden's face.

"Girls," Zack proclaimed with irritation. "You're both about to be kicked in your lady parts if you don't give it a rest."

Both men glared at him.

"If you don't mind," Zack announced with annoyance, "I have a suspect to interrogate." He again flipped the saw switch.

The saw buzzed loudly. The man screamed beneath the gag as the log rode the track, the saw cutting through it on its way to his crotch. Zack turned off the saw and eyed his prisoner.

"Something you'd like to add?" Zack asked while observing the bound man.

The man panted beneath the gag as sweat drenched his body and urine seeped through the crotch of his pants.

Zack eyed the urine stain and nodded. "I'll take that as a 'yes'."

Chapter Two

The three-story mansion encompassed several acres and seemingly branched out in every direction. It was nearly dark and almost every light was on inside and outside the multi-million dollar estate. A long curved driveway, secured by a guard at the gatehouse, led to the large fountain in front of the main house and also continued onward to the attached, eight-car garage in back. The garage only contained one bay door, but once inside, it held eight cars in what resembled a lavish room. It was more of a car museum than a garage. With a wide aisle, it contained four cars parked on each side to allow easy access. To the left side were classic cars and to the right were high-priced sports cars. Each car cost more than most residential homes.

A handsome, distinguished gentleman in his early fifties with a full head of moderately graying hair admired one of the new sports cars. Ross Madrid took his usual broad stance with his legs spread comfortably apart and his arms folded across his moderately muscular chest. Despite his age, he was an imposing figure. Beyond his charming smile, there hid a force beyond compare. He showed no reaction to the two large men watching him from the main entrance to the house. Although well-dressed, they were still just high-priced thugs.

A man dressed in a suit straight from the 'goodfellas' catalog entered the lavish garage with two other high-priced thugs on his heels. Cosmo Rembrandt, formerly Carlos Ruiz, grinned with his hands extended to greet Ross. Ross shook hands with the seemingly mousy man. Cosmo was the wealthy brains of the operation while pretending to be a recognizable force. His small stature and limited fighting skills meant he was almost nothing without his high-priced thugs to back him.

"I wasn't sure if you intended to follow through with our little transaction," Cosmo announced while remaining cheerful as he studied his guest.

"I can't say I'm thrilled with the ticket price," Ross casually replied then grinned, "but you have some hard to find items I can't pass up."

"Excellent," Cosmo announced and extended his hand along the broad aisle between the cars toward an area almost resembling a living room. "Your man can bring your transport van into the garage while we complete our transaction."

Ross glanced toward the bay door and signaled his man just inside the garage. Kirk Mandel gave a knowing nod then approached the black van he'd been leaning against for the last twenty minutes. Kirk was a large, muscular man who stood an imposing 6'4" with broad shoulders and biceps the size of tree trunks barely hidden beneath his black combat uniform. His buzz cut and thick facial stubble made him look moderately intimidating. Judging by his steely gaze, the man was incapable of showing emotion. The guards kept a close watch as the black van drove along the aisle between the expensive cars toward the living room area.

Cosmo removed a remote control from the bar and pressed a button. Several panels spun around to reveal military grade automatic weapons lining the walls. Ross stared at the assortment of weapons, grinned like a schoolboy, and shook his head.

"I have a friend who'd never leave this room," Ross announced. He then eyed Cosmo as his look turned serious. "But you said you could get me a dozen of each. For what I'm paying, I expect more than this."

Cosmo nodded and indicated the metal crates within a large opening. "They're all right there." He approached the containers and opened one to reveal the contents.

Ross eyed the neatly stacked weapons in each of the metal containers. He removed one or two, taking time to inspect them carefully, and then nodded his approval.

"Your men can load them up as soon as I see the cash in my account," Cosmo announced.

Ross replaced the weapons and shut the lids. He removed his cell phone and pressed a single button. Once the call was answered, he kept his message short. "Do it."

Cosmo approached a laptop computer sitting on top of the bar and pulled up his account. He waited only a moment before the enormous amount of money electronically appeared. He grinned and shut his laptop while looking at Ross.

"Load them up."

Cosmo's men helped Kirk load the four metal crates into the back of the black van.

"Can I offer you a drink?" Cosmo asked.

Ross nodded and flashed his usual charming smile. While Cosmo poured his drink, Ross glanced around the lavish garage.

"Some party you're having tonight, huh?" Ross asked then eyed the man. "I certainly hope I didn't keep you from your guests."

"That?" Cosmo asked then chuckled in his throat. "That's just a little something I have going on the side. Vices kindly provided to a select few for the right price."

"What sort of vices?" Ross asked then raised a clever brow along with a cheap grin. "What price?"

"For an important customer such as yourself," Cosmo announced, "consider it on the house. We have gambling, gorgeous women, and just about anything that'll make you feel good." He grinned almost deviously. "Why don't you leave your man to his work, and I'll take you on a little tour of the house? I'm sure we can find something to suit your taste."

"I'm in," Ross announced and again signaled Kirk.

Kirk nodded and finished loading the metal containers with two of Cosmo's men. Ross headed for the connecting door with Cosmo and his two guards.

Once Kirk finished loading the last crate, he removed a cigar and gestured to the guards. "Mind if I smoke?"

Both shook their heads.

"We'll join you," the first man replied and removed a pack of cigarettes.

The second man indicated the bar to Kirk in silent question. Kirk puffed on his cigar and nodded his acceptance.

"How about the good stuff?" the man suggested and held up an expensive bottle.

Kirk smirked at the men and chuckled softly. "When the cat's away--"

Both men chuckled as the second man poured them each a drink.

†

At the end of the mansion driveway, a black sedan parked near some large bushes, allowing it to blend in with the darkness between streetlights. The mansion gate remained closed with only one guard on duty. The amount of traffic entering and leaving the mansion through the main gate made it seem as if there was a party going on. Within the sedan, Holden sat in the driver's seat and kept close watch on those coming and going from the mansion. The man sitting in the passenger seat alongside him fiddled on his laptop then glanced at Holden.

"Ross was just invited inside the mansion," Beck announced then shut his laptop and looked at the main gate as well.

Beck Larue was a ruggedly handsome man in his mid-thirties. He stood over six feet tall and maintained an impressive athletic build. His light brown hair was moderately rumpled and his sturdy gaze lent a perfect balance between intimidating and cuddly.

"So what now?" Holden asked.

"We wait."

"Wait for what?" Holden questioned and eyed the man in the seat alongside him.

"Ross will do a quick guard count and let the others know how and where to enter," Beck replied while straining to see out the side window past Holden.

Holden sharply eyed Beck. "Others? Is he sending Jackie in there?"

Beck refused to look at Holden and maintained his gaze upon the closed gate. "That's how it works, Holden. Jackie's with Zack. You know that."

"Doesn't mean I have to like it," Holden muttered without looking back.

"I understand perfectly," Beck replied and finally looked at Holden as he relaxed in his seat. "You know, honestly, I don't get women." He made a face and shrugged more to himself. "I thought I did, but the moment you have them figured out, they go and change the rule book." He groaned and looked up at the ceiling. "I mean, what do they want?"

Nearly fifteen minutes later, Holden leaned his head back against the seat and listened while Beck continued to ramble on about women. He complained about what they wanted, and how difficult they liked to make things on men.

Beck seemed to take a break from his tirade then eyed Holden. "She has a stalker, you know."

Holden glanced at Beck and straightened in his seat, finally taking an interest in the conversation. "Who?"

"Pinto," Beck announced with a slightly irritated groan. "Haven't you been listening?"

"What do you mean 'she has a stalker'?"

"Jesus, Holden," he scoffed. "You're a frickin' fed. You know what a stalker is. Some guy." He waved him off then looked out the side window in silence. Unfortunately for Holden, it didn't last. He looked back at Holden and jumped right back into the conversation. "He's supposedly a friend. He's been coming to the club when she sings. Although she says he's a friend, he's definitely stalking her. He's stalking her, and she refuses to believe it." His eyes widened slightly. "I mean, this guy has made comments to me about *my girlfriend*. He says things even I don't feel comfortable repeating to her, and she still thinks I'm the one who's overreacting." He threw his arms in the air in a mild hissy fit. "*I'm* the one overreacting?"

Holden eyed Beck and raised a curious brow. "Didn't I get the same speech from you when Kirk was strutting around in my living room in his boxer briefs in front of Jackie?"

"That's different," Beck scoffed and waved him off. "Jackie's used to the guys running around commando."

"And that time I had to kick Zack out of my bed because he didn't want Jackie sleeping alone while I was working late one night?" Holden demanded.

"Seriously? You're comparing the two?" Beck demanded with irritation. "Zack is practically the family pet. He's not dogging your wife."

"Well, what about the time Monroe decided to use the bathroom while Jackie was in the shower?" he demanded. "You told me I was overreacting then."

"Because you were," Beck insisted then snorted a soft laugh and gave him a mocking look. "Come on, Holden. Monroe and Jackie had a thing once upon a time before you came into the picture. It's nothing he hasn't seen before."

Holden glared at Beck. "Gee, thanks for reminding me of that little fact. I'd nearly forgotten." He looked out the windshield. "For the record, I'd like to be paired up with Gil next time. I prefer sitting in total silence to this."

Beck touched his ear and listened through his hidden ear transmitter. "Ross is sending the guys in now."

"Why don't I have one of those?" Holden asked. "I hate hearing only half the conversation."

Beck groaned softly and eyed Holden. "For the same reason you're never paired with Jackie," he announced. "One little misspoken word, and you'll be running in getting us all shot while trying to save your wife who doesn't need saving."

"I have no idea why she likes hanging out with any of you," Holden retorted.

"Yeah, we said the same thing when she married you."

Holden glared at Beck.

Chapter Three

Within the estate grounds on the other side of the stone wall, a security guard patrolled the area. He passed a large tree towering over the wall from the opposite side. Zack dropped from one of the branches and softly landed on top of the stone wall in a crouched position. He wore his black combat fatigues, or his stalking outfit, as he fondly referred to them, which allowed him to blend into the night. He stared across the estate grounds and studied the distance to the mansion.

"Another guard at two o'clock," a female voice announced from within the tree.

"Yeah, I see him," Zack muttered softly.

"I thought you staked out this place," the female voice scolded.

"I did," he replied. "There's a little more activity tonight. Something must be happening."

Zack climbed back into the tree with little effort and straddled one of the larger branches alongside a young woman dressed in her finest prowling outfit, which revealed her toned, athletic body. Jackie Falcone was an attractive woman in her mid-twenties with her long, dark hair worn in a ponytail, as it usually was when she anticipated combat. She watched Zack while he studied the guard passing by their hideaway. Although he was nearly impossible to read, Jackie loved trying to figure out Zack's devious mind. Once the guard was out of earshot, she became curious.

"What are you thinking?" she asked while watching him as he studied the estate grounds.

"We have four guards patrolling the front grounds," he announced in a serious tone. "Our entrance is that second-floor balcony, which should be a bedroom." He didn't bother looking at her and wiggled his fingers as if anticipating her to hand him something. "Give me your bra."

Jackie stared at Zack with her mouth hanging open. "Pardon me?"

"Your bra," he reconfirmed and cast a look at her. "I need it."

"I'm not giving you my bra," she firmly insisted. "There's something seriously messed up with your mind if you actually think I'd ever give it to you."

He gave her a quick, disapproving once-over. "That's it," Zack snarled. "No more girls in my treehouse."

She groaned with annoyance then proceeded to unhook her bra and slip it out through her shirtsleeves without exposing any skin. Zack eyed her then the black lacy bra in her hand with moderate disappointment. She glared back sharply.

"Were you expecting a free show?" she demanded.

"No, I bet Monroe ten bucks you were wearing the red one," he remarked. "I'm out ten bucks."

She rolled her eyes and groaned while casting the bra into his face. He easily caught it but seemed pleased with the projectile nearly hitting him.

"Hmm," he cooed. "Satin and lace. Nice."

"I'd better get it back too," she snarled.

He eyed her then laughed softly. "Good luck with that."

The same guard passed the tree a few minutes later. He stopped and stared at the bra on the ground near the base of the wall. The guard hesitantly picked it up, ran his thumb across the lace, and then glanced up the tree. Zack somersaulted from the tree branch, wrapping his legs around the man's neck, and tossed him through the air before riding him to the ground. As Zack straightened, a second guard ran toward him with his shotgun aimed.

"On the ground," the guard shouted as he got within a few feet of Zack.

Zack casually raised his hands in the air then dropped to one knee. Jackie flipped from the tree and kicked the man in the chest with both feet, sending him flying several feet through the air. Zack casually picked up Jackie's bra and stuffed it into the leg pocket of his combat pants. He eyed Jackie with little reaction.

"That was okay," he critiqued her performance, "but if you'd take up gymnastics--"

13

"Don't start with that," she snarled.

"We'd better get these two out of sight," he announced and grabbed the man closest to him beneath the arms.

✝

The large kitchen bustled with cooks and wait staff preparing buffet style food for their guests. A tall, well-built man in his late thirties or possibly his early forties slipped into the kitchen through the rear door, leaving it partially open. Gil Rafferty was a ruggedly handsome man with short dark hair peppered with gray, giving him a slightly distinguished look. The seriousness on his face made him hard to read as he surveyed the busy kitchen then proceeded on his journey. He didn't slow or hesitate while passing through, snagging a tray of puffy pastries on his way, and followed another server through the 'out' door to the banquet room. Gil entered the informal banquet room, which was set up more like a lounge, and immediately set his tray on the nearby buffet table as he passed. He slipped into the crowd and easily blended within his expensive suit.

There were at least one hundred well-dressed guests, mostly men, socializing within the informal room. Approximately two dozen exceedingly gorgeous women in revealing dresses held drinks in their hands and seemed to 'work' the room. Their matching beauty and expensive attire were no coincidence. The women were high-priced escorts available for the men's entertainment. They flirted with nearly every man no matter how unattractive. The men put their hands on the women and even caressed their backsides without protest. Gil caught several glimpses of the working girls spreading the joy and raised his brows. He crossed the room, making eye contact with one or two of the working women, and offered an obligatory smile to keep appearances. He didn't stop long enough to allow them time to cozy up to him.

Ross stood in the center of the room with a glass of scotch in one hand and a sexy woman hanging off his free arm. It was obvious she initiated, forcing Ross to play along for appearances. Despite her obvious interest, he minded his hands. Ross had a moderately temperamental girlfriend back home, who wouldn't approve even for the sake of a mission. Ross met Gil's gaze from across the room. There was no secret signal, yet their eyes spoke volumes. Gil continued through the banquet hall and slipped through the side door

14

when no one was looking. Once in the hallway, Gil kept watch for anyone passing through. He didn't notice any cameras, at least none conspicuously located, and headed for the stairs. He passed an affectionate woman clinging to a sleazy looking man on their return trip from the second floor, which offered 'privacy' rooms.

As he walked along the second-floor hallway, he heard the faint sounds of women faking screams of pleasure through the doors on both sides of the hall. It was reminiscing of an old western brothel. Gil listened intently as he passed, seeking sounds that were somehow different from those common for the brothel atmosphere. A set of doors at the end of the hall caught his attention. They led into the west wing of the mansion with a sign clearly marked 'off limits'. He continued toward the doors with a faster, determined walk. That was what he was looking for. Gil entered the west wing, purposely leaving the door ajar, and hurried along the corridor, listening for any sounds coming from closed bedroom doors.

"This wing is off-limits to guests," a gruff voice informed him.

Gil stopped in his tracks and turned to face one of the mansion guards. As with all the mansion guards, he was a large, burly guy. Each guard was muscular and stood over six-foot tall. It was slightly amusing since tall and muscular didn't necessarily mean lethal. Zack was the perfect example with his little protégé Jackie coming in a close second.

"Sorry," Gil announced showing little reaction. "I must've made a wrong turn."

He attempted to walk past the guard. The guard caught him by the arm and stopped him. Gil didn't react, although he did eye the hand gripping his arm.

"You're not a guest, are you?" the guard demanded. "Show me your ID card."

"Oh," Gil replied and hesitated only a moment before patting down his pockets. He smiled innocently. "I must have left it in one of the rooms while I was, you know," he announced while grinning, "dressing."

The guard placed his hand on Gil's shoulder and kept him from advancing down the corridor. "You weren't in any of the rooms," he announced. "It's my job to know who's in what room and with which girl." The guard reached for his ear transmitter.

"I wouldn't do that if I were you," Gil announced with little reaction.

The guard glared at him. "Oh, you wouldn't, huh? Maybe I should just kick your ass around the mansion."

"Well, you could try," Gil casually replied, "but I doubt you'd be successful. I'm guessing I have ten years on you, but I can tell you're a little soft in the middle."

"Now I *am* going to kick your ass," the guard snarled and made tight fists.

Gil saw a shadow move in the nearby corridor. A tiny smirk crossed his face. "I think my partner may have something to say about that."

The guard caught Gil's glance toward the corridor behind him and saw the shadow of someone rounding the corner. The guard whipped out a nightstick and struck the man as he appeared around the corner. Another mansion guard took the hard hit and collapsed to the floor.

Gil laughed softly. "I think you just laid out your own man," he announced with humor.

The guard kept an eye on Gil while attempting to assess the condition of the guard he'd just knocked out.

"*My* partner is behind you," Gil informed him while smiling slyly.

"Do you really expect me to buy that--?"

There was a snarl directly behind the guard. He whirled around. A silver sable German shepherd dog leaped upward and grabbed the guard by his arm, keeping him from swinging with the nightstick. Darth snarled while tearing into the shirt and flesh of the guard's lower arm. Gil punched the man in the face, instantly dropping him. Darth leaped out of the path of the falling man then licked his bloodied muzzle and panted happily at Gil.

"We'd better tie up those two and hide them," Gil announced to the dog. "We've got a lot of ground to cover if we want to find that missing girl, and we don't need any unnecessary distractions."

Darth woofed in response while wagging his tail. Gil affectionately scratched the dog's scruff then proceeded with the mission.

Chapter Four

The second-floor bedroom on the east wing was mostly dark, revealing little of the expensive furniture. Monroe stood alongside the door just inside the darkened room and listened to footfalls passing in the hallway. Another man stood on the opposite side of the door and watched Monroe for his signal. Bogart was a well-built man in his late twenties. He was 'hunky actor' handsome with flowing golden-brown hair and sideburns nearly a shade darker. As a former conman, being handsome and charming were his biggest assets. There were times his charm was the only thing he brought to the team. When the footfalls passed the room, both men relaxed their stance.

Monroe tapped his ear transmitter and spoke casually. "We have a lot of security on the east wing second-floor," he announced in a soft tone. "Seems as if they're keeping watch over something. It could be our girl."

A voice came over both their ear transmitters. "Yeah, I'm on west wing second-floor," Gil informed them. "Darth and I are coming up with nothing. Only one guard and he's taking a little nap right now."

"Zack and I are on second in the main building," Jackie's voice came over their ear transmitters.

"Lots of beds squeaking," Zack's voice chimed in as well. "Other than some foul language and fake orgasms, we've got nothing."

"Thanks for the colorful update, Zack," Beck's voice was heard over their ear transmitters.

"Converge on second-floor east to assist Monroe and Bogart," came Ross's soft but commanding voice over their transmitters.

"Kirk, if you copy, bring the van to the staff entrance on the east wing and wait for my signal."

There was no response, but it was possible Kirk was in mixed company within the garage and was unable to respond. Monroe and Bogart exchanged looks, nodded, and then silently slipped into the second-floor corridor. They each took a side of the hallway and listened at the doors. None offered much. It was unusually quiet. Bogart suddenly stopped and listened to the soft singing from a little girl. He snapped his fingers, getting Monroe's attention, and indicated the door with a nod. Monroe joined him on his side of the hall then gently tapped on the door.

"Arianna?" Monroe announced softly through the door. "May I come in?"

There was silence as the singing stopped to the sound of his voice. Monroe and Bogart exchanged looks. Bogart shrugged. Neither was exactly great with kids. Monroe was about to tap on the door again when it unlocked. The door opened to reveal a five-year-old girl. She was a beautiful little girl with long black hair. Arianna stared at them with wide, dark eyes.

"Did my daddy send you?" she asked while eyeing each man with some apprehension. "Are we going to see him?"

"Actually," Monroe announced. "Your mother sent us. She wants us to bring you home to her."

The girl's eyes suddenly lit up. "Mommy? Is she back from her trip?"

Bogart and Monroe again exchanged looks. Bogart sneered his disgust.

Monroe managed a childlike smile while lowering himself to her level and nodded. "Yes, your mommy is back, and she wants you to come home right away," he replied.

Arianna became excited at the news. "I'll get my dolly," she exclaimed and ran back into the room.

Monroe and Bogart followed her into the room, gently closing the door behind them. The room decorated lavishly for a little girl had every toy imaginable. Arianna removed an old, worn doll from the bed then joined them by the door. They were about to leave when she hesitated and gave them a concerned look.

"What about Mimi?" the little girl asked.

Both men eyed her with puzzled looks.

"Who's Mimi?" Bogart asked.

"She's my friend," Arianna replied. "I'm not supposed to go downstairs, but I sneak down there to play with her in the morning when everyone is asleep."

"Downstairs?" Monroe asked.   "Is she one of the servant's little girls?"

"I guess so," she replied.   "Can she come along? I hate to leave her."

Monroe and Bogart again exchanged looks and groaned with defeat.   "Why don't we stop by her room on the way out, so you can tell her you're going away for a while?"

"Okay," the little girl replied, satisfied with the response.

Monroe tapped his ear transmitter.   "We have the kid. We're taking the back stairs toward the servant's quarters.   We should be out back in fifteen minutes."

"Everyone to the staff wing," Ross announced over their ear transmitters.   "I'll meet you at the bottom of the stairs, Monroe."

"Roger."

✝

Monroe entered the staff wing corridor from the back stairway with the little girl and Bogart in tow.   Arianna clung to Bogart's hand as if he were a longtime friend. He almost resembled a proud father while walking alongside her. Ross approached from the kitchen area to join them.   Monroe turned down the staff wing corridor, but the little girl suddenly pulled Bogart in the opposite direction.

"No, it's this way," she insisted.

Bogart eyed Ross and Monroe, uncertain how to respond to the little girl's insistence.

Ross appeared puzzled.   "Should I ask?"

"She wants to say goodbye to her friend," Monroe announced under his breath.

"We don't have time for this," Ross remarked firmly then watched the little girl practically dragging Bogart behind her.   Her insistence was curious.

When Arianna stopped before the basement door, all three men were puzzled. Ross stared at the basement stairs then turned off his ear transmitter.   Monroe followed suit.   Bogart saw them and immediately turned off his as well, although he didn't seem to understand the reasoning behind it.

"What's wrong?" Bogart asked.

"Let's meet this friend of hers," Ross muttered with noted concern in his voice.

Ross led the way down the stairs, removing his semiautomatic for the first time. Bogart and Arianna went next with Monroe bringing up the rear. He also removed his semiautomatic from his hidden shoulder holster. Something seemed wrong and all three men sensed it. They reached the bottom, where the little girl indicated a locked door. Ross studied the lock and reached for his small toolkit, but the little girl was already punching numbers into the keypad. The door electronically unlocked. Bogart held the little girl back while Ross and Monroe led the way. They entered a forty-by-forty foot room lined with cramped, dingy cells.

"Arianna," a little girl cried out.

Arianna pulled away from Bogart's hand and ran to one of the dark cells.

"Mimi," she cried out and hugged the six-year-old girl through the bars.

As Ross and Monroe uncertainly looked around the dark cells, little girls between the ages of five and ten years old emerged from the darkness and gravitated toward the bars. They stared at the three men with concerned and frightened looks. Some were already in tears at the sight of the strangers. Ross, Monroe, and Bogart stared with horror at the sight.

"Mother--" Ross began to curse then cut himself short. His overwhelming anger turned to concern. He removed his cell phone from his pocket and frantically typed into it while eyeing Monroe. "Call Holden. Tell him to get the feds here right away."

Monroe nodded and removed his cell phone. He paced the room surrounded by bars while Bogart just stared in silent horror at the little girls within the cells.

"What the hell?" Bogart gasped, not sure he understood what he was seeing. He then turned angry and looked at Ross. "Ross, what the hell?"

†

Jackie and Zack hurried along the first-floor corridor while keeping watch for any guards. Jackie felt her phone vibrate against her thigh, surprising her. It was a private phone and only the team and Holden had the number. She stopped and looked at the small pocket of her tactical yoga pants. She apprehensively removed the phone, pressed a button, and stared at it. Zack soon realized she wasn't behind him, looked back, and returned to her. Jackie saw the simple text: Remove Zack now!

As Zack approached, he saw her phone and his look became curious. "What is it?"

Jackie replaced her phone to the small pocket and looked at him with little reaction despite the chill that ran down her spine. "Ross's transmitter isn't working," she easily lied.   "He wants us to wait for them at the rendezvous with Kirk."

Zack eyed her a moment then nodded.   "They're on their way then?"

She nodded in response.   As Zack stared into her eyes a moment, she felt her heart racing.   For whatever reason, Ross wanted Zack removed from the mansion, indicating something had happened. Jackie had to sell it without him catching on.   Unfortunately, lying to Zack wasn't as easy as it sounded.   He nodded, although she wasn't sure he was convinced.   They continued along the hallway.   Rather than cross the busy part of the mansion, they were about to slip out a rarely used side door when Zack suddenly stopped and glanced back at her.

"Ross's comlink stopped working, huh?" he questioned, giving her a strange look.

"Can we discuss this at the rendezvous?" she snapped and immediately regretted her unfounded anxiety.

"Yeah, sure," Zack replied while shrugging.   She attempted to walk past him toward the door.   In an instant, his arm moved across the opening and stopped her.   "Why you?"

She stopped short of his arm, groaned softly, and looked at him, although she wished she hadn't.   "Why me what?"

He shrugged casually as if not the least bit bothered by the sudden change of plans.   "Just wondering why he would contact you rather than me?"   Zack seemed to consider his own question as if working out some secret plot where everyone was conspiring against him.   "I mean, I know you're more eye-pleasing, but I'm usually the contact."   His look then turned frighteningly demanding.   "So, again, why you?"

Jackie groaned, hoping it came off as irritation rather than concern.   "Beats the hell out of me, Zack.   Maybe you should ask him."

Zack stared into her eyes with a look that forced her heart to skip a beat.   He knew she was lying.   She didn't doubt he was watching her pupils or counting her heart rate by the vein in her neck.   She knew he had some secret super power to detect when someone was lying to him, and if he called her on it, she wasn't sure how she'd cover. He finally straightened and removed his arm from the doorway.

"Okay, so let's go," he announced in a casual, non-threatening tone.

Chapter Five

Zack and Jackie hurried across the side driveway and approached the van halfway between the staff wing entrance and the eight-car garage. Kirk stood outside the van casually leaning against the door as Zack headed for the side door.

"You're riding shotgun," Kirk informed him with little emotion.

Zack glared at Kirk and picked up his pace to the side door. He had to know they were hiding something from him. Kirk bolted from where he had been casually reclining and attempted to stop Zack, but it was too late. Zack pulled open the side door with added vigor. Fifteen bruised and battered little girls cowered on the van floor, clinging to one another and trembling when they saw him. Zack's expression momentarily shattered then morphed into something unrecognizable and frightening.

Ross jumped out of the van. "Zack," he warned firmly. "Holden has this under control."

"Glad to hear," Zack replied before turning and darting across the property.

Both Kirk and Ross were too late to stop him before he bolted. He disappeared into the darkness, forcing both men to stop.

Ross shook his head. "He's going to get his ass killed one of these days." He glanced at Jackie. "Think you can talk him off the bridge?"

"I've got this," Jackie announced while removing two tactical batons from her back belt holster and took off into the darkness after Zack.

Ross shook his head and glared at Kirk. "Zack's about to do something stupid. Fire up the van," he remarked. "We may need to make a hasty getaway."

"The feds will be here in twenty minutes," Kirk reminded Ross. "I think we can hold off Cosmo's men that long."

"It's not Cosmo's men I'm worried about," Ross remarked. "I don't want to hear another lecture from Holden about body count."

✝

Jackie cautiously entered the garage with a tactical baton in each hand. She was about to check the corners and behind the door for mansion security guards, but both men were already laid out on the floor. Despite that she was only moments behind Zack, he somehow managed to find the secret weapons compartments in just a few seconds and was playing with plastic explosives.

"Zack," she scolded and approached. "You're not solving anything by blowing up the uncle's hidden stash."

"Maybe not," he replied without looking at her, "but it'll make me feel better."

"Forget it," she remarked. "We need to go. You know the moment you entered this area, a silent alarm notified Cosmo's men. We have only a few minutes before they swarm this place."

"Then we're in luck," he replied. "I only need a few minutes."

"The FBI will be here soon," she insisted. "You can't be here when they arrive."

He cast a look at her. "In what world has a fed ever got the slip on me?"

"I know you go a little crazy when someone harms a child, Zack, but this is the wrong place and time to lose your head. We need to go."

Zack suddenly spun to face her with a look that sent a shiver down her spine. "Tell me, Jackie," he snarled. "When in your life have you ever collected scattered body parts of children blown up by their own government? And for what? Because we were *nice* to them? Gave them candy and toys? Made them smile for once in their short, miserable lives?" His look didn't soften any. "I once told a little girl there were no monsters, but there are. If I have to become a monster to stop others, so be it."

He finished setting up the plastic explosives and put it on a timer for ten minutes. Zack straightened proudly and faced her as the clock counted down.

"We can go now."

Two armed guards appeared from the outside entrance, cutting off their escape route. The main house door opened to reveal four more armed guards. Both looked at the guards closing in on them.

"I must be getting slow," Zack muttered.

As the men raised their weapons, Jackie and Zack dove to the floor in opposite directions, rolling behind expensive cars on either side of the aisle. The men fired their automatic weapons at them, missing their targets and hitting the cars.

"You idiot," one of the men from the house entrance cried out. "Don't wreck the cars!"

The six men split up, leaving one at each door, one along the left wall behind the sports cars, and one along the right wall behind the classic cars. The two remaining men walked the center aisle. Each man kept watch on his side. Jackie was practically wedged beneath one of the sports cars, hidden by the shadows of its tires. She watched shiny dress shoes pass on both the front and rear of the car, listening to the sounds their shoes made as they walked along the concrete floor. Someone needed to tell Cosmo's hired goons that fashion wasn't everything. A good pair of tactical boots wore better and reduced unwanted sound. Being silent and invisible had its advantages.

While keeping her tactical batons extended above her head, she rolled out from under the car and sprang into a crouching position. She heard a man let out a groan. The loud thump of his head hitting the car immediately followed, which subsequently set off the annoying car alarm. Like clockwork, the rapid gunfire followed. Zack successfully created a loud diversion. And the games would begin. Jackie saw her intended target several feet in front of the car. She leaped onto the car hood, causing the alarm to sound. As the man turned toward her, prepared to fire, she was already leaping through the air in a roundhouse kick as she dived off the car hood. She struck the man and knocked him backward against the car on the opposite side of the aisle.

The men not busy shooting at Zack's shadow turned their attention on her and opened fire, successfully driving the men away from either escape route. As they fired, Jackie was already landing from her flying kick and rolled between two luxury cars. The Rolls Royce had taken nearly a dozen hits before the men ceased fire to descend upon her. Zack slid over a car hood on his hip and struck one of the guards with both feet, knocking him into the next car and setting off more alarms. As soon as Zack's feet hit the floor, he was already punching the man and attempting to relieve him of his automatic rifle. Another guard fired at him. Zack spun the guard, allowing his man to shoot his own comrade in the back with several rounds and successfully shielding Zack. Zack held the dead guard against him, secured the automatic rifle, and fired back. Several guards went down.

Jackie jumped across one of the cars, setting off another alarm, and scaled the roof. She slid down the hood as a guard fired at her, but she was already pivoting her body and knocked the gun from his hand as she rode the hood. She landed softly and looked around. They successfully laid out the six men, but the car alarms were nearly deafening.

"Stop the bomb, Zack," she ordered.

He proudly carried the assault rifle over his shoulder while walking past her toward the outer door. "Nope."

She looked at her watch, groaned, and hurried after him for the outside door. The outer door opened to reveal another guard and Cosmo with their semiautomatics aimed at them. Zack allowed the assault rifle to fall into his hand and immediately shot the guard. Cosmo leaped to the floor. Zack tossed the assault rifle aside and practically jumped on top of Cosmo. He pulled him to his feet and held him in a fatal headlock, skillfully applying pressure. Jackie stared helplessly awaiting the fatal crunch. She had to stop him somehow even if the man deserved what he got.

"We need him alive," she shouted. "He's not the ringleader and you know that. Don't do it!"

Zack sneered and finally cast Cosmo aside. He fell to the floor and tried to catch his breath while Zack attempted to collect his emotions. Jackie knew he was pissed at her, but she had to stop him. Jackie approached them as Zack removed a zip tie from his thigh pocket. He reached down to grab Cosmo. Cosmo suddenly flipped over and struck Zack in the temple with a tire iron. As Zack collapsed to the ground, disoriented and bleeding, Cosmo grabbed the Bowie knife from Zack's boot and leaped on top of him. He rammed the knife downward for Zack's throat. Jackie grabbed the wrist holding the knife and caught Cosmo around the neck from behind. She attempted to keep him from impaling Zack, but she was losing her footing. He would soon toss her off him if she didn't overpower him.

Without a second thought, Jackie tore into Cosmo's throat with her hand, ripping his larynx from his neck in one swift motion. Cosmo gasped and wheezed, unable to catch his breath as blood poured from his throat. As the life seeped from his body, the knife fell from his hand. Jackie jumped off his back and tossed him off Zack. Zack lay motionless a moment while clutching his bleeding head. He seemed to have no idea where he was. Jackie stared at the man's bloodied throat in her hand, gasped, and dropped it. She trembled a moment then looked at Zack. He stared back at her, although unable to focus.

"Jackie," he gasped softly.

She didn't respond. She knew he was talking to her, but it didn't register.

"Jackie," he again gasped. "Snap out of it. We need to get out of here."

Jackie finally looked at Zack, pulled herself together, and helped him to his feet. He leaned heavily on her as they attempted to run from the garage. Jackie knew the explosion was about to come although it seemed to take forever. The explosion finally came and rocked the ground beneath them. A powerful force threw them to the ground, although she was uncertain if it was actually Zack tackling her to the ground. She looked back and saw the massive fireball that was once the garage. The ringing in her ears was almost more than she could handle. Ross and Kirk ran for them, finally seeing them as the flames brightened the entire area. When they realized Zack couldn't maintain his balance, Kirk tossed him over his shoulder and carried him toward the van. Ross grabbed Jackie, who could barely stand from the force of the explosion, and half dragged her alongside him.

Kirk tossed Zack into the van while the little girls watched the barely moving man. Ross helped Jackie onto the floor alongside him. Despite her ringing ears, she could now hear Beck cursing through her ear transmitter and Holden in the background demanding to know what the explosion was. As she sat on the van floor, she didn't have the strength to answer him, and she certainly wasn't about to explain things to him right now. Jackie sat mostly sedate on the floor alongside Zack where he lay. She stared at her blood-covered hand and relived what she had done to Cosmo in the garage. The horrible image played over and over in her mind. She couldn't believe she'd killed him with such violence and so easily. Her body subconsciously trembled. Zack attempted to stare at her as best he could from where he lay, unable to sit up. She could hear Zack speaking to her, but she wasn't sure what he was saying. When she finally snapped out of her trance, she looked down and realized Zack was holding her bloodied hand.

"It's okay," he softly repeated.

His words barely registered but his reassuring voice did stop the images from replaying in her mind. Several little girls collected around Jackie and Zack. They held frayed pieces of fabric from their worn, tattered clothes to Zack's bleeding head, attempting to nurse his injuries. Although Jackie would never mention it to anyone, she was certain she saw a tear in Zack's eye while the little girls took care of him. She knew, in his mind, it had been worth it.

Chapter Six

Zack sat on the exam table still fully dressed in his black combat fatigues with his arms folded across his chest. He wore a disgusted look on his face and refused to acknowledge or cooperate with the nurse attempting to take his blood pressure. Jackie sat in a chair near the door with her temple propped against her fist and stared at him with disappointment. The less than cheerful nurse eventually gave up.

"The doctor will be in shortly," the nurse huffed and left the exam room.

Jackie immediately straightened in her chair and received a firm glare from Zack.

"Don't," he scoffed.

"Don't what?" she muttered.

"Don't lecture me like I'm a child," he remarked without removing his arms from across his chest. "I don't even know what I'm doing here. I've lived through worse head trauma than this." He thumped the bandage taped to his temple. "Doesn't even hurt anymore."

"You've been hallucinating, Zack," she informed him. "I won't even mention the added irritability."

"You sound just like your mother," he scoffed and looked away. "She was a ballbreaker too."

Jackie rolled her eyes and ignored the comment. There was a soft tap on the door before it opened. A man familiar to Zack entered the exam room and adjusted his white lab coat.

"Zack," Dr. Sherman announced cheerfully. "It's been a while." He then glanced at his watch. "Almost a month since your last brush with death visit."

29

"Your bedside manner needs work, Doc," Zack muttered then shifted uncomfortably. "I don't need to be here. Ross is being a paranoid little bitch. He gets a girlfriend and suddenly he's Mr. Sensitivity."

The doctor chuckled softly in his throat. "I'm sure he'd appreciate hearing that."

Dr. Wade Sherman was a distinguished looking man in his late forties with gray throughout his once dark hair. He had served as a doctor in the Marines and became close to Whiskey Tango Foxtrot during their many missions. He was also the one they counted on to do most of their patch jobs without too many questions. Zack, in particular, had limited patience with the doctor on that score alone. He'd seen a little too much of the good doctor as well as the other way around. He shined his penlight into Zack's eyes, causing him to sneer with irritability.

"Hmm, you've got one beauty of a concussion," Dr. Sherman announced. "Bull riding or jumping out of a plane without a parachute?"

"Cut the bullshit, Doc," Zack grumbled. "Tell Ross I'm fine so I can get the hell out of here."

"Ross said you've been hallucinating," Dr. Sherman remarked while raising a brow. "That's pretty serious."

"I took a wallop two days ago," Zack remarked. "So my brains are a little extra scrambled. I'll be fine in a few days. Besides, Ross was exaggerating about the hallucinations."

"Zack," Jackie again scolded.

He cast a glare at her. "Stay out of my psychosis, Jackie dear," he snarled back. He shook his head and looked at the doctor. "Balls of brass Ross sends in Jackie whenever he thinks I'm being 'bratty'."

Dr. Sherman looked from Jackie to Zack and cleverly raised his brows. "Oh?"

"Yeah, he thinks I have a soft spot for the commander's daughter, so she gets all the shit assignments meant to keep me in line." He rolled his eyes and snorted a soft laugh. "I'm not saying she doesn't have a great ass and mind-blowing cleavage, but I'm not some hormone enraged sailor on shore leave. That's more Monroe's thing."

"So you don't have a soft spot for your former commander's daughter?" Dr. Sherman questioned while studying him.

Zack eyed Jackie. She just stared back, folded her arms across her chest, and raised a cocky brow waiting for his response. He looked back at the doctor.

"Of course not," Zack replied with little hesitation then straightened proudly. "That's absurd. I mean, sure, it's a bit of a turn-on that she can just about kick my ass. What guy wouldn't get a little hard from that?"

Jackie's mouth fell open with a nearly shocked expression. "Zack," she gasped while sitting forward then immediately appeared offended. "Who do you think you're kidding? I most certainly *can* kick your ass!"

"Yeah, when you cheat," he scoffed then looked back at the doctor. "Come on, Doc. Give me a note so I can return to active duty. This is bullshit."

Dr. Sherman straightened while studying Zack and sighed deeply. "Zack," he began gently without taking his eyes off him. "Jackie isn't here."

Zack stared at him a moment then eyed Jackie, who remained casually seated in the chair alongside the door.

"Well," she scoffed while raising an arrogant brow. "He's not the sharpest tool."

He looked back at Dr. Sherman, searching his eyes a moment, obviously considering the doctor had lost his mind. "She's in the chair by the door. Not sure how you can miss her."

Dr. Sherman grimaced slightly and shook his head. "I'm afraid not, Zack. Beck and Monroe brought you. They're in the waiting room."

Zack again looked at the chair by the door. It was empty. He stared at the chair a long moment with disbelief then looked around the room for Jackie. He uncertainly rubbed his sore temple then eyed the doctor.

"Am I here?" Zack finally asked.

"Yes, Zack," he replied cheerfully and offered a pleasant smile. "You're here."

Zack groaned and allowed his shoulders to sag for the first time possibly in his life then scratched his head. "I'm feeling a little confused now."

"It's understandable," Dr. Sherman replied. "I'm going to give you some pills which should take the edge off. Take it easy a few days, and you should be back to normal." He hesitated. "Well, back to your usual self." He routed through his cupboard and removed two bottles of pills then carefully marked each with his pen. "These are samples, so you won't need to visit the pharmacy. I know the drill with you guys by now. I'll leave the pills with Monroe. You'll take the first bottle for seven days and then the second for an additional ten after that. The first bottle will make you a little groggy, but I advise you to take them. You'll feel better while on the second bottle, but I want you to continue taking them until they're gone."

Zack frowned and nodded. "Yeah, okay."

✝

Monroe and Beck sat in the doctor's moderately bland, empty waiting room. It was after hours, which by design whenever they came to see Dr. Sherman. The guys attempted to keep their mission injuries beneath the radar of hospital doctors who would ask too many uncomfortable questions, particularly when it came to gunshot wounds. Monroe stared at the ceiling rather than his magazine and looked completely bored while Beck talked endlessly.

"I'm not kidding," Beck announced. "The guy's like a stalker or something." He indicated himself while raising his brows. "I can see it." He threw his hands in the air. "So why can't she?" He groaned with disgust. "She's letting this guy get too close. Something bad is going to happen, yet she won't listen to me when I try to warn her." He rolled his eyes. "I'm acting like 'the jealous boyfriend' and 'he's harmless'." Beck half turned in his chair to face Monroe. "Isn't that what all women say before some crazed lunatic kills them?"

"I don't know, Beck," Monroe groaned softly, tired of the conversation. "Why don't you try chaining her in the basement or something? Maybe that'll work."

Beck sharply glared at Monroe. "Now you're just mocking me."

"Yes, I'm mocking you," Monroe suddenly cried out and stared at him. "You've been ranting on and on about Pinto's non-existent stalker." He leaned closer to Beck and stared into his eyes. "She sings at a dive in the middle of nowhere. Where the hell would she even find a stalker? We're talking backwoods country boys here. They don't know how to stalk. They leer and drool."

Beck waved him off and straightened in his chair. "You're absolutely no help."

"That's because there's nothing wrong," Monroe demanded. "You're making a spectacle of yourself."

"In front of you?" Beck demanded then laughed. "I've seen you do worse."

32

Monroe indicated the camera in the corner. "Maybe so but never on candid camera. You know Dr. Sherman keeps close security watch on his office." He frowned. "He has too many clients like us."

Chapter Seven

The little town in Colorado was three hours north of nowhere and two hours south of far from nowhere. Far from nowhere was where the team owned an old lodge, which they considered their home base. Beck and Bogart were the only ones who actually lived at the lodge full-time. The remote town just two hours south of the lodge was where Beck's girlfriend, Pinto Romano, spent her weekends while she sang at the country lounge. During the week, she would return to the lodge to be with Beck. The small town had a population of nearly five thousand, making it larger than most places in the middle of nowhere. It had its own nightclub with country music and line dancing, several restaurants, a movie theater, bowling alley, and at least four bars.

Despite still being daylight outside, the lounge remained dimly lit with mood lighting on small, round tables. Larger tables and booths were off to the sides. A massive bar lined the back wall of the main room. A gorgeous woman in her mid-twenties with long, copper colored hair worn in a French twist stood on stage and sang for the nearly packed room of mostly men. Pinto Romano wore a form-fitting sequin dress that showed off her curves and a little more leg and cleavage than necessary, but it was what the crowd came to see. Beck sat at one of the small tables off to the side and watched his girlfriend as she sang. With the way he gazed at her and the smile etched on his face, he almost appeared to be under some magical spell.

Once the song ended, there was a roar of applause from the crowd. Beck clapped and cheered for his girlfriend. Pinto took a bow then left the stage and joined Beck at his table where a glass of mint iced tea awaited her arrival. Beck sprang from his chair and greeted her with a loving kiss then held her in a warm embrace. She returned the hug with a pleased sigh. He pulled away, grinned boyishly, and pulled her chair out for her before returning to his seat. Being their table was in a darker corner, Beck's hand immediately sought her leg beneath the long slit in her dress. She affectionately caressed his arm while his hand traveled her leg and met his loving gaze with her own.

"I wasn't sure you'd make it tonight," she announced cheerfully. "When did you get back?"

"I left Jackie's place this afternoon after Zack's appointment with Dr. Sherman," he informed her. "I thought I'd catch your set and drive back to the lodge with you tonight."

She swept a lustful gaze over him and grinned her approval. "I'd like that." Her look turned serious. "How is Zack?"

"Delusional," he replied. "Basically the same, in my opinion."

She frowned her disapproval. "You must have been worried, considering the entire team stayed at Jackie's for two days to keep an eye on him."

"Not really," Beck replied. "It usually takes six of us to get him into the doctor's office."

"Stop pretending you weren't worried," Pinto remarked while casually leaning across the small table as she caressed his lower arm. "If you thought he was fine, you would have brought him back to the lodge rather than leave him with Monroe and Kirk at Jackie's place."

Beck avoided looking at her and shrugged. She shook her head at his reluctance to acknowledge his concern for his teammate. A man in his late twenties approached their table and paused near Pinto. Beck saw the familiar man and immediately sank back in his chair while snorting a soft laugh, although it was obvious he wasn't humored.

"Hey, Pinto," Will announced cheerfully. "Great set tonight."

Pinto glanced at the man alongside their table and shifted slightly, appearing uncomfortable. "Thanks, Will."

Will was a moderately attractive man although not nearly as lean and athletic as Beck was. He had light brown hair that fell to his brow, giving him the appearance of the lead singer in some boyband.

"Mind if I join you?" he asked, almost completely ignoring Beck's presence.

Beck chuckled softly and shook his head while placing his hand over his eyes. He refrained from commenting at the boldness of his girlfriend's stalker.

Pinto shifted in her chair, looked at Will, and attempted a polite smile. "Beck just came back from his business trip," she informed the younger man eager to join her. "I haven't seen him in a week, so--"

Will reluctantly took the hint and fidgeted slightly while backing up a step and finally casting a look at Beck. "Uh, yeah, sure. I understand. I'll call you later." He turned and walked away from their table.

"He's unbelievable," Beck muttered and finally sat forward, glaring at Pinto. "Is he really that naïve? He honestly didn't know I was gone an entire week?"

"Please, Beck," she announced with a dreary sigh. "Let's not start this again. He's just a friend, and he's not a stalker."

"So he's just naturally creepy," Beck remarked, unable to control his sarcasm.

"He's never made one inappropriate remark or even asked me out," she insisted. "Can we just drop it?"

Beck shifted and attempted to control his emotions. He forced a smile and nodded. "Yeah, I don't want to discuss Will tonight. We have better things to talk about."

She grinned slyly and nodded. "Absolutely."

His hand again returned to her leg as he leaned across the table and kissed her warmly but passionately. Fifteen minutes later, the owner again introduced Pinto on stage for her last set. She kissed Beck quickly on the lips then hurried for the stage. As Pinto started her second to last song, Beck's cell phone vibrated. He removed the phone from his pocket and saw the new test message from an unknown caller. Curious, he viewed the text message. It simply read, 'Your girlfriend cheated on you while you were gone'. Beck stared at the message. His horror soon turned to hostility as he scanned the lounge. He saw Will at the bar laughing with one of his friends. Beck leaped up from his chair, crossed the crowded lounge, and approached Will. He grabbed Will by the arm and spun him to face him, showing him the text on his cell phone.

"What the hell is this?" he demanded.

Will eyed the message, appeared surprised, and then looked at Beck while shaking his head. "No idea."

"Bullshit! You sent this," Beck shouted loud enough for half the lounge to hear him.

"What?" Will gasped then chuckled softly. "You're insane. Why the hell would I send you something like that?"

"To put a wedge between Pinto and me," Beck snarled with an icy glare. "I know she'd never do something like this, so that leaves you!"

They received several looks, including a stray look from Pinto while she attempted to continue singing, although she was clearly distracted.

Will again laughed and shook his head. "You're delusional," he remarked as his smile mocked him.

Beck punched him in the abdomen, causing him to clutch himself and double over in agony. There were several gasps from within the lounge. Beck grabbed Will by the back of the neck and forced him to make eye contact. He pointed a warning finger in his face.

"That was the warning shot across your bow," Beck snarled. "Disrespect Pinto again and I won't pull any punches." He released Will and straightened.

Will gasped while clutching his abdomen and seemed to overplay his injury while looking past Beck. Beck realized the singing had stopped. When he looked behind him, he saw Pinto standing only a few feet away with a horrified look on her face.

"Beck," she gasped in a scolding tone.

"He sent me a text," Beck informed her then extended his phone to her.

Pinto eyed the text then looked at him with surprise. "And you actually believed this?"

"No, of course not," Beck replied then indicated Will, who still milked the punch to his gut. "He sent it to piss me off, and it worked."

She returned his phone while shaking her head. "That's not even his number.

"I didn't send it, Pinto. I swear," Will proclaimed while still doubled over. "Your boyfriend's had it out for me since the beginning."

Beck stared with surprise at the look on Pinto's face and immediately read her expression. "You aren't honestly going to believe him over me?"

"I don't know what to believe," she launched back then placed her hand to her head. She finally looked at him. "I need to be alone. Please, just go home."

"Pinto--"

"I need some time to sort this out," she reiterated. "Please, just go."

Beck frowned and nodded. "I'm sorry, babe," he announced softly. "Call me when we can discuss this." He left the lounge without further comment or incident despite the looks he received.

Chapter Eight

Three days later. It was early morning just before sunrise.

Holden was spooned against Jackie from behind in their king-sized bed. He woke and nuzzled his wife. His eyes opened partway, allowing him to view her wildly mussed, dark hair. A sly smirk crossed his face and he allowed his hand to caress her bare leg beneath the sheets. She groaned softly, took his hand, and pulled it closer to her panties. Holden flipped Jackie onto her back, nearly causing her to gasp with surprise. She giggled softly as he partially moved on top of her and kissed her warmly and lovingly on the lips. As his hand traveled her thigh, there was a soft knock on their door. Holden broke off the kiss, groaned softly, and eyed her.

"It's like he knows," Holden snarled softly. "He's killing our sex life."

She sighed as Holden rolled off her and collapsed onto his back. He allowed his arm to cover his eyes. Jackie stared at the ceiling a moment and waited.

"Jackie," came Zack's soft call through the door. "You're out of bread and milk. Is it okay if I borrow your car?"

"No, Zack," she called back. "You may not borrow my car. You can't see straight." She then considered the comment. "And there's plenty of bread and milk."

"Um, no, I beg to differ," Zack responded through the door.

"I just--" she began then groaned. "Kirk."

"When are they going home?" Holden demanded.

t

39

Later that morning, Jackie entered the kitchen and found Monroe preparing a crockpot dinner for that evening. It wasn't as if she was surprised to find him cooking. Monroe was domesticated and had exceedingly high standards on many things from his wardrobe to the meals he ate. She felt that sometimes he was more of a woman than she was. The thought made her laugh a little. She glanced around the kitchen.

"Where's Zack?" she asked.

"He went outside to get the morning paper," Monroe replied. "Assuming he can find his way back inside."

"Is he still acting weird?"

"He only killed one imaginary spider this morning," Monroe informed her. "Unfortunately, there's a snake living in your guest toilet bowl."

"Not a real one, I hope," she gasped.

"Unless he flushed it, I didn't see it," Monroe replied.

"I didn't flush it," Zack announced from behind them.

Both suddenly turned and saw Zack standing in the kitchen doorway with an offended look on his face.

"But I assure you, it was there," he announced firmly then looked at Jackie. "Although there is the off chance I'm seeing things now. There's a platoon of little women soldiers standing in your living room foyer. I'm not sure what they want, but I'm positive they're up to no good."

Jackie attempted a smile, although it was tough keeping up with some of his hallucinations. "Zack, I assure you, there are no little soldiers in my living room."

"Fine," he replied casually, "but I'd appreciate it if you asked them to leave all the same. I don't like the way they're staring at me."

Jackie groaned softly then attempted a polite smile. "Okay," she replied. "Show them to me, and I'll ask them to leave."

Zack left the kitchen with Jackie following. Once they entered the foyer, Jackie suddenly stopped and stared at five Girl Scouts in their green uniforms with their green berets and badge sashes. Each girl had a rolling cart behind her with boxes of cookies for sale.

"We're selling cookies to support our troop," one little girl announced.

"Cookies," Zack scoffed under his breath to Jackie while folding his arms across his chest. "That's how they always sucker you in."

"Zack," she scolded. "They're Girl Scouts. You've seen Girl Scouts before."

"Like Boy Scouts but without--"

Jackie placed her hand over Zack's mouth to silence him. "Behave in front of the kids." She removed her hand from his mouth and smiled at the little girls. "I'm sure I could find use for a few boxes of cookies around here."

"It's a trap, Jackie," Zack muttered while eyeing the girls suspiciously.

One little girl stared at Zack. He stared back through narrow eyes meant to intimidate her. She returned the look, moderately startling him. They heard thundering footsteps on the stairs, causing all five girls to jump with surprise. Kirk slowed as he reached the bottom and acted casual. He approached one of their carts and began removing half a dozen boxes of cookies, stacking them in the crook of his left arm. He handed the girls a wad of cash and headed back up the stairs.

"Poor bastard," Zack muttered while shaking his head. "Someone should warn him."

Jackie raised her brow and watched as Zack walked up the stairs. She shook her head and groaned softly. "Heaven help the nursing home that takes him."

✝

Four days later. The helicopter landed in the massive clearing before the old lodge nestled in the middle of nowhere. Once an impressive resort, the fifty bedroom hotel showed years of neglect. There were several boarded windows, the paint was peeling, and the wraparound porch appeared to be eroding. As the helicopter rotors slowed, Monroe, Kirk, and Zack got out. Kirk removed their gear from the bottom the helicopter as Jackie climbed out of the pilot's seat. She eyed the lodge and grimaced slightly as Beck approached to greet them.

"You know, a fresh coat of paint would go a long way," Jackie remarked.

Beck was within earshot and glared at her. His mood seemed to be lacking. "Sorry," he muttered. "We have other things on our plate right now."

Jackie eyed him with surprise to his hostility. "Someone woke up on the wrong side of their blowup doll. What's your problem?"

"Pinto broke up with him," Kirk offered while handing Monroe his duffel bag.

"She didn't break up with me," Beck snarled at Kirk then eyed Jackie and fidgeted slightly. "She needed a little space, that's all."

"He decked her boyfriend," Monroe added casually.

Beck's jaw tensed as he glared at Monroe. There was about to be bloodshed. He turned to Jackie and smirked. "Maybe you should keep them a few more weeks."

"Oh, no," she insisted. "They're all yours. It's vital to my marriage that I get them out of my house."

Beck groaned softly and attempted to put on a false front. "So Zack's back to himself then?"

"Yeah, he's fine," she replied. "He hasn't had any hallucinations or incidents in nearly four days. Monroe has his second bottle of pills that he starts tonight."

Beck nodded, although it was obvious he wasn't in a good mood. "So you're off to pick up Ross?"

"I'm collecting them on my way back and dropping them off at the airport," she replied. "Two weeks in Rio. I wish I were going."

"Good for Ross," Beck announced with a dreary sigh. "I'm glad someone's having a good time. Are you staying for lunch?"

"Thanks, but my schedule is a little tight," she replied. "Holden's taking off early, so we can have the entire evening to ourselves."

Beck couldn't help but frown. "Sounds romantic," he remarked with little enthusiasm then watched his three friends head for the lodge. He suddenly turned toward Jackie and seemingly came to life. "Think I should call Pinto again?"

"I think you should give her the space she asked for," Jackie replied casually while leaning against the helicopter. "What's going on between you two?"

"It's this guy," Beck announced now wildly enraged. "He's trying to drive us apart, and I think he's succeeding. He's successfully making me out to be the bad guy while he plays innocent."

42

"I don't know this guy, Beck," she informed him, "but I doubt he's smarter than you."

"Unfortunately, I need to keep my distance from him," he replied. "If Pinto sees me anywhere near him, all he has to do is cry wolf, and I'm totally screwed. I don't know if she'll forgive me as it is."

"I'm sure she will," Jackie announced while straightening. "Pinto loves you. She just needs time away from you to remember how much she misses you. It'll all work out in the end."

"Yeah, but this guy--"

"Oh, Beck," she groaned with a sigh. "You're playing your hand all wrong." Jackie grinned and gently patted him on the chest. "You're failing to use the ace up your sleeve."

"Which ace is that?"

"You've got Bogart, the conman, and Zack, the invisible man," she informed him. "They can handle this stalker, check him out without her ever knowing, and report back to you."

"Isn't that sort of against the rules?" Beck asked.

"It's sort of a gray fuzzy area," Jackie replied. "Besides, if they find evidence that this guy has been setting you up, they can handle it, and Pinto will never have to know."

Beck smiled for the first time and laughed softly. "You know, Jackie, you're sometimes a little too much like your father. It's almost scary."

She smiled and shrugged. "I'd like to believe I would do him proud."

Chapter Nine

Early Saturday evening, Pinto sat at the bar within the mostly empty lounge. The Saturday crowd wouldn't show up for another hour, at which time she would need to change for her first set. She had too much time to think about recent events. Pinto stared at her cell phone with Beck's name displayed. She tapped her finger on the edge of the phone and seemed to be debating whether she wanted to press the call button or not. She pushed the phone across the bar with frustration and held her head. The tears in her eyes revealed her torn emotions.

"Honey," came a familiar male voice from a few feet behind her.

Pinto turned on the bar stool and stared at her father only a few feet from her. Salvatore Romano was a robust man, although not necessarily overweight. He held his weight well. Despite being in his mid-forties, his face had a youthful appearance and almost cherub in nature. His baby face and moderately balding head gave him an almost innocent appeal. Pinto allowed a heavy sigh escape while springing up from her bar stool. She hurried to greet her father and his loving, outstretched arms. He held her in a long, warm embrace. Although they once had a falling-out that lasted a few years, their relationship was back on track, mostly due to Beck and his teammates, but that was a different story. She pulled away from him and struggled to hold back her tears.

"I didn't expect you to fly all the way out here," she announced, although she was obviously glad he had.

He guided her to one of the nearby tables and sat with her. "You sounded so upset on the phone yesterday; I thought I'd better come out and see how you were doing." He smiled timidly. "You must be going through hell. I never thought Beck would break my little girl's heart."

She stared at the look on his face and practically read his eyes. Pinto managed a smile and wiped a tear from her eye. "It's not over yet," she remarked. "You can relax." Pinto laughed softly and attempted to keep from crying. "I know how much you adore Beck, Dad.

Sal allowed a deep sigh to escape while gently rubbing his bald head. "That's a relief." He reached across the table and held her hand. "It'll work out, I promise. He's a good man. He'll renew your faith in him." Sal then shrugged. "If not, I'll have him bumped off."

She pulled her hand from his and groaned. "Don't even tease," she scolded.

Sal's reputation as a mob boss had been circulating for decades. It was never proven, although it was also never disproven either. The fact that he openly teased about it was slightly concerning. Sal laughed softly at her expense.

"You certainly don't have your mother's sense of humor," he teased. His look turned serious. "You know what you need?"

"No, Dad," she muttered not wanting to hear another lecture. "What do I need?"

"A relaxing cruise to Columbia," he announced cheerfully.

She eyed him sharply then groaned. "Are you seriously trying to get me to go along with you to that island wedding?"

"You need a break, and I need a date," he insisted while grinning. "Come on, honey. You need to get away for a while and clear your head. A cruise and some time at an exclusive island will do just that."

Pinto stared at her father a long moment then reluctantly sighed. "Maybe you're right," she announced while straightening. "I can sort things out while traveling in the lap of luxury. Sun, sand, and solitude may be just what I need."

Sal clapped his hands together enthusiastically. "Fantastic! I'll send 'G' a text and let him know you'll be attending as my plus one."

"So when does this cruise leave?" she asked.

"Monday morning. If we leave right after your last set tonight, we'll have just enough time to stop off at the house in Chicago. We can leave Sunday morning, spend the day in Florida, and catch the ship first thing Monday morning," he informed her.

She stared at him with surprise. "I won't have time to pack."

He waved her off. "I'll slip off to your apartment and pack a few things for you. Anything else you need, we'll buy along the way."

Pinto pondered his suggestion a moment then offered a pleasant smile. "You know, that's a wonderful idea. Did you bring your key to my apartment?"

He dangled the key and smiled. "I'll head to your apartment right after your first set and be back before your last set."

She sank into thought and appeared to drift out. Sal studied her with concern.

"Something wrong, honey?"

"Should I tell Beck?"

Sal leaned back in his seat and studied her a moment. He smirked and shook his head. "No, you shouldn't tell Beck," he informed her. "He needs a little jolt of reality in order to get his priorities straight. I'll leave a message with the staff at the house, and if he calls, they can tell him where you went."

"Sounds almost cruel."

"No, you're making your point," he insisted. "Trust me, honey. I know men like Beck. He'll appreciate what he has if he's afraid he's lost it."

"Fine," she replied with a sigh. "We'll do it your way. I have to change for my first set."

Sal stood while grinning. "And I'll have just enough time to stop by that little deli and grab something to eat. I'll be back before you're on."

As Sal turned, Bogart disappeared out the lounge doorway. Bogart hurried along the sidewalk and darted into a nearby alley. He removed his cell phone and pressed a button then waited for an answer.

"Do you have eyes on Will?" Beck asked over the phone.

Bogart shifted uncomfortably while casting looks to the alleyway entrance. "No sign of him, but you'll never believe who's here."

"Who?" Beck asked.

"Sal Romano," Bogart informed him. "I guess he decided to visit your girl. Should I abort?"

"No," Beck announced firmly into the phone. "Wait until Pinto's on stage and get eyes on Will. He'll be there I guarantee it. Just make sure he stays there long enough for Zack to search his apartment."

"What if Sal sees me?"

"You're not doing anything wrong," Beck replied over the phone. "Say hello. Have a drink with the guy. Just make sure Will doesn't leave during Pinto's set."

✝

It was nearly eight o'clock when Bogart entered the crowded, dimly lit lounge. He scanned the room several times then changed location and searched again. He found a dark area along the back wall and removed his cell phone. He pressed a single button and waited for an answer.

"He's not here," Bogart announced into the phone. "The little rat didn't show up."

"That's impossible," Beck exploded. "He's there every night lurking in the corner. Look again."

"Unless he's in her dressing room, he ain't here," Bogart snarled into the phone. "Want me to warn Zack?"

"Yeah, you'd better call him," Beck replied, sounding defeated.

Bogart disconnected his call and pressed another number. He heard a phone chirp alongside him. Zack removed his phone from his pocket and placed it to his ear while looking at Bogart.

"Yeah?"

Bogart glared at him, frowned, and disconnected the phone. "I thought you were checking out the weasel's apartment?"

"I already did," Zack informed him while replacing his phone to one of many pockets. "Looks like he split town." He handed him a wedding invitation. "I found this with next Saturday's date on it. Looks like our boy rushed to make reservations on a cruise ship for Monday, so he's probably already on a flight to Florida."

"So he's not even in town," Bogart announced then grinned. "That's perfect. Did you search the rest of his apartment?"

Zack glared his disapproval. "Of course I did. That *was* the point."

"And?"

"And Beck's not going to like what I found."

"What did you find?"

"Nude pictures of his girlfriend," Zack remarked. "They look like they were taken without her knowledge. I'm guessing they were from a spy cam."

47

"Really?" Bogart gasped then turned serious. "Let's see them."

Zack glared at Bogart then revealed the flash drive. "For Beck's eyes only." He returned the flash drive to his pocket. "We'd better return to the lodge and report this to Beck."

Chapter Ten

The ten-passenger Grand Caravan, single engine prop plane set down at the private airfield early Sunday morning just outside Chicago. Five of the guys from Whiskey Tango Foxtrot disembarked the plane as it shut down. Beck was already on his cell phone then disconnected it with disgust.

"I still can't reach Sal or Pinto on their cell phones," Beck announced with concern. "My calls keep going to voicemail."

"I hope you didn't leave any irate messages," Bogart casually commented. "That won't get you any return calls."

"No, I took your advice," he replied with defeat then muttered, "If you can believe that."

Monroe disconnected his cell phone. "Still no answer at Sal's house either. It's strange that the answering machine isn't picking up," he announced. "I know it's early, but you'd think the staff would be up by now."

Jackie, Gil, and Darth were the last to step off the plane only moments after the guys. Gil enjoyed piloting larger private planes, so Jackie played co-pilot this time. They joined the others.

"So what's the big plan?" Jackie asked Beck while raising her brow. "Are we going to storm Sal's house?"

"Been there; done that," Zack muttered.

"I know searching the jerk-off's apartment was my idea," Jackie informed him, "but you do realize you have no proof Will took those pictures. She's liable to hand you your balls."

Zack eyed Jackie and grinned. She caught his look and rolled her eyes. She knew Zack enjoyed it when she talked like 'one of the boys', and she'd been trying hard to break that habit, particularly around him. Zack only had four moods. Sleepy, hungry, horny, and kill everything in sight.

"I don't have a plan," Beck replied. "I just need to get her back for now. I need to keep her as far from Will as possible. Once I know she's safe, the rest of you can get the proof we need on her stalker."

"Well you're certainly not going to Sal's house alone," Monroe announced. "You'll say or do something stupid. One of us needs to go along to make sure you mind your manners."

"That rules out Zack and me," Kirk muttered.

"Jackie and I will go with you," Monroe replied.

Beck then frowned. "Bogart should come along too," he remarked. "For some odd reason, Sal likes him."

"That's because I'm charming," Bogart announced while grinning, pleased with the compliment.

"Just shut up and get in the car," Beck snarled.

✝

Sal Romano's country mansion was nestled on a large parcel of land beyond tall, stone walls. The professionally landscaped estate didn't have a hedge out of place. Weeping willow trees and faux split rail fencing lined the long driveway. The driveway split off to circle a large fountain outside the front door, while the remaining driveway branched off to the left. The driveway led to the kitchen, staff wing, and eventually to the massive, detached, eight-car garage. Jackie approached the front door with Beck, who seemed unusually nervous.

"What if I can't get her to take me back?" he asked almost timidly.

"She loves you, Beck," Jackie insisted. "She's not dumping you forever just for hitting her guy friend. You guys fight with Holden almost every time you see him."

"That's different," Beck remarked while nervously straightening his jacket. "He's one of us. It's expected."

"It's a wonder she dated you at all," Jackie muttered.

He glared at her. "What was that?"

"Nothing," she replied and rang the bell.

"I wasn't ready."

"You're ready," she snarled without looking at him. "Stop primping like a girl."

They heard heavily thumping feet within the mansion as if someone were running. They exchanged looks. The door quickly opened to reveal Rosa, a plump, older maid. She stared at them with surprise then relief.

"Oh, Mr. Larue," she gasped. "Am I glad to see you!" The short, plump maid ushered them inside.

"What's wrong?" Beck asked with concern.

She shut the door behind them, leaned against it, and held her chest. "After Mr. and Miss Romano left this morning, someone must have broken into the house. Both their bedrooms were trashed, and I know some things have been stolen."

"Just the bedrooms?" he asked with confusion. "Not the study?"

"No, not the study."

"So they weren't interested in the safe?" Beck asked then sank into thought.

"No," she replied. "The police filled out a report and left. They didn't even check the estate for intruders. I was so scared. What if they're still here?"

"I doubt it," Beck replied while removing his cell phone, "but we'll take a look around for you." He held the phone to his ear. "Monroe, call the guys. Tell them to get here right away. You and Bogart need to search the grounds for trespassers." He disconnected the call and looked at Rosa. "You said Sal and Pinto left this morning? Where did they go?"

"On a cruise ship to Costa Rico, but they were getting off in Columbia to go to a wedding on some island."

Beck's eyes widened. He looked at Jackie. "Cruise? Didn't Zack say Will booked a cruise?"

Jackie stared back at him with the same concern. "That can't be a coincidence."

He looked back at Rosa. "Everything will be okay, Rosa," Beck informed her. "The guys will search the mansion and the grounds. Did you call Sal?"

"I tried, but he's not answering," she replied while wringing her fingers together. "I left a message, but he didn't call back. He may still be in the air."

"I don't know what you're thinking," Jackie announced, "but tread lightly, Beck. We don't know anything yet."

"I know," he muttered then looked at her. "Find Monroe. We're going to need to do a little undercover work on that cruise ship, and I need him to do his magic."

Jackie nodded and hurried from the house.

Beck looked back at Rosa, who seemed to be settling down now that she knew the guys were there. "I need to use Sal's computer then speak to the security guards and have a look at the security footage."

"Yes, of course."

✝

Within the windowless security office, Beck stood over the security guard's shoulder and watched the security camera playback on one of many screens. The footage revealed nothing of particular interest and certainly nothing to indicate anyone had been casing the place.

"Shortly after Sal left, the cameras went haywire," the guard announced while keeping his attention on the monitors. The images on every monitor turned to static as if on cue. "The system's been a little glitchy this past week but nothing like this. After the interruption, we walked the grounds but found nothing out of the ordinary. The doors seemed secure. Thirty minutes later, Rosa's screaming about a break-in."

"Whoever did this knew what they were doing," Beck informed him. "How many guards on the grounds?"

"Just the two of us."

"Two?"

"After that incident with Sal's trusted men, he decided to rely more on automation and less on human intervention," the guard informed him then gave a knowing look.

"I can't say I blame him," Beck muttered, recalling the recent events.

The security office door opened with added vigor as Monroe entered in a slight rush. Beck straightened and eagerly awaited his response.

"Othello will have everything waiting for us at the private airfield in Florida," Monroe announced although he seemed unusually uncomfortable. "Are you sure you want to do this? We don't know that any of this has anything to do with Pinto's stalker. If she finds out you're following her, she may never forgive you."

"Only if I'm wrong," Beck replied. "If either Pinto or Sal is in trouble, we need to intervene."

"Maybe we should call Ross--"

"No," Beck practically cried out then ran his fingers through his hair, held his breath, and attempted to relax. "We're not bothering Ross on his romantic vacation with Lee. We can handle this."

"If there's even anything to handle," Monroe remarked slightly under his breath.

"I'll take full responsibility."

Chapter Eleven

The cruise ship, *Andrea Maria*, sailed along the calm, peaceful waters of the Caribbean Sea on her voyage that Monday morning from the United States to Costa Rica. Although small in comparison to other luxury cruise ships, the power yacht was a well-appointed, ten-ton ship with six decks and every amenity offered by ships twice her size. Her capacity was a mere two hundred passengers with a crew of approximately one hundred and twenty-five. She wasn't a newer vessel, but she had her charm.

Jackie entered her luxury cabin with her rolling bag behind her. She looked around and nodded her approval. The studio-style cabin had its own balcony, a king-sized bed, small wet bar, and open living area. She couldn't help but wonder who was paying for all the little extras on this trip. She filled her bag with some of her personal items from home usually kept in her emergency flight bag, but most of the items she purchased yesterday in a mad rush to prepare for their unexpected voyage. Even the rolling bag was new, considering her flight bag didn't fit the part. She removed her cell phone while stepping out onto the balcony and called Holden. He answered almost immediately.

"Hey, I'm just settling into my room now," she announced. "Someone sprang for the platinum package."

"It's nice, huh?" Holden remarked. "Are you sure I shouldn't have come along?"

"Honestly, Beck's off his rocker," Jackie replied. "We have an asshole stalker and a random house break-in. I don't even know why *I'm* here."

"A buffer to keep Pinto from killing Beck when she finds out *he's* stalking her," Holden teased. "So what's the plan?"

"I don't have a clue," she replied with a sigh. "Frick and Frack are working out our cover stories now."

"Remind me," Holden announced. "Which ones are Frick and Frack?"

"Beck and Monroe."

"Ah, yes, the masterminds," Holden teased with sarcasm in his tone.

There was a knock on her room door, alerting her. "Oh, gotta go."

By the time she turned and entered the room, the door opened to reveal Monroe with his bag. She eyed his bag then gave him a slightly puzzled look.

"Should I ask?"

"It's our cover," Monroe announced. "We're Mr. and Mrs. Arlington."

Horror crossed her face. "You made us married?"

He released his bag, glared at her, and leaned against the wall. "No, Beck made us married."

"So he wants to save his relationship by killing mine?" she demanded.

"Relax," Monroe muttered and flopped onto the sofa. "I already know where I'll be sleeping."

"Let's just get on with the assignment," Jackie announced with a groan. "Where are the others?"

"Gil and Zack are employees, which will give them access to 'off-limit' areas," he announced. "Kirk's above us on the Pacific Deck, Bogart is below us on the Caribbean Deck, and Beck is on the upper Riviera Deck."

"And Pinto and Sal?"

"They're also on the Riviera Deck in some lavish suite," Monroe replied.

"And how do we avoid Sal and Pinto?"

Monroe smiled and flashed a laminated card. "They made an itinerary with the cruise director," he announced while grinning. "We'll know where they're going to be just about every hour."

Jackie eyed him with skepticism. "That's awfully convenient, don't you think?"

"You'd think, but it turns out a few dozen wedding guests are booked on this cruise," Monroe remarked. "Apparently, Sal's friend is richer than rich. They have special events for the wedding guests, and they were able to pick which events they wanted to attend while onboard. Fortunately, Sal is quite the social butterfly. His dance card is pretty full."

"So where are they now?"

He glanced at the itinerary. "They're at a cocktail party in a private room on the Riviera Deck. That puts them in Beck's court, so he'll keep an eye on things from there."

"I'd like to get my bearings straight," Jackie announced. "I'd like to explore the ship."

"I'll join you," he announced and sprang up from the sofa while grinning, "Mrs. Arlington."

She groaned softly and headed for the door. "Holden's going to kill both you and Beck."

✝

O n the outskirts of Denver, Colorado, in the early morning hour, Holden returned his cell phone to his inner jacket pocket and received a look from another neatly dressed man leaning against the nearby building. Holden eyed the cable and internet van parked alongside the curb a few feet away then seemed to realize the man by the building was still staring at him. He groaned softly and looked at the man.

"I know what you're thinking, Parker," Holden remarked. "You don't need to say it."

"I'm not saying anything," Parker announced while grinning. "None of my business that your super-hot, spy wife is conquering the world while you're on the streets of Denver chasing after the dregs of society."

"First off," Holden announced, "she's not a spy." He then frowned. "And she's not conquering the world; she's passing love notes on the playground to Beck's girlfriend. This is one time she absolutely doesn't need my protection."

"Let's see," Parker announced while grinning. "She can kick the entire department's collective ass without breaking a sweat." He held back his laugh. "I think it's safe to say the only protection she needs from you is the kind that keeps your swimmers away from her fertile feminine parts."

"That's so romantic, Parker," Holden announced while raising his brows. "Honestly, you should write greeting cards." He then indicated the van. "Can we get this show on the road?"

"Yeah, anything you say," Parker replied with a chuckle.

They approached the van, looked around, and then climbed inside. Holden and Parker entered the back of the van where six men in FBI swat gear sat and waited.

"So how reliable is this tip?" Holden asked the lead man in combat gear.

"Well, his phone number is registered to an apartment across the street, and we're pretty sure he's a guy," the man replied. "Other than that, he's your typical anonymous caller."

"Cute," Holden muttered. "Everyone's a comedian today."

"There was a lot of activity coming and going throughout the night," the man in charge continued. "Our eyes in the building across from the warehouse reported two known arms dealers went into the building early this morning, and they're still there."

"If it's good enough for the judge," Holden announced, "that's good enough for me."

Holden and Parker slipped into their official vests and helped themselves to automatic rifles.

"We're looking at no more than six heavily armed men," the man continued. "Apart from our arms dealers, the identities of the others are unknown."

"We'll ID them after we arrest them," Holden announced with a sigh. "Let's knock on the front door. Tell the second team to move in through the rear."

All eight filed swiftly from the van and headed for the warehouse across the street. The first two men carried a battering ram. The man in charge gave the signal, and they plowed the door inward with one strike. The eight men filed into the warehouse. Two man teams hurried through the corridor checking vacant areas within the office before heading into the abandoned warehouse. They entered the large holding area and met with their two men, who had entered from the back. Dozens of crates filled the warehouse, which was supposed to be empty.

"Boys, I think we've hit the jackpot," Holden announced. "Two man teams. Proceed with caution."

They swept through the warehouse, carefully passing stacks of crates while keeping an eye out for the six perpetrators. Several men dressed in black suddenly dropped on cables from the ceiling while firing at the FBI swat team. Despite their protective vests, two men went down from headshots. Holden fired back at the men dropping to the floor behind crates surrounding them.

"It's a trap," Holden announced through his ear transmitter. "Fall back!"

Although there were only six men, they came at the ten-man swat team from behind, trapping them in the center of the warehouse. They exchanged automatic weapon fire in catastrophic shootout. Holden fired back while watching his men drop one-by-one. Two shots struck him dead center in the chest, dropping him despite his bulletproof vest. Another shot found his leg. Holden pulled himself along the floor and behind a crate. He sat against the crate and fired back, but most of his team was already down. Parker stood from behind the safety of his crate and unloaded several rounds into a man nearly on top of Holden from behind. Holden took another shot to his vest and one to his shoulder beyond the vest. The force of the shot threw him against the crate, where he struck his head.

The room was spinning as shots were echoing from every corner of the building. Holden attempted to raise his weapon but could do little more than watch Parker take several shots to his body and ultimately one to his head. Holden saw the masked man across the warehouse standing near his fallen friend. He raised his weapon at Holden and squeezed the trigger. A shot rang out.

Chapter Twelve

The elegant lounge on the Caribbean Deck was cozy and intimate with a piano, small bar, pool table, and a few sofas and chairs. A bored young bartender, Grant Peters, prepared a couple of drinks. Grant was a classically handsome man in his late twenties, who seemed more interested in his hair than his job. Jackie and Monroe entered the lounge and looked around. Since it was early afternoon, the lounge was practically dead. They approached the bar and immediately received Grant's full attention. He smiled charmingly and gazed over Jackie a moment longer than he should have.

"What can I get you?" Grant announced cheerfully.

Monroe gave him a disapproving stare after seeing the way he looked at Jackie, his pretend wife. "I'll have a glass of bourbon and a seven and seven for my *wife*."

Grant seemed to take the hint and prepared their drinks. Despite the new knowledge, he still checked out Jackie. Monroe nudged her and headed across the lounge to one of the cozy sitting areas. Both sat with their backs to the wall and watched the doorway, as if on a stakeout.

"Is Beck crazy?" Jackie finally asked. "Are we doing this for nothing?"

"Beck's crazy in love," Monroe muttered then sighed. "I've been there once."

"I swear," she remarked firmly while glaring at him with limited patience. "If you finish that sentence with 'but she was my commander's daughter', I'll throw you overboard."

Monroe frowned and looked away. "Someone's sensitive today." As he looked toward the lounge doorway, something caught his attention and he suddenly laughed, although attempting to contain it. "Oh, this should be fun."

Jackie looked in the direction he stared. Zack stood in the doorway wearing his neatly pressed white uniform with shoulder embalms indicating he was a porter. The look on his face was somewhere between psychotic and deranged. He saw them and headed across the lounge.

"Someone is going to die," Zack snarled while subconsciously tugging on his uniform. "I feel like a sissy teenage Navy boy minus the raging hormones."

Monroe held back his laugh. "I can't remember the last time I saw you in clothes with so many pressed creases."

"And you'll be the first to go down," Zack growled through gritted teeth.

"I think you look very handsome," Jackie announced although she had a tough time not laughing.

He glared at her. "You're next, princess." Zack snatched Monroe's glass and drank the entire contents, surprising him. He set the glass down with added vigor. "Who the hell starches brief underwear? I'll be scratching my ass all night."

They watched Zack turn and walk away. Monroe groaned softly and shook his head. "Well, we're all going to die in our sleep tonight."

$$†$$

Gil patrolled the Pacific Deck in his crisp, white security officer uniform and neatly polished badge upon his chest. Darth proudly walked alongside him wearing his official security vest. Gil looked at home and even smiled at passing couples.

"Gil," came Beck's commanding voice through his ear transmitter.

Gil secretly touched his hidden ear transmitter. "Yeah, Beck," he announced softly so no one would hear his conversation seemingly with himself while passing. "How's stalking your girlfriend going?"

"Very funny," Beck snapped, clearly agitated. "Pinto and Sal left the private party. I'm going to keep an eye on them. Might be a good time for you to check out the other wedding guests traveling onboard."

"As you wish, Beck," Gil replied while casually looking around. "I'd just like to remind you that this isn't going to end well if you're wrong about her stalker."

"Yeah, thanks," Beck snarled. "I've gotten enough lecturing from mother hen."

"You should listen to mother hen more often," Gil casually announced then smiled and nodded to a passing couple. His serious look immediately returned. "She knows a thing or two about relationships."

"I'll keep that in mind," Beck snarled through Gil's ear transmitter. "The same way you listen to her in regards to your on-again-off-again relationship with the future ex-Mrs. Rafferty. Incidentally, how's that working out for you?"

"Someone's a little snarky today," Gil muttered. "You weren't nearly as snarky before you became a stalker."

"Beck out."

✝

The private party in the lounge on the Riviera Deck was elegant and decorated with all the glitz and glamor of a Hollywood party. Gil and Darth entered the room and remained practically invisible along the back walls. Although Darth received a few snotty looks for entering their fancy, high-society party, others were eager to comment on the handsome dog. Some of the attractive younger women were quick to comment on the handsome security guard as well. There was no denying Gil rocked his excessively pressed uniform. He wore it well, particularly around the buttocks region, and the women noticed. Two fairly large men dressed in expensive suits approached Gil. It wasn't difficult to make the men as personal bodyguards to one of the guests. They weren't Sal's men since Gil had met what was left of Sal's personal guards on a past mission. If recall was correct, he'd beaten a few of Sal's remaining personal guards. Whether they would have a sense of humor about it remained to be seen.

The two burly men, attempting to blend in with the guests, paused before Gil. Darth snarled softly at them. Gil gave a gentle tug on the leash to remind Darth they had to play nice. Neither man seemed to have a personality, although it sometimes seemed Gil didn't either. He could maintain a frozen expression for hours. He eyed the two guards and showed little reaction to their size. Sealy was attractive by most standards and had a full, thick head of dark hair. Allen, on the other hand, wore his light hair in a buzz cut, giving a certain military look, although Gil was certain he'd never been in the military. Allen's features were harsh and almost Neanderthal in nature, which gave him a slightly intimidating look. He resembled a less cuddly version of Kirk.

"We appreciate your service," Allen gruffly announced, "but we have security at this party under control."

"Just doing my job," Gil announced without a hint of emotion in his voice. "I'll make my rounds and then leave you to your party."

"I don't think you're paying attention," Allen snarled.

Another man approached, although judging by his expensive clothes, he was more the man in charge type. Nelson Banks was a wealthy man in his early fifties, indicated by his outward appearance and professional hair transplant. He wore a suit that almost made Sal look poor in comparison. Far from a handsome man, Nelson's only redeeming quality was his firm, stocky body mass resembling a tank. Ironically, it wasn't his physical appearance most people feared about the intimidating man.

"Everything okay?" Nelson asked.

"Ship's security wants to case the party," Sealy informed his boss.

"So let him," Nelson replied then smiled at Gil. "I'm happy he's doing his job." He then shooed his men away. Both men left on command. "You have to forgive my men. They forget this is a pleasure cruise and not a war zone."

"I have a similar friend," Gil replied.

An attractive, much younger woman approached. Nelson's wife, Emily Banks befitted the term 'blonde bombshell' with curves barely contained in her moderately revealing dress. Despite only being in her mid-thirties, she was already past her prime for someone like Nelson Banks. His lack of attention toward his large bosomed wife was apparent in the way she ogled other men, particularly men younger than her husband.

Emily Banks gave Gil a lustful once over. "Aren't you going to introduce me, dear?"

"Honey, this is one of the ship's security guards," he announced then looked at Gil for further information.

"Gil, ma'am," he announced politely and offered one of his few pleasant smiles.

She kept her eyes on him and again swept her gaze over his body. "It's a pleasure to meet you, Gil." Emily looked back at her husband. "Nelson, dear, would it be okay if Gil escorted me back to our suite." She indicated her expensive jewelry. "I'd feel safer with him and his dog by my side."

"If Gil doesn't mind."

Gil hesitated with some awkwardness then managed a smile. "It'd be my pleasure, ma'am," he replied and politely extended his hand toward the door.

Despite his attempt at mere politeness, Emily captured his arm, linking onto him, and walked with him from the lounge. As she clung to his arm, she pressed her bosom against it. Gil raised a brow and eyed the woman clinging to him.

✝

Emily remained linked onto Gil's arm as they leisurely walked along the deck. Gil had attempted to increase their pace, but Emily constantly held him back, turning his escort service into a romantic stroll. She seemed a little too at home linked onto his arm while enjoying the evening air.

"Wouldn't your suite be on this deck near the lounge?" Gil finally asked.

"Yes, but I thought I'd enjoy the evening ambiance and take the scenic route," she replied then eyed him while grinning slyly. "Are you married, Gil?"

"I'm divorced," he replied then seemed to think better of it. "My wife and I are trying to work things out."

"So you're technically a free agent," she almost cooed while studying him, her breasts firmly pressing against his arm.

Gil glanced at her and the look on her face. He fidgeted slightly from her breasts pressed against him, reading her intentions loud and clear.

"I wouldn't say that," he replied.

His words disappointed her, but she didn't appear ready to give up on the handsome man just yet. They finally entered the nearby corridor and approached her suite. She reluctantly released him and removed her card key. Emily unlocked the door, opened it partway, and leaned seductively against it.

"Want to join me for a drink?"

Gil managed a smile. "Thanks, but I'm on duty," he announced and gave a tiny salute with his index finger to his brow. "Have a pleasant evening, ma'am."

As Gil turned and walked away with Darth by his side, Emily watched him leave with disappointment then studied his backside and smiled slyly.

Chapter Thirteen

The small village outside Rio de Janeiro, Brazil was one of the less traveled tourist spots. Charming shops lined the streets with vibrantly colored flowers, clothing, and foods from different cultures. Friendly locals exchanged pleasantries with a few dozen tourists passing through. Ross placed a white fedora hat on his head, tilting the brim for a menacing look. He glanced across the hat table to a dark-haired beauty nearly half his age. Leeann Whitley dressed the part of a world traveler, but she had more of a country girl appeal. Lee's gaze fell upon Ross with the making of a schoolgirl in love. She eyed him across the table, grinned her approval of the hat, then flashed a thong bikini bottom and suggestively raised her brows.

Ross groaned softly then turned to the shopkeeper. They haggled in Portuguese over the price of the hat. One might assume Ross just enjoyed arguing with people in different languages. Lee seemed to enjoy it as well. Ross indicated Lee while handing the man some local currency. The man eyed the beautiful woman then grinned at Ross. He said something that sparked a fire in Ross. Another round of arguing ensued. In the end, both men laughed. Ross motioned to his girlfriend.

"It's yours," he announced.

She approached him with her new purchase and stuffed it into her bag. "What was all the arguing about?" she asked.

"He offered to let you have it for free if you modeled it for him," Ross remarked casually. "I politely told him I'd gouge his eyes out with a spoon."

"Hmm, that's pleasant," she cooed while affectionately clinging to his arm.

"Yes," he replied. "Although I did change the body part and the method in which I'd remove it for your comfort."

Lee groaned softly and rolled her eyes. "You're terrible."

"Here I thought I was initiating foreplay," he announced with a teasing grin.

She playfully smacked his arm then hugged it. "It's like I'm seeing another side of you," Lee informed him. "Maybe a small peek into that former Navy SEAL life."

Ross suddenly laughed and patted her hand on his arm. "Oh, my darling, if no one's suffered a throat punch; you're seeing nothing from my SEAL past."

They casually walked through the market attempting to decide what to have for dinner. Ross glanced at several items on stands they passed while Lee talked endlessly about their romantic beachfront accommodations. Ross no longer seemed to be paying attention to her as his muscles tensed against her hand. Lee eyed him with a curious look.

"Ross? Are you listening to me?"

"No," he replied gently and lowered the brim of his hat. "Would you allow me one small moment of paranoia?"

Her expression dropped as she stared at him.

"Don't look at me and keep smiling," he ordered softly through slightly gritted teeth that almost formed a smile.

Lee looked at the stands and the food that suddenly didn't seem appealing. "What's wrong?" she asked while attempting to keep up a jovial appearance.

"We're being followed," he remarked. "If we keep heading straight for three blocks, there will be taxis. I want you to keep walking and get in the first taxi you see. I'll meet you back at the hotel."

"What are you going to do?" she nervously asked, no longer able to maintain her false smile.

"I'm just going to talk to the men following us," he replied simply.

"I'm not leaving you, Ross."

"We're not debating this," he growled softly. "Three blocks. First taxi you see. You don't look back, and you don't stop no matter what."

"Ross--"

"I'm serious, Lee."

Lee slowly released his arm and looked along the aisle in front of them. She nervously touched his arm. "Ross--?"

Two men approached them from the opposite direction, cutting off Lee's path to the taxis. Neither man bothered hiding that they were staring directly at them. They must have known they had Ross trapped.

"Change of plan," Ross announced gently while stopping her in the middle of the mildly busy market area. "To your right. Through that door. Don't stop. Just run." There was a strange pause. "Now!"

Lee turned to her right and ran for the door between the outdoor shops. Ross bolted after her. As the men pursued him, he toppled a stand in their path, stalling them. He ran into the building after Lee. The men scrambled over the scattered market items and ran after them while removing their automatic weapons. The men ran through the kitchen and looked around. Any cooks in the kitchen were already gone. The first two men walked cautiously with their weapons aimed.

The first man suddenly fell to the floor. Ross slid out from under the counter and jumped on top of him. He grabbed him around the neck and flipped their position. The second man fired at Ross, riddling his own man with a spray of bullets. As he shot his own man, Ross remained behind his human shield, raised the man's weapon and returned fire. The man took several shots and flew to the floor. Ross jumped to his feet with the assault rifle in his hand and ran after Lee. As he ran through the kitchen, the men who had been following him now entered and pursued him. Ross fired at the men and dove into the doorway as they fired back.

"Lee," he cried out while facing the kitchen then glanced back to check her position.

Lee was already on her knees with a heavily armed man standing behind her. He held a gun to her head. She stared at Ross with fear in her eyes. A second man appeared behind the man holding Lee hostage and fired at Ross. Ross dove to the floor, avoiding the barrage of bullets. He rolled into a sitting position and fired back. The man removed the gun from Lee's head and shot at him as well. Ross fired upon both men, tearing into them with multiple shots each. Before they had a chance to go down, their rifles fired through the opening in the doorway. Ross's expression dropped as he looked back and saw the propane tanks just on the other side of the door. He leaped for Lee and took her to the floor. There was a familiar pop followed by a hiss.

Ross looked into Lee's frightened eyes. "I'm sorry," he whispered.

Outside the building, there was a tremendous explosion that rocked the entire marketplace. Vendors and tourists screamed and ran from the area without looking back. The old, fragile looking building collapsed in a cloud of dust and debris that quickly swept through the market.

Chapter Fourteen

The following evening, the room service cart squeaked as it rolled along the carpeted corridor of the Pacific Deck. Zack, in his neatly pressed, over-starched, brilliant white uniform, pushed the cart with little enthusiasm. His hand twitched with every squeak of the wobbling front wheel. There was little doubt if he'd been carrying a weapon, he'd have shot the cart by now. He glared at the stateroom number before him, stopped in front of the door, and cursed under his breath before knocking.

"Room service," he announced without emotion.

The door opened only a moment later to reveal a man in his plush, cruise line bathrobe. He held the door open and gave Zack a stern look.

"Well, it's about time," the man grumbled.

Zack somehow managed to ignore the man's attitude and pushed the cart into the room. He pulled up the cart leafs to create a table.

"Not here," the man snarled demandingly and pointed. "In front of the balcony."

Zack moved the rolling cart closer to the balcony without comment, despite the grumbling of the man in the robe. He turned toward the passenger and managed his best Hannibal Lecter smile.

"Will there be anything else, sir?" Zack asked beyond the grin that suggested he might gut the man.

"Think you can manage to light the candles and open the champagne?" the man demanded with limited patience, not even noticing the way Zack was staring at him.

The shower within the bathroom turned off, indicating the passenger had company. More than likely, his company was the opposite sex. Zack eyed the man while listening to someone move around within the bathroom.

"Shall I dim the lights?" Zack asked, almost sounding professional.

"Yeah, sure," the man grumbled and waved him off. "Just make it quick. I want you gone before she comes out of the bathroom." He then muttered under his breath. "This isn't a peep show."

Zack snatched the bottle of champagne as if prepared to strangle it. He eyed the label and made a slight face at the cheapness of the bottle. He swiftly removed the foil paper as if he'd opened hundreds of bottles before and wiggled the cork while aiming it in an odd direction. The man in the robe took a step back and watched him with uncertainty. The cork popped from the bottle, shot across the room, and struck the dimming switch. The room became considerably darker. He returned the bottle to the ice bucket while simultaneously removing the lighter from his pocket. A foot long flame shot out from the lighter and lit both candles horizontally. Zack turned toward the man, grinned, and clicked his heels together while bowing slightly.

"Have a pleasant evening, *sir*," he scoffed and headed for the door.

†

*Z*ack walked along the service corridor heading toward the kitchen via the back way to avoid disturbing the ship's passengers. He maintained his usual, expressionless gaze, but it was obvious he was unhappy with his assignment. Angry voices came from one of the kitchen linen closets. Zack paused near the door and listened a moment.

"We continue as planned," one man announced in what sounded like a loud whisper.

"What about *him*?" another male voice demanded.

"Get rid of him," the first man snarled.

There was a loud, abrupt grunt. Zack opened the door, attempting to maintain a casual stance, but he was actually in attack position. He'd perfected casual combat stances after years of practice. Two men in crewmen's uniforms stood over a third crewman, who was sprawled unnaturally across the floor. The position of his head indicated his neck had been broken; one of Zack's many areas of expertise. Both men lunged for Zack, expecting him to run, but he was already snap kicking the first man under the chin. He then threw himself into a roll across the floor to avoid the flying fist of the second man. Zack sprang up just behind the man in the tight quarters. As the man turned, Zack thrust his knee twice into his ribs then grabbed him by the head and dropped him to the floor alongside the man they'd just killed. The first man recovered and removed a switchblade knife, swiftly opening it with some level of skill. He lunged for Zack, prepared to slash him with the razor-sharp blade. Zack blocked his hand with the knife then swiftly grabbed the wrist and twisted his arm backward. The second man attempted to subdue Zack while he was busy with his accomplice.

Zack whirled the first man around and forced his wrist upward, causing the second man to impale himself on the switchblade in his friend's hand. He gasped as the blade pierced his abdomen and clutched his bleeding midsection, his once white uniform quickly saturating with bright red blood. Zack released the first man's wrist, grabbed him by the head, and swiftly broke his neck. He allowed the man to fall to the floor alongside his accomplice and the dead crewman. Zack stared at the three dead men and cursed softly. It was true. Dead men tell no tales. There would be no way of knowing why the two men killed the other crewman, if they actually were crewmen, and what deed they would continue as planned.

"Nice going, Zack," he muttered under his breath.

He removed his cell phone and realized he had no signal so close to the kitchen. He frowned and left the linen closet. Zack headed for the first stairwell he found and ran up the steps with his cell phone in his hand, watching and waiting for the first sign of a signal.

†

Jackie and Monroe hurried along the staff corridor attempting to keep up with Zack as he headed toward the linen closet not far from the kitchen.

"You can't keep doing this, Zack," Monroe scolded while only a few steps behind him. "There's no need to kill everyone you meet."

"Shit happens, Monroe," Zack muttered.

He opened the linen closet door and looked inside. To Zack's surprise, there was no one within the closet. All three

71

crewmen were gone without a trace of blood or a scuffle. Jackie and Monroe stared into the empty linen closet then exchanged strange glances. Zack turned toward them and pointed a warning finger.

"I'm not hallucinating," Zack growled with conviction. "Two crewmen killed another crewman. They were plotting something. We need to find out what it was."

"Are you taking your pills?" Monroe asked while raising his brows.

"I just told you," Zack lashed out. "I'm not hallucinating!" He then searched his white cuffs. There was a tiny spot of red on the right cuff. "There! That's blood!"

Both looked at the small red stain. Jackie fidgeted and finally turned away. Zack's expression shattered while watching her reaction.

"You don't believe me," Zack gasped with horror. "Jackie, you know I'm not making this up."

Jackie turned to face him and offered a timid smile. "I know you're not making it up," she announced gently. "I'm just not sure you really saw what you think you saw."

Zack groaned and shook his head. "I expected that much from him," he announced while indicating Monroe, "but you're my partner. You're supposed to have my back."

Without another word, he stormed past them and headed for the stairs. Monroe groaned softly while running his fingers through his hair then eyed Jackie.

"You're his partner?" Monroe finally asked.

Jackie smiled weakly and shrugged. "It certainly never came up before," she remarked then threw her hands down with frustration. "I'm worried about him, Monroe. What if he stopped taking his meds?"

"If he's hallucinating again," Monroe remarked, "he's pretty much a ticking time bomb."

She fidgeted a moment then stared into Monroe's eyes. "We need to get him off this ship," she announced. "At our first port of call, one of us needs to take him back home."

"I hope you don't think that's going to be you," Monroe announced.

"I'm the logical choice," she replied. "I can handle him and he'd never hurt me."

Monroe laughed almost nervously. "Jackie, if Zack ever goes off the deep end, none of us are safe. Don't let his psychosexual fantasies about you cloud your judgement. If anything, you're more vulnerable."

She glared at him and folded her arms across her chest. "Oh, really? Because I seem to recall endless hours of martial arts training with Zack, and I'm pretty sure I'm the only one who could take him down."

"Hand-to-hand, you're probably right," Monroe announced then eyed her sharply. "But you're also the only one who wouldn't put a bullet in him if it came down to it."

Jackie stared at him with a look of horror. "Why would you even say such a thing--?"

"Because, Jackie," Monroe softly lashed out. "Zack is Zack. The little guy in his brain who flips the switch between right and wrong isn't exactly reliable. He's been through a lot. He's *done* a lot. Dr. Sherman has suggested numerous times we retire Zack. He's concerned about his mental state."

"Why's that?" Jackie asked. "I know he's, well, different, but he seems like the same guy I knew when I was a little girl."

"Zack never uncorks his emotional bottle," Monroe informed her. "We've all let it out in either sorrow, anger, or a drunken stupor, but not Zack. He keeps it buried deep inside him. That's what the doc fears about his personality. You can't keep all that bottled inside. Eventually, it's going to explode."

"You know, ever since I was a little girl, I've heard my father and the rest of you tell me, 'don't worry about it' or 'I'll deal with it'," she informed Monroe. "Well, now it's my turn. You just leave Zack to me. I'll deal with it."

Jackie turned and headed down the corridor for the stairs. Monroe held his head and groaned softly.

Chapter Fifteen

The sun was setting on the ocean, lending a romantic backdrop for lovers taking a stroll along deck. Bogart and Kirk leaned on the railing staring into the ocean with uninspired frowns chiseled on their faces.

"I'd forgotten how much I hate being confined to a boat," Kirk muttered. "Why the hell would anyone choose a cruise as their vacation?"

"I'm thinking the company makes the difference," Bogart remarked. "Believe me; I'd rather be watching the sunset with a gorgeous woman than share it with you."

Kirk cast a sideways glare at Bogart, his lips curling into a strange sneer. "I'm working with a team of lonely hearts," he scoffed then looked back across the ocean. "There's no room in this outfit for sappy romantics. You're better off severing romantic relationships in this line of work."

Bogart turned sideways while leaning on the railing and stared at Kirk with disbelief. "You, amigos, are a tight ass."

A couple passed by and gave them a strange look. Bogart attempted a smile and gave them a slight wave. Once they passed, he gave them the middle finger then returned his attention to Kirk. His comment drew Kirk's undivided attention.

"Tight ass?" Kirk demanded while facing him and straightened to his full 6'4". "Who are you calling a tight ass?"

"You and your macho 'boys only club'," Bogart announced, refusing to back down. "There's nothing wrong with having someone to share your life. You're just afraid to open up your heart in fear of having it broken, because then, heaven forbid, you'll realize you have emotions."

"Do you ever shut up?" Kirk demanded.

"I'll tell you something," Bogart continued without missing a beat. "I've had my heart broken, stolen, stomped on, and put through a meat grinder, but I'll never let that stop me from searching for my soulmate."

"Oh, God," Kirk groaned and leaned on the railing. "Not the 'soulmate' bullshit."

Bogart stared at Kirk and frowned. "You were never close to your mother, were you?"

"Can I interrupt this Freudian moment?" Gil announced from behind them.

Both men turned and saw Gil with Darth only a few feet away.

"Yes, interrupt," Kirk announced. "Anything?"

"Dead end so far," Gil replied with a bored sigh. "I think Beck's off his rocker on this one. I think we should throw a hood over his head, duct tape his wrists, and take him on the next flight back to Colorado."

"I'll get the duct tape," Kirk announced and attempted to walk past Gil.

"Not so fast," Gil scoffed, stopping him.

Kirk frowned and leaned his back against the railing, obviously knowing it was too good to be true.

"We owe it to him to see this through until they disembark the ship at the next port," Gil remarked. "We'll survive another day."

Zack stormed past them. "Speak for yourself."

They watched him disappear around the corner then exchanged looks. All three shrugged and didn't give it a second thought.

"Darth and I are going to make our final round then our shift is over," Gil informed them. "A few of the party guests made their way to the lounge on the Caribbean Deck. Apart from scoping them out, I doubt there's anything more either of you can do tonight. Beck will keep tabs on Pinto's cabin throughout the night."

Gil and Darth left in the same direction Zack had gone. Bogart and Kirk glanced at each other.

"Buy you a drink?" Bogart offered.

"You're on."

t

The Caribbean Deck lounge was slightly crowded that evening, mostly with guests attending the same wedding as Sal and Pinto. Their private lounge on the upper deck was only reserved until eight o'clock, so that left some free time. Young people and loud music filled the nightclub bar. The main bar was crammed full with the rest of the ship's passengers who weren't into modern music, which just left the lightly traveled lounge on the Caribbean Deck. Grant struggled to serve the large number of passengers flooding the small lounge, but he seemed more than equipped to handle the attractive women who came with that flood.

Bogart and Kirk played a friendly game of pool while checking out the crowd of both younger and older men and women. It was easy to spot those who were attending the wedding on the private island. Almost all were recognizably wealthy, making Kirk and Bogart look like outcasts in their casual jackets and khakis. Bogart stood out a little more, refusing to change out of his cowboy boots.

"Well, son-of-a-bitch," a man exclaimed, alerting half the lounge.

Bogart and Kirk instinctively looked up from their pool game along with half the lounge. A large man stood only a few feet inside the lounge and stared directly at them. Kirk tensed, obviously knowing the man. Bogart remained happily clueless. Corbin was an imposing man standing nearly as tall as Kirk but with a slightly less muscular build. He kept his light hair in a buzz cut, increasing his intimidating appearance. His moderately expensive suit was the only difference between him and Kirk. Corbin approached them by the pool table and grinned while extending his hand to Kirk. Kirk managed a slight smile and gripped his hand in a half-hearted chest bump.

"Good to see you, Kirk," Corbin announced cheerfully then eyed Bogart. "Friend, acquaintance, or *other*?"

Kirk eyed Bogart and frowned at his own answer. "Somewhere between acquaintance and other," he replied.

Bogart glared at Kirk and appeared slightly offended. "Now that's just plain mean."

Corbin laughed at Bogart's expense. "Don't worry," he remarked. "Kirk doesn't have many friends. I wouldn't take it personally."

"What brings you here?" Kirk asked then looked around. "You with a girl?"

"Me?" Corbin chuckled softly. "No, I still haven't found one crazy enough to tolerate me, although I hear Ross has finally reeled one in."

"Yeah," Kirk replied with little emotion. "They're doing okay."

Bogart listened to the conversation with great interest. Despite the clueless country boy act, he had a knack for reading people. It's what made him a good conman for so many years.

Corbin leaned in closer to Kirk and rolled his eyes at the other guests. "I'm going to that snobfest of a wedding."

"You?" Kirk asked with genuine surprise. "Doesn't seem like your scene. If there's no woman involved, how'd someone like you get invited?"

"It's a good thing we're cut from the same cloth, or I'd take offense to that," Corbin remarked then laughed softly. "I'm working security for the wedding guests onboard. I volunteered for the shitty night shift detail. Most will be in bed before ten, but some of the younger ones are tying one on in the nightclub."

"Security for wedding guests?" Kirk asked with surprise. "Is that common for the insanely rich?"

"Hell if I know, but we're not talking any ordinary wedding either," Corbin remarked. "There are six of us working this ship and about two dozen on the rich guy's island. We're looking at some highly connected people with deep pockets and a list of enemies as long as your arm." A grin suddenly crossed his face. "Hey, if you're between jobs and want to get off this floating morgue, you and your colleague would probably be welcomed as additional security. Fast, easy money."

"Until you realize you're stuck between two rival mobs," Kirk remarked.

"Well, no one lives forever," Corbin remarked then excused himself.

Bogart watched the man head into the crowd of wedding guest passengers then eyed the way Kirk stared after the man. "I assume he's not your bosom buddy."

"Definitely not," Kirk muttered. "That's what's known as a 'bottom feeder'. A merc."

"Mercenary?" Bogart gasped softly and cast another look at the man. "He didn't look unstable."

"Mercenaries aren't unstable," Kirk informed him. "They're high-priced hitmen. That particular one has zero ethics."

"Seemed friendly enough."

"That's what he's selling," Kirk remarked. "He'll slit your throat while telling you to have a lovely day."

"Makes me wonder about this wedding," Bogart announced while sinking into thought.

"It's going to be one for the books, that's for sure." Kirk returned to their game and sank the two-ball. He no longer paid attention to Corbin. "I wonder who else we'll know at this little gathering."

Chapter Sixteen

Despite continuing activity on the ship well after midnight, the decks were mostly peaceful. A stray couple or two would stroll the deck while returning to their staterooms, but most of the activity remained centered around the bars and the casino. Zack sat high upon his perch overlooking a large portion of the stern. He'd made himself at home on a small overhang encased in shadows. Exactly how he got there was one of those little Zack-style mysteries. He grew tired and found it difficult to keep his eyes open. Before he fell from his perch, it was time to come off it and head back to his cramped quarters in the crew cabins.

As he was about to straighten, he witnessed a woman dressed almost entirely in black slip along the shadows of the deck below. Something familiar about the way the woman moved caught his attention. Her tactical attire and stealthy movements were enough to pique his curiosity. Zack easily shimmied down the support beam, slipped into the shadows, and hurried after the woman. He couldn't let her get away without getting a look at her face at the very least. He kept his distance, so she wouldn't realize he was following her.

The suspicious woman hurried down the stairs to the Caribbean Deck, her black boots making little sound on the steel steps. Zack waited for her to reach the bottom then scaled the railing near the top and shimmied his way down the more direct route. He saw her disappear around a corner and had to pick up his pace if he didn't want to lose her. He checked the corner before proceeding and realized she'd given him the slip. She couldn't possibly have known he was following her. Even Jackie couldn't detect him when she *knew* he was following her.

He proceeded in the logical direction a woman sneaking about might head. He passed an employee's only door and heard the faint sound of the door opening. Zack spun around but was already too late. The woman kicked him in the side and spun into a high roundhouse kick for his face. Despite initially catching him off guard, Zack blocked her flying foot and came back at her with his own karate punch. The woman blocked his punch and attempted to kick him a little lower. Zack blocked the groin shot and attempted to take her down.

Both fell to the floor, each trying in vain to subdue the other. She seemed to know all his moves, causing him to hesitate, because he knew his attacker! She pinned him to the floor while straddling his waist and prepared to strike him when they finally saw each other's faces. Zack stared at the attractive woman with her long dark hair worn in a sleek, neat ponytail. She had incredibly dark eyes that pierced through him.

"Katya?" Zack gasped while staring at her.

She stared back, equally surprised to see him and straightened without moving off him. "Zack?" Anger quickly replaced her surprise. "What the hell are you doing here?" she demanded in a thick Russian accent.

He stared at her, stunned by her reaction. "Me?" he countered. "What are you doing sneaking around like some filthy Russian spy?"

Katya stared at him with a strange expression. It was unclear whether she intended to hit him after the comment. She leaned down, kissing him passionately and aggressively on the mouth. Zack barely had time to return the kiss before she broke it off and straightened, springing to her feet. She stared at him where he remained laying on deck peering up at her.

"Stay out of my business and stay the hell out of my way," she launched. "I have no problem going through you." She then ran along deck, disappearing into the shadows.

Zack sat up and stared after her with a look of surprise. "The guys are never going to believe this," he muttered then considered the comment. "Looks like I'm flying solo on this one."

†

$\int$al's spacious two-bedroom suite was located on the Riviera Deck along with the rest of the VIP suites mostly occupied by the wedding guest passengers. The suite contained a wet bar, sunken hot tub, and three private balconies. It was nearly one o'clock in the morning. Sal and Pinto were still dressed from their earlier private party. Sal looked classically handsome in his excessively expensive suit and bold, red tie. Pinto dressed less formal in a flattering pale blue, thin-strapped dress barely reaching her knees. They entertained two wealthy looking men. One was close to Sal's age and the younger was a little older than Pinto.

Their guests were the bride's father, Matt Whitehouse and his son, Luke. Matt was slightly taller than Sal, although somewhat thinner. He had a full head of thick dark hair, which may or may not have been his own. If the hair was natural, the color certainly wasn't. Luke was lanky and almost awkward looking. Despite his age, he still looked like a gangly teenage boy who hadn't quite matured. Although he came from a wealthy family, his posture was less than impressive. He mostly sat hunched. His unusually thinning hair gave insight to what Matt probably looked like at his age.

Luke took in sweeping gazes of Pinto in her stunning dress. She shifted after the last look rested on her cleavage longer than it should have. She glanced at the grandfather clock, as it was about to strike one, and then cast a look at Sal.

"It's late, Dad," she announced while standing. "I think I'll be turning in now."

All three men stood respectfully. Luke continued to stare at her, paying particular attention to her cleavage.

"We'll see you again tomorrow afternoon, won't we?" Luke eagerly asked.

"I'm not sure--"

"Absolutely," Sal announced cheerfully. "We're entered in the skeet shooting contest. Then there's the formal dinner at seven and the lounge party at nine." He eyed Pinto and winked. "I'm hoping to coax my daughter into singing for the masses."

"Dad," she protested. "We discussed that. The ship already has entertainment. I don't want you using your influence to get me on stage. I'm strictly small town entertainment; not cruise ship ready."

"Don't be ridiculous," Sal protested. "You're amazing!"

"I know I'd love to hear you sing," Luke announced.

Pinto managed a smile, but she was obviously growing tired of the man's display of interest.

"We should probably be going too," Matt announced as he remained standing. "It's late."

"Yes, of course," Sal replied and escorted both men to the door.

Sal opened his suite door to reveal a large man standing guard just outside in the corridor. The bodyguard gave a slight nod, indicating everything was quiet. Sal shook both their hands and bid them goodnight. Matt and Luke walked along the corridor with the large guard following behind them. As they passed one of the nearby rooms, the peek hole appeared to dilate. The small webcam followed them as they passed the room. On the other side of the door, Beck sat in one of the comfortable chairs now positioned in front of the door. He watched the two men and the guard head down the hall on his screen.

The camera angle turned to reveal Sal's door down the hall. Beck pulled up pictures of all three men from his private security footage and entered their images into face recognition. He waited for the information to process while eating nuts from the minibar. Little of interest came up on Matt and Luke, revealing nothing more than parking tickets. It would appear Luke had a bit of a lead foot with his sports car. The bodyguard, on the other hand, showed a police rap sheet. Most of the charges were assault and battery, although none went to court. Either deep pockets or some form of intimidation must have been at play. Beck groaned softly and leaned back in his chair. It was going to be a long, boring night.

✝

Matt's bodyguard saw the two men safely to their two-bedroom suite at the opposite end of the hall. Once Luke entered their suite, Matt handed the guard an envelope.

"I want you to do a little checking on a few of the new guys in the morning," Matt informed him. "My eyes only. If there's something underhanded going on, I want to know about it."

"Yes, sir," the guard announced.

Once the door closed, the bodyguard headed to his room just next door, ran his card through the reader, and entered his suite. The door automatically closed behind him. The suite was unusually dark, considering the small alcove light usually remained on for the passenger's return. He flipped the light switch, brightening the alcove and some of the living area. He cast the envelope aside and immediately headed for the wet bar. As he poured himself a drink, there was a strange metallic click. The bodyguard stiffened then reached inside his jacket for his concealed gun while spinning around. He had his weapon drawn but didn't have a chance to aim when nearly silent shots were fired. He took both shots to the chest, throwing him backward against the bar. The glasses and bottles rattled from the heavy jolt, but it didn't make nearly enough noise for anyone to hear. The large man collapsed onto the floor.

The balcony door opened, allowing the sounds of the ocean and the ship enter the suite. A black gloved hand removed the envelope from the bar and stuffed it into the dead guard's inner jacket pocket. The bodyguard was then pulled along the floor by his ankles toward the open door.

Chapter Seventeen

A shotgun blast echoed across the calm ocean in the late morning sun. The special edible skeet pigeon made from compressed feed shattered over the water, pelting it with the remaining particles while simultaneously feeding ocean life. Sal lowered the pump action shotgun and grinned at Pinto, who stood several feet away with noise reducing headphones on. She gave her smiling father a proud thumbs-up. They removed their headphones and turned to Matt and Luke, who stood near them.

"It's been a while," Sal announced.

"Eight out of ten," Matt remarked cheerfully. "Not too shabby."

"My turn," Luke announced then grinned at Pinto. "See if I can impress the ladies."

Sal glanced back at Pinto with a strange smirk on his face. Pinto raised her brow in silent conversation. Not surprisingly, both had to keep from laughing. Everyone positioned their headphones to drown out the blasts and watched as Luke shot nine out of the ten skeet pigeons, one-by-one. He beamed at his handy work and removed his headphones.

"Bet you've never seen that before," Luke announced to Pinto. "Want to give it a try?"

Pinto hid her smile and shook her head. "No, I'm good, thanks."

"I'll teach you," Luke informed her. "I promise you won't even ruin your manicure."

Pinto eyed her fingernails and the manicure she'd just gotten yesterday in the ship's spa. Something inside her suddenly twitched.

A strange smile crossed her face, and she approached the instructor holding the shotgun.

"You know," Pinto announced. "Maybe I will give it a go."

The instructor handed her the shotgun after loading it with ten shells. He grinned with pleasure as she took the shotgun. "You let me know when you're ready by saying 'pull'. No pressure to go fast."

She nodded knowingly then positioned the shotgun against her shoulder and looked through the sights. Pinto exhaled softly. "Launch them as fast as you can," she informed the instructor, surprising him. "Pull!"

The instructor seemed surprised but did as instructed. He sent one skeet pigeon after another with only a second between each. Pinto shot each one, skillfully pumping the shotgun without any hesitation. She shattered all ten skeet pigeons then lowered the shotgun and returned it to the instructor. She removed her headphones and looked at the shocked expression on Luke and Matt's faces.

"My boyfriend is a bit of a badass," she informed Luke then grinned and walked away.

Sal kept his hand to his chin while secretly covering his humored smile. "I think that's lunch," Sal announced and held back his laugh.

†

Once changed into something a little less casual, Sal and Pinto entered the private dining room on the Caribbean Deck and found their assigned table. Both remained amused by the earlier skeet-shooting contest and Pinto's ability to show up the boys. When the novelty wore off, Pinto's mood turned serious.

"I think I've had enough of Matt and his son," Pinto finally informed her father. "I hope they're not at our table this afternoon. I can't keep up the pleasantries."

Sal groaned softly and sank back in his chair. "Oh, thank God," he announced with relief. "I was worried you were enjoying their company."

"Me?" she asked. "I was just putting up with them because I thought you were getting along with Matt."

Her father laughed. "I guess we need to work on our communication."

Pinto giggled along with Sal. Her father's expression suddenly dropped, alerting her to something he must've seen. She followed his gaze. A woman in her mid-thirties approached their table, an expression of disbelief on her face.

"I don't believe it," the woman shrieked cheerfully.

"I don't either," Sal remarked and failed to breathe. He managed an uncomfortable smile. "Hello, Val."

Pinto stared at the woman a moment longer then held back her gasp. She quickly covered with a failed attempt at a smile, but she was obviously uncomfortable.

"I didn't know you were attending the wedding," Sal announced.

"I'm sure you didn't or you would have sent your regrets," Valerie announced with a humored look.

"We're adults," he replied. "I think we can be at the same gathering and live to tell about it." He gently cleared his throat. "I don't believe you've met my daughter, Pinto."

Pinto uncertainly extended her hand to her father's ex-girlfriend.

Valerie shook her hand while grinning. "No, I wasn't aware you two were on speaking terms," she remarked and eyed both. "How wonderful."

Pinto shifted in her seat and avoided looking at the woman. It was unclear whether the remark intended to sound as snide as it had.

"This should be an interesting lunch," Valerie announced and pulled out the chair before her, surprising Pinto and Sal. "I wonder whose idea it was to put us at the same table?"

Sal again shifted in his chair and gently rubbed his temple. "I'm wondering the same thing myself."

"My date will be along shortly," she informed him cheerfully.

"Oh, you brought a date," Sal announced then chuckled softly in his throat. "That's nice."

Pinto sprang up from her chair and looked at her father. "I'm going to find that nice lady with the drink tray."

Beck darted away from the open doorway to avoid Pinto seeing him as she crossed the room in search of a drink. He nearly collided with another man. Their eyes locked. Beck's mouth fell open with surprise.

"Dr. Sherman?" Beck nearly gasped then managed a nervous laugh. "What, uh, are you doing here?"

Wade stared at Beck with the same stunned look then smiled and extended his hand. Beck hesitated then shook his hand but maintained his surprise.

"Beck," Wade announced cheerfully. "What a surprise. Are you here for the wedding too?"

"Oh, you're attending the wedding," Beck stammered while staring at the doctor. "I, uh, didn't know you were friends of the family."

"Long story," Wade announced then offered a soft chuckle. "Are you going to the wedding too?"

"Yeah, uh, that's a long story too," Beck announced then gently scratched his brow. "Could you, uh, not mention to anyone that I'm here?"

Wade stared at him a moment then smiled knowingly while nodding. "Oh, I get it," he announced. "You're on an assignment." Wade laughed softly. "How I envy you. I hate parties when I don't know anyone. Being undercover must make it more interesting at least."

"Yeah," Beck muttered. "Something like that."

"No one will hear it from me," Wade announced while chuckling. "You know our relationship is completely confidential. Actually, I prefer if no one knew of our relationship also."

"I can understand that," Beck replied while appearing relieved. "Between us, okay?"

"Absolutely," Wade assured him without hesitation. "Catch up with you later."

Beck nodded then watched Wade cross the private dining room and head toward Pinto's table. Beck groaned while placing his hand to his temple then quickly left. Dr. Sherman paused before Pinto's table and smiled cheerfully.

"Hey, honey," he announced cheerfully.

Valerie sprang to her feet and greeted Wade with a quick kiss then took his hand. "Wade, I'd like you to meet Sal Romano and his daughter, Pinto." She then looked at Sal and Pinto. "This is Dr. Wade Sherman, my boyfriend."

Sal stood and shook Wade's hand with a somewhat pleasant greeting.

Pinto stared at the doctor a moment with a puzzled look. "Dr. Sherman?" she questioned. "Don't you have an office in Denver?"

"Yes," he replied and eyed her. "Have we met?"

"No, I don't think so," she replied. "But I know I've heard your name before. Maybe one of my co-workers has been to your office."

"Small world, huh?" he replied and joined them at the table.

"Gets smaller every day," Sal muttered and sipped his champagne and orange juice.

Chapter Eighteen

Katya remained hidden on top of crates piled high within the cargo hold. Her dark stalking outfit allowed her to remain practically invisible while listening to four men having a discussion in the tight aisle between the piled crates. She suddenly tensed and looked alongside her. Zack lay on his stomach next to her and watched the men as well.

"Zack," she scoffed softly in her thick Russian accent. "I thought I smelled napalm and gunpowder."

"I'm happy to see you too," he teased and watched the four men across the cargo hold. "So what's the ops?"

"None of your business," she scoffed while keeping her eyes on the men.

"You realize it's easier on you if you just tell me what you're up too rather than play spy games," he remarked. "Saves you the embarrassment of me finding out on my own."

"Same old Zack," she remarked. "Sacrificing the foreplay and getting right down to business."

He cast a glare at her where she casually lay on her abdomen next to him. "You're the one who always sets the pace, my dear Katya," Zack remarked. "I've never missed my mark."

She snorted a soft laugh. "That's a good one," Katya informed him. "You're a merciless killer. You haven't got a passionate bone in your body."

"Well, now, that's the AK-47 calling the Uzi black," he scoffed.

"I'm working here," she snarled. "Go away."

"I'm working too," he remarked. "I have to think about my client. What are those guys up to?"

"Some sort of assassination plot," she informed him. "I've been stalking them since before we boarded the ship." Katya sharply eyed him. "And I need them alive for interrogation, so don't get involved. I know you don't play well with others."

"Unlike you," he scoffed, "I've never sacrificed my own team."

"That's because you're the pawn," she remarked. "You're the idiot throwing himself on the grenade to save others. In my business, I'm the important one. I'm the one with the intel. I'm the one for whom others sacrifice themselves."

"You always did overvalue yourself," he replied. "We're all expendable in this game. We're all just pawns."

"Including Jackie?" she asked while glancing at him and raising a mocking brow.

Zack's look turned hostile. "Leave Jackie out of this," he snarled. "You don't know anything about her."

"I know you fantasize about screwing her while banging other women," Katya remarked. "I dare you to deny it."

"Can we just focus on the bad guys?" he demanded.

"You *are* the bad guy, Zack," she replied while smirking. "You're just too stupid to realize it."

Before he could defend himself, they heard the men discussing their assignment.

"We'll coordinate the attack as planned," one of the men announced. "We wait until after the last of the guests have been served dinner. An hour afterward should do it."

"Are they talking about the island wedding?" Zack asked with surprise.

"If my sources are correct," she announced, "I believe so. There are some heavy hitters attending that wedding."

"I have to warn the guys," Zack remarked. "It was never about Pinto. It's always been about Sal Romano. Those men intend to carry out a hit on him."

"You may be right, but we have to be sure," she replied. "We need to take those men down quietly and question them about the hit. You take point. I've got your back."

Zack nodded and was about to get up. She grabbed his arm forcing him to look into her eyes.

"We need them *alive*."

"I'm not a two-year-old," he scoffed. "You don't need to keep reminding me."

Zack and Katya easily climbed down the crates and crept along the cargo bay, keeping hidden until they reached the four men. They went their separate directions around another stack of crates for a surprise attack from both ends. Zack somersaulted across the floor and swept the first man's legs out from beneath him, signaling for Katya to attack from the other end. She expertly fought the two men on her end with amazing martial arts skills, although Zack was too busy with his own company to notice. With the first man down, Zack sprang upward and immediately threw his entire body into a roundhouse kick, taking down the second man. As the second man went down, Zack punched the first man as he attempted to make it to his feet.

The third man jumped him from behind. Zack easily flipped him over his shoulder and into a crate with a loud crash. He captured the second man as he straightened and slung him over his shoulder and into the first man, who again attempted to stand. When the fourth man came at him, it became obvious Katya wasn't holding her own and left him to fight the entire battle. Zack kicked the man in the gut and then in the face as he doubled over, throwing him backward into more crates. Zack finally straightened and glared at Katya, who hadn't even broken a sweat.

"Thanks for the backup," he snarled.

Katya approached one of the men on the floor. She stood over the dead men, shook her head, and glared at Zack. "Which part of 'taken alive' did you not understand?"

Zack looked around and realized all four men surrounding him were dead. The outcome surprised him as he met her disapproving glare. "I don't know what's gotten into me lately," he muttered shamefully. "I've lost control over my own strength. It must be from the concussion."

"Well, get your head on straight," she snarled. "I'm not taking responsibility for your blunders."

†

Zack leaned against one of the crates within the cargo area only a short while later, his arms folded across his chest and an unpredictable yet frightening look on his face. Bogart and Kirk looked around the empty area where the four men once lie dead then exchanged strange looks.

"I know what you're thinking," Zack snarled, about ready to strike.

Jackie leaned against one of the crates not far from Zack and silently watched him. He refused to look at her, but she could almost feel his gaze upon her, although indirectly. She watched his hand twitch several times. His rage was evident, at least to her. Monroe's famous words echoed through her mind and now sounded accurate. 'Ticking time bomb'.

Monroe approached from one of the nearby aisles and shook his head. "There's no one here, Zack," he protested. "Dead or alive. No blood; no bodies."

"I'm not fucking hallucinating," he launched as his hands fell from his chest and he took a quick step toward Monroe.

The look in his eyes was psychotic and beyond unpredictable. Jackie took a step toward him and caught his hand. He shot a glare at her hand on his then met her gaze with frightening hostility. Jackie locked eyes with him, showed no judgment, and wrapped her fingers around his hand, holding it in hers. His hand gently squeezed hers and his look immediately softened. Jackie looked at the others, who now stared at them with moderate surprise.

"Zack and I are going to the gym for a little workout," she informed them. "We'll catch up with you guys later."

Monroe tensed at the suggestion but didn't comment. Jackie turned while holding Zack's hand and effortlessly led him from the cargo hold.

"Christ," Bogart scoffed while shaking his head. "She's like a Zack whisperer or something."

"If she ever has that sort of hold over me," Kirk remarked, "please, shoot me."

†

Within the ship's gym, Zack and Jackie had their shoes off while on the mats as they blocked each other's kicks and punches with amazing speed and aggression. Despite all that had happened, Zack remained focused while sparring with Jackie. She was aware his heart wasn't into it as much as usual. Given the opportunity to spar with Jackie, Zack was usually aggressive yet playful. For him, it was more like foreplay to some sexual fantasy she'd never understand. Today, he was just working out aggression, which was unusual. She expected some sexual innuendoes, but he just wasn't in the proper mood. It almost worried her. He offered no challenge and didn't seek any from her. After nearly an hour of unleashing punishment on each other, Zack sank against the wall while breathing heavily then slid down it. Jackie crawled across the mat and sat alongside him, leaning her back against the wall. He handed her a towel while both worked on slowing their heart rate and breathing after their intense sparring match. He cast a quick glance at her.

"I'm not hallucinating," he informed her.

"I believe you."

He eyed her and appeared surprised. "You do?" Zack released an uneasy laugh. "Everyone else thinks I'm crazy. Why would you think differently?"

Jackie took his hand in hers and held it up, revealing his scraped knuckles. "You gave someone a beating," she replied then released his hand.

He eyed his knuckles then allowed his head to fall back against the wall. "I'll admit; my methods are unorthodox, and I lack compassion at times, but no one's ever questioned my intel before. When I reported back, it was taken at face value. I know my job and I do it well."

"Yes," she replied. "Your knowledge and skills are legendary." She inhaled deeply and eyed him. "I don't suppose you got a look at any of their nametags."

"Their name badges only have first names," he replied. "There was a Don and a Sigmund. I didn't see the other two. Although, they were all galley crewmen. I did take note of their insignias."

"They worked in the kitchen?"

"That's what galley means, Jackie."

"I'm familiar with the term," she muttered then sank into thought. "We reach port in the morning. That doesn't give us much time to figure this out."

"If they aren't legitimate crewmen, they'll probably get off the ship with us," Zack informed her. "Katya was convinced they were sent to assassinate someone at the wedding. I think they're after Sal."

Jackie tensed and stared at Zack. "Katya?" she asked with surprise then gently cleared her throat. "You mean your Russian spy girlfriend? Are you saying she's onboard?"

"Yeah, I ran into her last night," he replied and turned on his hip to face her. His look was serious. "What if Pinto's stalker isn't really interested in her? He could be behind this entire assassination plot to kill her father."

Jackie shifted slightly then attempted a smile. "Then we need to keep an eye on Sal at the wedding," she replied. "I'm sure you can manage that without being seen."

"Of course," he confirmed without hesitation. "So you believe me, right?"

"We don't have any proof that anyone wants to kill Sal," Jackie informed him. "This may have nothing to do with Sal or Pinto." She hesitated while staring into his eyes, attempting to remove any indications that she didn't believe him. "If you run into Katya again, I'd like to talk to her."

"I'm not sure that's a good idea," Zack announced and seemed to tense. "She has a terrible temper, and she can be somewhat territorial."

"Territorial? Of what?"

"She's a little jealous of our relationship," he admitted. "She knows we're close, and I think she has a problem with it. She's not exactly stable. I don't know that I want you around her."

Jackie shifted slightly then smiled while nodding. "Okay, if you think it's best."

Chapter Nineteen

Pinto stretched out on one of the lounge chairs at the pool on the ship's stern later that afternoon. Although she wore a conservative black bikini, it still revealed plenty of leg and cleavage, gaining attention from other male passengers. As she soaked in the sun, Sal sat at the poolside bar with a few acquaintances and laughed over drinks. Beck leaned against the alcove near the outside stairs. His eyes remained hidden behind dark sunglasses to keep anyone from noticing his over-attentive stare at the sunbathing beauty. He finally fidgeted and frowned, giving up. Beck turned to leave and nearly collided with Corbin. Beck took a step back and maintained his calm demeanor despite his surprise.

Corbin grinned and looked past him toward poolside. "Considering the sausage fest on that side of the pool, I'm assuming you're checking out the redhead." He nodded his head with approval while giving Pinto a lengthy once over then met Beck's gaze. "Nice."

"Not that I hadn't noticed," Beck casually announced with little emotion, "but I was actually trying to place the two men at the poolside bar. The bald man is Sal Romano, but I don't know who the other man is."

Corbin chuckled in his throat. "That's Matt Whitehouse," he informed him. "Father-of-the-bride."

Beck cast a quick glance toward the distant bar then looked back at Corbin with a bewildered look. "I thought the bride's name was something Italian."

"Agosti?" Corbin questioned then grinned. "Yeah, his ex-wife married Bruno Agosti, and he adopted Whitehouse's daughter. Some real bad blood there."

"Why did he consent to let Agosti adopt his daughter then?" Beck asked.

"You *are* out of the mafia loop," Corbin teased. "Rumor has it Bruno Agosti had the goods on Whitehouse. The only way he'd keep from going to prison or worse was to allow Agosti to adopt his little girl."

"But wasn't there a son?" Beck questioned. "Lucas or something."

"Luke? Yeah, he's here with his father," Corbin replied. "The redhead insulted him half an hour ago, and he took off with his tail between his legs."

"Agosti didn't want to adopt Luke?"

"No," Corbin practically gasped. "Luke is a few years older than his sister. He wanted to live with his father after the divorce. He wanted nothing to do with Agosti or his mother for that matter. He's devoted to his sister though." He held back his grin. "Of course, everything changed once Bruno Agosti got himself whacked. The wife too. Now the daughter is back in his life."

"Almost sad I'm going to miss this wedding," Beck announced then grinned. "Sounds like it could be explosive."

"Yeah, someone's going to lose their head, that's for sure," Corbin teased then laughed. "Come on. I want you to meet the big man himself. My boss, Mr. Banks."

"Okay, sure."

"You'll need to dress up a little," Corbin informed him. "They won't let you into the high-stakes section of the casino dressed like that."

"Why don't I change and meet you there in twenty?" Beck suggested.

"You're on."

Once Corbin walked away, Beck removed his cell phone and walked along deck, putting distance between him and the pool. He waited for Gil to answer his cell phone.

"Gil, were you aware that Matt Whitehouse and Nelson Banks are onboard?" He listened then nodded. "Yeah, and they're all going to the wedding." He stopped near the railing. "Bruno Agosti was step-father to the bride." He paused and listened to Gil on the other end. "Yeah, tell me about it. Can you get some of the guys into the high-stakes area of the casino?" He hesitated then grinned.

"Meet me there in fifteen minutes." He disconnected his call and hurried along deck.

✝

Bogart stepped out of the bathroom within Jackie's suite and straightened his expensive jacket while grinning proudly. The country boy cleaned up nicely.

"I look pretty sharp," he announced then checked himself out in the mirror.

Monroe sat on the sofa with his temple resting against his fist and shook his head with irritation. "Try not to ruin my threads," he remarked.

Monroe and Jackie were also dressed for the occasion. Monroe wore an expensive suit with a brilliant red, multi-colored vest while Jackie wore an elegant black dress that barely made it to her knees and offered plenty of cleavage.

"Don't forget your tie, double-o-negative," Jackie remarked and handed him an expensive silk tie.

Bogart looked at it and frowned. "I never could tie one of these."

"Not surprising," Monroe muttered.

Jackie took the tie from him then glared at Monroe. "Meet Beck in the casino and tell him we're running late," she announced. "I don't need him calling again."

"Fine," Monroe groaned then stood and left.

Jackie stood before Bogart and put the tie around his neck. As she worked on adjusting the tie, Bogart snuck a peek down her dress and hid his boyish grin.

"You really rock that dress," he teased. "I guess it's a good thing Beck paired you with Monroe and not me. Know what I mean?"

Jackie shifted uncomfortably while tying his tie. He again looked down her dress and grinned. Jackie took a quick step back and glared at him.

"Stop that," she ordered with hostility.

He stared at her with surprise. "What? I'm the only one not allowed to ogle you?" Bogart grunted with humor. "Sort of hard to do, considering I caught a peek of you naked once. I love telling that story. Never gets old."

Jackie flinched and then ran her fingers vigorously through her hair. She finally met his gaze. He stared back at her and his mood immediately changed.

"What's wrong?" he asked with a strange look on his face. "Was it something I said?"

Jackie immediately tensed while thinking of the best way to bring up the uncomfortable conversation. "Ross recognized your mother from that picture I'd found," she informed him while fidgeting. "It turns out your mother knew my father's team before you were born. When I asked Zack about your mother--" She hesitated and held her breath. "He told me she partied with them during their week on shore leave."

Bogart stared at her a moment with a baffled look. "You mean--?"

Jackie exhaled deeply. "Your mother slept with my father, Ross, and Zack at some point during their shore leave." She again fidgeted. "Less than a year later, you were born."

Bogart stared at her with his mouth hanging open. He seemed at a loss for words as he processed the information. "You mean one of them could be my father?" His eyes suddenly widened as he took a step away from her. "You could be my sister?" He suddenly cringed. "Ah, hell! I saw you naked once! That's just wrong!"

"Yeah, so could you refrain from looking down my shirt and making lewd comments?"

He held his hands up in the air defensively. "Consider it done!" Bogart lowered his hands then stared at her while taking in the new information. "Is that why you were asking all those questions about my birthday and my mother?"

Jackie nodded.

His look suddenly changed as hostility took over. "You were sitting on this information for some time now and never said anything?"

"I'm sorry," she replied while running her fingers through her hair. "I didn't know how to bring it up. I certainly wasn't going to ask Zack or Ross so they could either confirm or deny it. Without a test, we'll never know."

"Then let's do it," Bogart announced boldly with conviction. "Let's take the test. If you and I are brother and sister, it'll show up, right?"

"I think that's how it works."

"Then I want to do it."

"Are you sure?"

Bogart stared at her as his anxiety faded away. He offered a warm smile. "Finding out you're my sister would be one of the greatest moments of my life. I always wanted a sister, especially one like you." He then considered the comment and eyed her with a curious look. "Is that why you've been defending me so much lately?"

Jackie smirked then straightened his tie. "We'd better get going."

Chapter Twenty

Just outside the high-stakes casino, Gil and Darth stood near the doorway while talking with the casino sentry. It was his job to ensure those who entered the high-stakes area were properly dressed, the appropriate age, and looked wealthy enough to afford the high minimums. They joked around and had a good time while simultaneously allowing Kirk to slip in, now miraculously changed into a waiter's uniform. Where he located one to fit his massive frame was an interesting question. Beck and Monroe had already found their way inside, dressed the part and accepted by the wealthy crowd. Jackie approached the high-stakes area while linked onto Bogart's arm, despite the premise that she was traveling with Monroe. The sentry on duty gave them a polite nod, assuming they could afford high-stakes gambling.

The handsome couple crossed the room and casually looked around. The high-stakes casino was surprisingly full; indicating many of the passengers fell into a higher tax bracket. Bogart maintained his charming grin while casing the place.

"I hate ties," he muttered.

"Quit whining," Jackie scoffed through her teeth without breaking her smile.

Beck and Monroe were already with Corbin near one of the empty poker tables. Judging by the look on Monroe's face, he had a difficult time pretending he was happy to see Corbin.

"So who is this guy?" Bogart asked softly as they worked the room.

"I've never met him," Jackie announced while casting several looks in their direction, "but I've heard enough unpleasant stories about him to know I wouldn't care for him."

"So basically he's Zack."

"Mind your manners," Jackie scolded without looking at him.

"Sorry," Bogart remarked then grinned boyishly. "So he's *Dad*."

Jackie eyed Bogart and the cheap grin on his face. She groaned softly and shook her head. "I'm putting my money on Ross being your father," she remarked. "You two have the same charming disposition."

"Was that a backhanded compliment?"

"It wasn't any sort of compliment," she muttered.

Kirk signaled them with a look from across the room, catching their attention. He stood behind Nelson Banks at one of the blackjack tables and indicated the man with a single look.

"That's Banks," Jackie announced softly.

"Tables a bit crowded," Bogart remarked as they made their way closer.

Kirk tilted his tray and spilled a drink on the man sitting alongside Nelson. The man jumped up and cursed at Kirk. When the man saw Kirk's size, he controlled his hostility. Kirk apologized and handed him a napkin. The man collected his chips and stormed away. Bogart pulled Jackie along a little faster and claimed the vacant seat. Kirk politely wiped the spilled drink from the seat and the padded table bumper. Bogart grinned at Kirk.

"Scotch on the rocks," Bogart announced and gave Kirk a polite slap on the shoulder.

Kirk sneered then forced a smile. "Certainly, sir." He then looked at Jackie. "Anything for the lady?"

"Chardonnay," she replied pleasantly.

Kirk managed a polite smile then walked away. Jackie knew they'd probably never see those drinks. While Bogart played blackjack, loose and free with Monroe's money at one-hundred dollars a hand, he made small talk with Nelson. True to form, the conman Bogart was a hit. Corbin approached their table and spoke into Nelson's ear. He finished his hand and left with Corbin. His wife took his seat and continued playing in his place. She was quick to make small talk with Bogart, and he was willing to play along.

"And is this your wife?" Emily asked, indicating Jackie.

"Her? No, that's just my sister," Bogart announced, practically waving her off.

Emily smiled as her interest increased.

Bogart suavely took her hand in his and admired her ruby and diamond tennis bracelet. "That is exquisite," he announced while grinning his approval as he lightly turned her wrist to admire the bracelet.

She leaned closer to him, squeezing her cleavage together and practically displayed it in his face, revealing the matching necklace. His attention strayed to the necklace and then the ample cleavage below.

Jackie watched Bogart ogle Emily's bosom and immediately looked away. "Oh, boy," she muttered, knowing where this was leading.

As she looked across the room, she saw Gil and Monroe now talking with Corbin and Nelson Banks. The couple near them caught her attention. Jackie's expression suddenly dropped as she stared at Dr. Sherman with an attractive woman in her mid-thirties attached to his arm. Jackie leaned closer to Bogart's ear.

"I think we have a situation," she whispered. "I see an old friend."

Bogart glanced across the room, but Jackie was already gone. He shook his head. "Jesus, she's turning into Zack."

Jackie approached Beck and Monroe while they talked with their new acquaintance, Nelson Banks. Jackie linked onto Monroe's arm and played the role of his trophy wife. Oddly enough, he didn't even flinch, instead, just patted her hand on his arm.

"Monroe and I would be happy to help out at your resort this weekend," Beck announced, surprising Jackie, although she didn't respond.

Monroe attempted a smile but it came off more like a smirk. He obviously wasn't thrilled with Beck's new plan to stalk his girlfriend either.

"That's wonderful," Nelson announced cheerfully. "You can meet us at my private dock once we reach shore."

"If it's okay with you," Beck announced, "we'd prefer renting our own helicopter and do a little fly-by of the place. Get a lay of the land, so to speak."

"Excellent idea," Nelson cheerfully replied. "I'll see you tomorrow afternoon at the resort."

Beck nodded then watched Nelson walk away. Corbin grinned, patted Beck on the back, and then hurried after Nelson.

"What was that about?" Jackie suddenly demanded. "I thought we were heading home when we reached Columbia."

"Change of plans," Beck informed her. "There's something big going down around here, and Pinto's going to be sitting in the middle of it. I can't leave her unprotected." He straightened proudly. "After you drop me off at the resort, the rest of you can go home if you want, but I'm staying."

Monroe and Jackie groaned softly. "We're not leaving you," Monroe announced with limited enthusiasm. "If you're right, you're going to need all the protection you can get."

"We'll need to discuss this someplace less public," Jackie announced. "I just saw Dr. Sherman in the casino. He's here on the ship. If he sees us--"

"I already ran into him," Beck replied. "He's one of us, sort of. It's fine."

"You're digging your hole deeper," Monroe informed him. "If you're wrong about any of this, Pinto's going to bury you."

"Rather she buries me than the other way around," Beck remarked. He then looked around and appeared puzzled. "Where's Bogart?"

Jackie looked back at the blackjack table. Bogart and Emily Banks were gone. She groaned softly. "Oh, great," Jackie muttered. "Our charming country boy is about to do something stupid."

"You mean Bogart and Mrs. Banks?" Monroe suddenly gasped and looked around. "No, no, no. You don't mess around with a mob wife. He'll be floating face down by morning."

"We better go after him," Jackie replied with a soft sigh. "Once the blood leaves his head, he lacks morals and judgment."

Jackie walked away leaving Monroe and Beck staring after her with their mouths hanging open.

"Can you believe the mouth on that one?" Beck huffed.

"She's been spending too much time at Zack's finishing school for wayward girls."

Beck chuckled at the comment. Monroe laughed with him then indicated the door. Both men left the casino.

Chapter Twenty-one

Zack stood outside the stateroom suite with his rolling dinner cart and stared at the familiar number from his last room service visit. He groaned softly, straightened proudly, and promptly knocked on the door. The door opened to reveal an attractive woman in her early thirties dressed in a sexy nightgown with matching satin robe hanging open, allowing him a generous peek at her toned body. She smiled pleasantly and stood aside, allowing him to enter.

"Good evening, ma'am," he announced with renewed cheerfulness.

"Good evening," she replied and shut the door behind him.

The arrogant man stepped out of the bedroom while attaching his expensive cufflinks to his overpriced shirt. He saw Zack and immediately frowned.

"You can put it by the balcony," he snarled.

The woman darted a disapproving look at the man. As Zack pushed the cart toward the balcony, the man glared at the woman.

"What's wrong with you?" he demanded. "Close your robe. You don't need to be giving the hired help any ideas."

Zack twitched but continued converting the cart into a table. He lit the candles then turned, forcing an unsettling smile. "Will there be anything else, sir?"

The man stood directly in front of Zack, folded his arms across his chest, and stared down at him, standing at least four inches taller.

"Yeah, you can stop ogling my girlfriend," he snarled.

"I don't recall ogling the young lady," Zack remarked, "but I'll be sure to mind my eyes."

"He wasn't looking at me, Glenn," she protested from across the room.

"Stay out of this, Rhonda," he barked back without looking at her. "I know how these horny cruise ship guys operate."

"Will there be anything else, sir?" Zack repeated with a snarl in his tone as his eyes locked onto the man blocking his path.

"You've got a problem?" Glenn demanded and waved him on. "Take your best shot, little man."

"Best shot?" Zack questioned, allowing a throaty laugh to escape. "You don't want my best shot." His eyes narrowed, resembling a rattlesnake about to strike. "Too much blood. Very messy."

"You think you're funny?"

"Glenn, that's enough," Rhonda insisted.

"Funny? No, I'm not the funny one," Zack replied then sneered. "I'm pretty fucking serious." He eyed the woman. "Pardon my language."

As Zack looked back, Glenn threw a tight fist for his face. Zack blocked the punch with his left hand and smacked him across the face with his right, stunning the man with the hard slap. Zack grinned, pleased with himself. The man became upset and threw another punch. Zack caught his wrist then backhanded his crotch with his free hand. Glenn gasped and writhed with discomfort, although he was lucky Zack hadn't put him on the floor. Zack released his wrist and smirked.

"Are we done here?"

"You asked for it," Glenn snarled and attempted to snap kick Zack.

Zack caught his ankle and held his foot in the air while Glenn tried to keep his balance. Zack appeared baffled while glaring at the man. "What the hell what that supposed to be?"

Rhonda folded her arms across her chest. "He thinks he knows karate."

Zack released his foot, waited for him to catch his balance, and then kicked him lightly in three places along his body in one kick. Glenn groaned from each shot, even though they weren't very hard.

"Like that?" Zack demanded and glared at Glenn. "Or--?"

Zack spun into a roundhouse kick and struck Glenn in the chest, sending him into the sofa. Glenn hit the sofa and fell to the floor while groaning.

"More like that?" Zack teased with an amused chuckle. He then eyed Rhonda and gave her a serious look. "I think you should consider finding a better man. Eventually, this one is going to strike you, and you'll end up putting a steak knife through his chest."

As Zack headed for the door, the woman hurried after him and stopped him. He glanced at the odd expression on her face. She grabbed his shirt and kissed him passionately on the mouth, startling him. She broke off the kiss and smiled lustfully at him.

Zack remained slightly surprised, stared at her a moment, and then smiled politely. "Good evening, ma'am."

As he left the room, she sighed dreamily.

✝

Now changed into his basic black combat outfit, Zack made his way undetected through the belly of the ship. The noise from the engines was near deafening. He moved into a dark alcove and blended in until one of the workers passed then continued on his way in search of answers. The crewman he followed never saw him, despite seemingly looking for anyone tailing him. His behavior was moderately suspicious, but his reason for being in the engine room was what made Zack follow him. A wine steward had no business in the engine room, yet there he was. He met another man in a secluded area far from the activity. The other man was with the maintenance department. They talked too softly for Zack to hear and getting closer would be next to impossible. The maintenance man indicated a drum toward the back. They continued their conversation then went their separate ways.

Zack waited a moment then approached the area containing the drums. He searched each drum. It wasn't until closer inspection that he noticed something was off with the drum toward the back. He pried open the drum to reveal two suitcases. He didn't have to open them to know what they contained. They were bombs! He returned the lid to the drum and was about to leave when he heard movement from nearby. He darted for the nearest crow's nest and easily climbed up and out of sight. The same two men returned and noticed someone had tampered with the drum. They looked around then immediately retrieved some hidden weapons. They cocked their semiautomatics containing silencers and scanned the area.

A handprint on the once dirty pipe was enough to force both men to look up to Zack's perch. Zack dove off his perch into a forward flip and landed just past the men. He no sooner landed before spinning into a roundhouse kick, taking out the first man. The second man attempted to shoot him, but he spun for the return kick and knocked the gun from his hand. He punched the man twice in the face and grabbed him by the head. Zack suddenly hesitated. He had to take them alive. He needed answers.

Zack held him in a headlock. "Who do you work for?" he demanded while squeezing the man's neck. "Who wants to blow up the ship?"

The man gasped what sounded like a response. Zack felt the man twitch. When he looked down, the man was dead and he could feel his broken neck beneath his grip. Zack released the man and watched him fall lifeless to the floor. He didn't mean to kill him yet somehow he did. When Zack looked back at the second man, he was also dead. It appeared as if he hit his head against the metal and either crushed his skull or broke his neck. Possibly a combination of both. He stared at both men with confusion while running his fingers through his short hair. He couldn't make sense of what just happened. He'd purposely tried to keep the men alive, yet they seemed to drop dead on their own.

"Not again," came the familiar Russian voice.

Zack looked up and saw Katya standing only a few yards away. She shook her head in disbelief.

"We needed them alive," she insisted. "What's wrong with you? Are you turning into some sort of bloodthirsty psychopath?"

Zack drew a deep breath and collected his emotions. "It wasn't as if I did it on purpose," he growled while collecting their weapons. He stuck them into cleverly concealed pockets on his tactical jacket. "I need to bring the guys down here to see this," he informed her. "Once they see the briefcase bombs, they'll believe me."

"And I'm sure the bombs and the bodies will be gone by the time you get back," Katya informed him. "You're going to look like a nutcase again."

"So you've been spying on me as well?" he demanded. "How else would you know the bodies were gone when I brought the others back?"

"Of course I've been spying on you," she remarked. "It's in my job description. It's all part of the whole spy gig." She reluctantly groaned. "Fine. I'll wait here and keep watch on the bodies and the bombs while you get your team together."

Zack eyed her suspiciously. "We go back a long way, Katya," he announced simply. "I've allowed you to violate my body three ways from Sunday, but I don't trust you at all."

She didn't even seem fazed by the insult. A sly smirk crossed her face as if the comment pleased her. "So we'll move the bombs," Katya replied. "If we hide them, they can't remove them. The bombs will be enough to convince your team that you're not crazy."

"And it'll also keep whoever is responsible from being able to use them," Zack added.

"Unless they have a remote control," she informed him. "Then they could simply blow them whenever."

"Wrong type of bomb. I know bombs," he informed her then smirked. "It's in my job description."

"There's a job description for deranged lunatics?" she asked without cracking a smile.

He glared at her. She grinned then chuckled softly.

✝

*Z*ack and Katya stood outside Kirk's stateroom door and waited for an answer. While they waited, Zack removed his cell phone and attempted to call each of the guys. He shook his head with annoyance then returned his phone to his pocket.

"I don't know why I can't reach any of them," he remarked.

"They're probably tired of playing cat and mouse with you," Katya muttered. "They think you're crazy, remember?"

"You're not helping."

Zack removed his official master key card and ran it through the lock on Kirk's door. He opened the door and eyed Katya.

"I'll leave Kirk a note," he informed her. "Then we'll wait for them within the perimeter of the hidden briefcases."

Katya followed Zack into Kirk's room. Zack headed for the table and the notepad. Katya casually flipped the bolt across the closed door. Zack heard the clunk and immediately turned toward her. Katya smiled lustfully as she approached him and ran her hands along his chest.

"It's been a while," she cooed softly while slipping her arms around his neck as she moved her mouth closer to his. "You know you want to take me right here and now."

Zack groaned softly, grabbed her around the waist and by the back of the neck, and kissed her aggressively. She returned the wild passionate kiss and immediately ripped at his shirt. She spun him into the dresser, scattering items to the floor and toppling the chair as she practically climbed his body. She attempted to pull him away from the dresser, knocking over a lamp. It hit the floor and shattered, although neither cared. Zack tossed Katya over his hip and onto the bed, landing roughly on top of her. They wildly pawed at each other while writhing around the bed, attempting to rip each other's clothes off.

Katya ran her hands along his abdomen beneath his open shirt and dug her nails into his side. Without breaking off the kiss, he kept her from drawing blood and held her hand to the bed, partially restraining her. As her hand caressed his, he saw a flash of a bloody hand. Zack's thoughts strayed back to the assignment a little over a week earlier and the incident in the van outside the mansion. He stared at Jackie's catatonic state and took her blood-covered hand in his. Her eyes met his. Her traumatized expression caused him to tremble. Zack suddenly broke off the kiss and stared at Katya beneath him.

Katya stared back at him with a strange look of surprise. "This is usually the part where you impress me," she remarked and continued to stare when he didn't react. "Can't get the soldier to salute?"

Zack moved off her and sat on the edge of the bed. He breathed heavily while running his fingers through his slightly mussed hair. Katya sat up behind him and stared at him.

"Zack?"

He repeatedly rubbed his hand against his chin while staring at nothing in particular. "This isn't right," he whispered then drew a deep, shaken breath. "You're not real."

Katya stared at him then faded away. Zack gently allowed his head to fall into his hand and clutched his forehead while staring blankly at the floor.

Chapter Twenty-two

Monroe and Jackie followed the irate Beck in their futile search for Bogart. When they checked a few minutes earlier, Bogart wasn't in his room with the mobster's wife. Gil and Kirk went to Banks' suite on the upper deck, but they weren't there either. Jackie often wondered if Bogart thought much before he followed his hormones into strange women's bedrooms. Didn't he realize Emily Banks was married to a notorious mobster who'd have him killed just for looking at his wife the wrong way? No, she supposed he didn't think of that. Perhaps he hadn't even been paying attention when they were discussing Banks. If he were her brother, he certainly didn't get her father's intelligence. Beck stopped them before the corridor leading to his room not far from Pinto's room. He made certain the hallway was clear before they proceeded to his room to retrieve his laptop.

They stopped before his room and waited while Beck ran his card key through the card reader. The door hummed. He attempted to open it, but it caught on the bolt across the door. Beck stared at the jammed door with surprise then pushed harshly against it, succeeding only in straining his shoulder. All three came to the same conclusion.

"Bogart," Beck scoffed then shoved his shoulder against the partly open door with a bang. "Damn it, Bogart! Open this door!"

All three could hear movement from within the room. Something thudded. Bogart peered through the partially open door held in place with the dead bolt. He grinned boyishly with some embarrassment.

"Hey, uh, Beck," he announced in a soft tone. "I'm sort of in the middle of something. Could you come back in half an hour?"

Beck shoved his shoulder against the door, causing it to thud loudly then glared at Bogart through the small opening. "Open this door or I swear I'll kill you when I get my hands on you," he snarled through gritted teeth.

"Okay, okay," Bogart announced then shut the door.

There was an unusually long pause followed by hushed voices on the other side of the door. Beck was seething with rage now, thinking Bogart had purposely locked him out. Bogart removed the bolt and opened the door. He stood in the doorway wearing only his pants. His shirt and shoes were missing. Beck shoved him aside and stormed into the room. The bed was mussed but empty. Despite the absence of Emily Banks, one of her shoes was on the floor among Bogart's shirt and shoes. Beck looked at the closed bathroom door and shook his head.

"Tread lightly," Jackie muttered.

Beck sneered then knocked on the bathroom door while attempting to control his hostility. The bathroom door opened to reveal Emily, now back in her dress. She readjusted her severely mussed hair.

"Bogart didn't say he was expecting company," Emily announced while managing a smile.

"Bogart should have gone to his own room," Beck informed her then glared at Bogart. "Do you have any idea who she is?"

Bogart indicated the attractive woman. "Yeah, that's Emily," he replied then smirked. "It would be rude not to ask a woman her name."

Emily smiled sweetly, approached Bogart, and seductively patted his chest. "I think he's asking if you know who my husband is."

"Husband?" Bogart questioned with surprise. "I thought he was your father."

She shrugged without care. "Why do you think I came on to you?"

Bogart groaned and shook his head. "Damn it," he cursed softly then threw his hands in the air. "I've been trying to avoid married women."

"Her being married is only the beginning of your problems," Monroe remarked. "Her husband is a mob boss."

He stared at Monroe a moment almost frozen then tilted his head. "A what?"

"Totally overblown," Emily informed him then eyed the others. "I'm guessing our romantic interlude has passed. Maybe another time, Bogart."

She slipped into her high heels and left the room. All four stared after her until the door closed. Once it closed, the three turned their heads and glared at Bogart.

"Are you out of your mind?" Beck exploded.

"This isn't going to solve anything," Jackie announced. "She's gone. Nothing happened."

Bogart considered the comment and hid his grin. "I wouldn't say nothing--"

Jackie wanted to smack him but resisted the temptation. He wasn't helping. "She's certainly not telling her husband."

Beck's laptop beeped at him. He became alert and hurried for it. "That's the motion detector I have on Pinto's doorframe," he announced then looked at the computer screen.

All four stared with surprise when they saw Will leaving Pinto's room.

"He's been on the ship the whole time?" Monroe suddenly asked. "Why haven't we seen him?"

"Because he doesn't want to be seen," Beck muttered while staring at the screen. As Will passed Beck's room, Beck looked at the door and listened to the footfalls in the hallway.

"You know how I feel about Pinto," Monroe announced while staring at Beck then appeared defeated, "but if he was in her stateroom, isn't it possible there's something more between them? How do we know what we found wasn't just him being creepy around his girlfriend?"

Beck glared at Monroe and appeared ready to explode. "She's not seeing him," he snarled. "She wouldn't cheat on me. She loves me." He straightened and stood proudly. "She's not even in her room. She's with Sal in the lounge."

"Do you think he was in her room uninvited?" Jackie then asked.

"It's the only explanation," Beck informed them.

Beck's cell phone vibrated inside his jacket pocket. He removed his phone, eyed the caller ID, and then answered it. "Yeah, Gil."

"Zack wasn't answering his phone," Gil announced from the other end, "so we tracked it. We found his cell phone in Kirk's room, but he's not here. Someone trashed the room."

"What?" Beck gasped with surprise. "Does it look as if someone was searching the room? Or does it seem like a struggle took place?"

"I'm going with struggle," Gil responded. "Usually Zack only makes this sort of mess during mating season."

Monroe, Jackie, and Bogart stared at Beck while attempting to put together the entire conversation from the fragments they were hearing.

Beck made a face and lightly scratched his head with bewilderment. "Okay, that's not weird," he muttered.

"That's not the worst part," Gil continued over the phone. "Darth found a semiautomatic within the scattered sheets. Even if he had smuggled a weapon onboard, it's nothing from Zack's arsenal. I'm almost positive."

"All right, okay," Beck announced and drew a deep breath. "We need to find Zack. You and Kirk check the kitchen and retrace his room service deliveries. We'll split up and check the passenger areas."

"You've got it," Gil announced then disconnected the call.

Beck eyed the others while replacing his phone. "Zack's MIA. They found his cell phone in Kirk's room along with an unfamiliar firearm. The room's been trashed, so something went down," he informed them. "Jackie and Monroe will check the casino and the lounge on the Caribbean Deck. Bogart and I will scout the dining room and dance club."

"I don't get it," Jackie remarked. "If he found something, why wouldn't he call us on our cell phones? He didn't try calling me."

"Why would he?" Bogart announced while glaring at them. "It ain't like any of you believed him the first few times. Why start now?"

Bogart's words crushed Jackie, but she knew he was right. She was just as guilty as the rest of the team. If something happened to Zack, she probably wouldn't be able to forgive herself.

"We need to find him ASAP," Beck announced with concern. "If he found one gun, he may have found two. The last thing we need is Zack running around a cruise ship armed and delusional."

Chapter Twenty-three

It was a little after two o'clock in the morning when they called off the search for Zack. Everyone knew it would be impossible to find him if he didn't want to be found. Monroe felt it best to stay in Zack's quarters, in case he returned, giving Jackie the suite to herself. She slept restlessly beneath the covers then seemed to wake for no reason. Jackie turned over in bed and saw Zack peacefully reclined against the headboard with his legs stretched out on the bed and crossed at the ankles. He at least had the decency to remove his dirty combat boots before making himself comfortable. Jackie jerked with surprise then groaned softly while sitting up and ran her fingers through her mussed hair.

"We've been looking everywhere for you," she informed him then stared at him with concern. "Where were you?"

Zack sat quietly in the dim lighting and barely reacted. "I tried calling you and the others earlier," he informed her without emotion. "No one answered."

She was surprised to hear him say that. "No one got your calls, Zack," she replied while attempting to handle the situation delicately. "Kirk's room was trashed. They found your cell phone among the mess." Jackie stared at him a moment with a curious look. "What happened?"

He drew a deep breath then groaned softly. "I can only assume I'm the one who trashed Kirk's room."

She continued to stare at him and observed his unusual behavior before reaching for the bedside light.

"Can you leave that off?" he asked in the same unemotional tone.

Jackie hesitated, glanced back at him in the dim lighting, and then turned on the light anyway. She turned in bed and looked at Zack, briefly scanning him for injuries or signs of blood. He allowed his head to fall into his hands and held his temples.

"I asked you to leave it off."

She didn't take her eyes off him. "Are you okay?"

"No, Jackie," he grumbled softly as he looked down at his legs while holding his head. "I'm not okay." He finally lifted his head and looked at her. "As a matter of fact, I'm completely fucked up."

She slipped out from under the covers and moved closer to him while sitting on her feet. "Whatever you're going through, we'll deal with it, Zack."

He stared at her a moment then returned his head to his hands and held his temples. She watched as he trembled. What Jackie witnessed concerned her. He was on the edge and slipping fast. She gently took his hand and removed it from his temple, holding it in hers.

"I won't abandon you," she firmly announced. "You don't need to talk about it if you're not ready but promise you'll stay by my side until we get back home. I'm renting the first plane I can and taking us home."

He searched her eyes and was almost at a loss for words. Zack managed a slight nod. He drew a deep, shaken breath but didn't look away. "Nothing I've seen is real," he informed her. "It's all been in my head. Hired killers, Katya, briefcase bombs. I've been taking those pills the doc gave me, but they're not helping. I feel like I'm going out of my mind."

She warmly caressed his hand, calming him. "It's okay, Zack," Jackie gently replied. "You're with me now, and I'm going to take care of you."

He stared into her eyes a moment then managed a tiny laugh. "Your compassion astounds me," he remarked while shaking his head. "I'm a horrible person, yet you always find a reason to look after me."

Jackie smiled and gently touched his face. "That's because I love you, you stupid jackass." She allowed her hand to fall from his face. "I'm going to get you a drink from the bar, and then I want you to get some sleep. You'll feel better in the morning."

"I doubt it," he muttered, "but as long as it makes you feel better--"

Jackie sprang from the bed and hurried across the room for the wet bar. Zack allowed his head to fall back into his hands. He again trembled and concentrated on his breathing. Jackie handed him a glass of scotch. He eagerly accepted it and drank the entire contents of the glass while Jackie climbed over his legs and returned to the spot on the bed alongside him. He set the glass on the nightstand and drew a deep breath, allowing the alcohol to numb his senses. Jackie warmly caressed his hand as he relaxed. He finally looked at her and took her hand between his.

"Do you think it'd be okay, just this once, if I could hold you while I sleep?"

"Under the circumstances, I think that'd be fine," Jackie replied then turned out the light on her side of the bed.

She no sooner slipped under the covers before Zack nestled against her. His hand warmly caressed her side and immediately traveled along her hip and to her thigh. He couldn't seem to help himself, but it seemed odd that she didn't stop his wandering hand. He stared at her through the dim lighting. She stared back and still didn't stop his hand. He removed his hand from her leg and gently touched her face. When there was no protest, he leaned in closer and kissed her warmly on the lips. Jackie returned the kiss without hesitation and ran her hands along his body. He needed little encouragement to prompt bad behavior. Zack tackled her to the bed, pinning her beneath him, and kissed her aggressively. He suddenly hesitated and slowed the kiss, taking his time and displaying great passion.

As the couple rolled around beneath the sheets, Zack remained reclined on the bed against the headboard. He'd managed to separate himself from the hallucination, although it was unclear why. It was obviously one of his more pleasant hallucinations. He watched the couple making love, feeling everything they felt, and his body aching the same, yet it wasn't him. It wasn't real.

"You should be ashamed of yourself," a familiar male voice announced sternly.

Zack looked away from the couple making love and saw Jackson Remus sitting casually in a chair near the bedside with his large booted feet propped on the nightstand not far from Zack. He was a moderately intimidating looking man with a shaved head and stern features.

"Commander?" Zack gasped softly while straightening on the bed. He then looked back at his other self making love to Jackson's daughter and panicked for the first time. Zack looked at the Commander with horror in his eyes. "I can explain," he announced. "This isn't how it looks."

Jackson chuckled softly in his throat. "I'm sure it's not," he replied. "You're just having a sexual fantasy about my daughter. Nothing wrong with that."

Zack stared at the Commander with his mouth slightly open, the surprise clearly across his face. "Why are you taking this so well?"

"Why do you think, Zack?" he responded.

Zack looked from the couple beneath the sheets to the Commander. "It's not real."

"Of course it's not real," Jackson blurted out. "If this was real, I'd kill you." He hesitated then considered. "Providing I was still alive, but, well--"

"I don't understand," Zack replied. "Am I losing my mind? First Katya, then Jackie, and now you."

"You had a concussion," Jackson informed him. "You remember what the doc told you. You're hallucinating, that's all. Why are you so worked up over it?" A twisted smile crossed his face. "Why aren't you under the covers enjoying your hallucination?"

Zack stared at him with a slightly bewildered look. "Something just doesn't feel right," he replied. "I mean, other than you telling me to jump your daughter."

"It could be because you're not in control for the first time in your life," Jackson replied. "If you were honest with yourself, you'd admit you've never been in control. Your demons have always controlled you."

"Confession is good for the soul, huh?" Zack remarked. "Isn't that what you were always trying to drill into my head? I'm not like you, Jackson. I don't have a wife to bare my soul to."

"No, but you have Jackie," he replied.

Zack glanced at the beautiful, naked woman entangled in a compromising position with his alter ego. He stared a moment longer. Jackson cleared his throat. Zack looked back at him.

"She's not mine," Zack replied. "She's Holden's wife."

"She's Holden's wife, but she's your partner," Jackson informed him. "She loves you as much as she loves him. It's just a different kind of love."

"I've never been real good with sharing my emotions," Zack informed him.

"You'll learn," Jackson replied and smiled. "I can't think of a better person to start with than my daughter."

Zack considered the comment then nodded. "You're probably right," he replied. "You usually were."

Jackson stood and placed his hand on Zack's shoulder, locking eyes with him. "You need to trust your instincts," he announced. "They've never been wrong. As for me, well, I'm just an extension of you. Someone you pulled from your subconscious to help guide you through this."

"So you're not really the Commander's ghost?" Zack questioned.

He shook his head.

Zack indicated the couple moaning beneath the covers. "And I'm not really making love to Jackie?"

"I'm pretty sure the term 'only in your dreams' applies more than ever on this one," he replied.

Zack unbuttoned his shirt. "Sorry, Commander, but you need to take a hike," he announced with confidence. "I have something more important I'd like to be doing."

"You should probably hurry," Jackson remarked. "Jackie's going to be waking you in five, four, three--"

Zack jerked awake and looked at Jackie where she sat on the edge of the bed holding a glass of scotch before him.

"I'm sorry," she announced gently. "I didn't mean to wake you. Drink this. You'll feel better. Then you should get some rest."

Zack stared at her a moment then eyed the empty bed alongside him with disappointment. He looked back at Jackie, held his breath, and then accepted the glass. His hand trembled slightly as he drank the entire contents in one gulp.

Chapter Twenty-four

A little after five o'clock on Thursday morning, Zack wandered through one of the private lounges. It was already set up for the elegant farewell brunch for those leaving the ship for the island wedding. The room was almost deathly silent, as was most of the ship in the early morning hour. Zack checked under tables, looking for anything suspicious. He heard the door open, but there was little time or space for Zack to make himself disappear. He casually straightened and faced whoever had entered.

"You're not supposed to be in here," Allen announced as he briskly crossed the large room toward Zack. "What are you doing here?"

Zack shrugged and leaned against one of the expensive chairs covered with a white satin liner. "Looking for my imaginary girlfriend, so I can apologize," he replied without care. "What are you doing here?"

Allen gave him a puzzled look then appeared irritated. "I'm Nelson Banks' personal guard," he replied. "It's my job to be here."

"Oh?"

Allen groaned softly and shook his head. "I'm tired and it's too early to get into trouble. Do us both a favor and leave," he announced with disinterest. "I don't have time for guessing games. I've got a lot of work to do."

"I've heard of Nelson Banks," Zack announced casually. "He's that lowlife mob boss, right?"

Allen sighed and scratched his head. "Yeah, that'd be the one."

119

"Don't care much for your boss, I take it."

"At five in the morning, I don't care much for anyone," Allen muttered while sighing then appeared annoyed. "He's had me running around since we boarded the ship looking for imaginary hitmen."

"Imaginary hitmen?" Zack announced cheerfully while straightening. "Well, you're in luck. I've already taken care of them, so you can go back to bed."

Allen stared at Zack as if uncertain what to make of him. He suddenly smiled and chuckled. "You're a little wrong in the head, aren't you?"

"Most days," Zack admitted then gingerly rubbed the scar on his temple, "but the concussion has made that worse. Apparently, I'm Batman."

Allen just stared at Zack.

Zack marveled at the look he received then chuckled. "That was a joke." He sighed and looked around. "This place is clean. I don't think you're going to find any imaginary bad guys here. I'm sure they're hanging out in the cargo hold."

"Good to know," Allen replied and held back his chuckle. "Want a cup of coffee? We can look for your imaginary girlfriend on the way to the lounge. Maybe she has a friend for me."

"Doubtful," he replied. "All her friends are assassins. You don't want to mess with those crazy bitches."

Allen laughed as they left the private room and headed into the upper-level corridor. "So how does your imaginary girlfriend know so many female assassins?"

"She's a Russian spy," he casually replied.

"Really?" Allen remarked and held back his laugh. "How did you meet?"

"She tried to kill me," he replied then made an imaginary gun with his fingers and stared down his index finger, which was the barrel. "It was love at first sight."

"Uh, huh."

✝

Allen and Zack entered the only lounge open that time of morning serving coffee and pastries for the early rising passengers. The lounge was empty, as were most of the passenger areas onboard for such an early hour. Both men helped themselves to some coffee and pastries then sat at the bar. Even the wait staff was suspiciously missing.

"So these imaginary people wanting to kill your boss," Zack casually began, "how badly do they want him? Have you ever actually caught one?"

"Now and again," Allen informed him. "I don't think there's any onboard this ship though. Sealy and I have been over every inch of this ship, and we screened the crew and passengers a week prior to the voyage."

"I wouldn't rely too heavily on the ship's security," Zack informed him while grinning. "I'm practically a stowaway myself. They'll let any nutcase on this ship without proper credentials." He stood while looking around the empty lounge. "I guess one of the imaginary bad guys I'd killed was supposed to be on duty here. We seem a little light in the wait staff department. If you find someone, see if you can secure a blueberry muffin. I'll be in the little boys' room."

"You've got it," Allen replied.

Zack headed into the bathroom and paused just inside the doorway. He eyed the frilly restroom then double-checked the sign just outside the door to make sure he had the right bathroom. He shook his head, returned inside the bathroom, and ventured into the first stall. Once he finished, he flushed the toilet and stepped out to wash his hands. A faint sound alerted him. Zack peered beneath the stall doors and saw a pair of neatly shined, white shoes in the last stall. The man's foot slid and turned out. Zack removed the gun from the back of his pants and approached the last stall. He gently pushed open the door and aimed the gun. A ship's server was propped on the toilet. His eyes remained open while staring transfixed at nothing. His neatly pressed white uniform had a large spot of fresh blood covering the chest. Zack straightened while staring at the dead man.

"Okay, that's not real," Zack remarked while replacing his gun. He left the stall and headed for the bathroom door. As he opened the door, he called out. "Hey, Allen, could you check something for me?"

Zack stopped and looked across the lounge. Allen was gone. Zack again removed the gun from his pants and crossed the lounge. He paused near the bar and peered over it. Allen lay dead on the floor behind the bar. Zack jumped back from the bar and looked around the empty lounge. There was no one within the room. Zack hurried for the door, checked outside to make sure there were no surprises, and rushed from the lounge onto deck. He kept his gun concealed close to his chest and kept an eye on a nearby dark area beneath the steps. He heard something move behind him. Zack spun around, prepared for anything. Several nearly silent shots fired from the darkness further down deck. Zack took two bullets to his chest and flew backward over the ship's railing from the force of the shots. A loud splash followed.

Chapter Twenty-five

Gil and Darth entered the lounge while following the exceptionally loud voice of an irate woman. It was a little before seven in the morning. The lounge was still set up for early morning passengers, but there were several empty coffee cups on the tables and lining the bar. The pastries hadn't been replenished and the woman from the kitchen was complaining to a security guard that the excessively large coffeepot was empty. Gil approached the guard and the woman.

"What's the problem?" Gil asked.

"Rick took off and left the lounge in this condition," the woman informed him while gesturing wildly with her hands. "Passengers were complaining about the state of the lounge. There's no coffee and the pastry plates are empty. Look at all the dirty dishes!"

The guard eyed Gil. "It's not the first time Rick skipped out on his duties," he announced. "Usually it's just an extended cigarette break." He looked back at the woman. "We'll find Rick and deal with him accordingly. Would you mind filling in for him?"

"Yeah, whatever," the woman balked. "But this is the last time I'm covering for him."

She began cleaning up the dirty dishes then tended to the coffee machine.

Gil looked around suspiciously. "Anything odd about what you found so far?"

"Odd?" the security guard questioned then chuckled softly. "No, nothing odd. We searched the lounge but didn't find anything. He's probably been gone a couple of hours, considering the coffee machine is empty. I'm going to check his quarters then search the kitchen. Would you check the nearby area?"

"Yeah, sure," Gil replied but remained deep in thought.

He took a moment longer to look around the lounge then headed onto deck with Darth. They only walked a few feet when Darth started sniffing the nearby railing. Gil carefully searched the railing to see what had Darth's attention and discovered a recently splintered section of wood. Considering it was on top, maintenance would have almost certainly found it on their early morning inspection. Gil removed a pocketknife and dug into the hole. He stared with moderate surprise at the bullet he held between his fingers.

"Oh, that's not good." Upon closer inspection of the railing, he found a fragment of black cloth. Gil removed his cell phone and pressed a button. "Hey, we may have a problem. One of the staff is missing from his post inside the lounge, and I found a bullet matching the caliber of that gun we found in Kirk's room. It's fresh. Only an hour or two." He hesitated. "But it gets worse. There's some black fabric that is the same as Zack's combat uniform."

†

Beck paced his suite with his cell phone to his ear and a concerned look on his face while listening to Gil's report.

"We'll see if Darth can track Zack," Beck announced to Gil over the phone. "Meet me in Zack's room in the crew's quarters." He disconnected his call as someone knocked on the door.

Beck looked out the peek hole and saw Bogart standing before the door with an anxious look on his usually calm face. Beck opened the door, already irritated with Bogart.

"What is it--?"

He suddenly hesitated when he saw Pinto casually leaning against the wall with her arms folded across her chest.

Bogart frowned and looked ashamed. "She cornered me in the stairway."

Beck stared helplessly at Pinto and barely heard a word Bogart said. "I can explain everything," he immediately blurted out.

She straightened and allowed her arms to fall to her sides. "You've been following me," Pinto snapped hotly. "I was thinking I'd overreacted, and now I find you on some covert mission to spy on me. You're unbelievable!"

Pinto turned and stormed down the hall. Beck stared after her but couldn't force himself to run after the irate woman.

"What's wrong with you?" Bogart demanded and pointed. "Go after her!"

"No, she's in a fighting mood," he replied. "I need to let her calm down. She has an unbelievable temper."

✝

Bogart and Jackie sat with Sal on his private balcony while he sipped coffee and stared out into the ocean. They watched him without saying a word. He finally sighed, adjusted his glasses, and then looked at them. He was clearly disappointed but there was something else beyond his eyes.

"Beck definitely crossed a line," Sal informed them, "but I understand his concerns."

"So he should show Pinto the photos Zack found?" Bogart asked, satisfied he was right.

"Oh, absolutely not," Sal announced as his eyes widened and he shook his head. "Will is a sensitive subject, and admitting they searched his apartment without justification will send her over the edge."

"There's definitely something going on, Sal," Jackie informed him. "I know Zack is known for his disappearing acts, but something is different this time."

"Yes, the bullet Gil dug out of the railing," Sal replied then sighed. "That's troubling. Someone would have heard a gunshot and reported it, which means the gun most likely contained a silencer." He raised his brows and eyed both. "Guns are prohibited, so one with a silencer was certainly brought onboard with foul intentions. And you found another gun containing a silencer in Kirk's room, but it hadn't been fired?"

"Zack was suffering a concussion from another assignment, which was causing hallucinations," Jackie informed him, "but I think he may have actually stumbled upon something. If he believed he was hallucinating, he may have underestimated the situation."

Sal again sank into thought and stared at the ocean. He sighed softly without looking at them. "My first priority is my daughter," he informed them. "I want to see her happy and more importantly, I don't want something to happen to her because I underestimated what you're telling me." He again looked at them. "I trust the instincts of your team. If you believe either of our lives are in danger, I'm willing to suffer her wrath if you're wrong. You

125

say Banks already hired Beck and Monroe as additional security guards for the wedding, so they're covered. I'll see that the rest of you receive accommodations at my friend's resort. Completely under the radar stuff. My friend will keep your identity between us. He'll trust my judgement."

"Thank you, Sal," Jackie replied.

"What about Beck and Pinto?" Bogart asked. "Can you help smooth things over with her?"

"You can't tell that girl what to do," Sal announced. "There was a time she barely spoke to me. I don't have any influence over her decisions. I'm afraid she'll have to come to her own decision about Beck." He groaned softly. "Believe me, no one wants to see her get back together with Beck more than I do, but it's out of my hands."

"She's going to realize we're at the wedding reception," Jackie informed him. "We can't fly that low under the radar."

"I'll handle that," Sal informed them. "She'll be mad, naturally, but I doubt it can get much worse."

Chapter Twenty-six

The *Andrea Maria* docked at the port in Cartagena, Colombia. Most of the passengers disembarked the ship to explore the shops and countryside. The wedding guests left the ship and immediately headed for Nelson Banks' luxury yacht, which would take the nearly fifty guests to Giovanni's private island just off the coast of Columbia. The team remained on deck and watched the wedding guests board a rented bus to take them to the dock where their yacht awaited. The six exchanged looks and frowns, their concern for Zack growing.

"He should have been here by now," Gil remarked and again checked his watch.

"In his current state--" Jackie began but Beck interrupted her.

"He's fine," Beck snarled, a little more on edge than usual. "He's gotten into worse situations. I sincerely doubt he met his demise on a cruise ship."

"Should we search the ship again?" Bogart asked, showing the same concern as Jackie.

"Darth couldn't pick up his scent," Monroe muttered with an oddly defeated look while slumped over the railing. "If he doesn't want to be found, we're not going to find him."

Kirk straightened and showed no emotion. "He's fine," he announced boldly. "He'll show up later like always."

Bogart eyed the four men then raised his brow. "If you're all so damned confident he's fine, why are we still standing here?"

When they didn't acknowledge Bogart's sarcastic comment or even bother giving him their usual annoyed look, Bogart straightened with concern.

"You actually think something happened to him," Bogart announced with surprise.

Jackie placed her hand on Bogart's lower arm and gave it a slight squeeze, silencing him. He shook his head with disbelief and some hostility.

"I'm going to his room to pack up his things," Bogart announced boldly. "I'll meet you guys on the dock." He turned and left with disgust. Jackie eyed the guys then hurried after Bogart.

Monroe straightened and glanced at his friends. "We should probably collect our things and head to the airfield."

They nodded in agreement, yet none made a motion to move away from the ship's railing.

✝

The older helicopter had seen better days, leaving the five men clinging to their seats on the nearly thirty-minute journey to Giovanni's private island. Despite the term 'private island', Sal's friend had a luxurious hotel resort along the beach, which offered many amenities to its guests. The mansion was further down the beach and nearly inaccessible from the hotel. A manmade rock formation created a natural looking barrier to keep guests from wandering onto the wealthy owner's property. The wedding guests were staying at the resort, which remained closed the entire week to accommodate the nearly two hundred wedding guests. It allowed them sole access to the resort and its facilities. They were holding the wedding at the hotel for convenience and security reasons.

Jackie flew the helicopter with Gil as her co-pilot. Despite Gil's piloting experience, Jackie was the better helicopter pilot. She circled the island, allowing the guys to scope the area below. The island interior was mostly wooded jungle terrain, although they could make out a roadway directly through the center of the island. The shoreline on the other sides of the island contained some beautiful beaches, but not nearly as large as the one where the resort was located. They could see old docks on remote beaches but none contained any boats.

Once they had a lay of the land, Jackie found a quiet spot to land the helicopter. It was a short walk to the hotel, although they

128

were anticipating a moderately unfriendly greeting. As the helicopter shut down, the guys unloaded their gear. Beck gave Jackie several annoyed looks as she finished shutting down the craft. She finally climbed out of the pilot's seat, glared back at him, and folded her arms across her chest.

"Something you'd like to say, Beck?" she demanded.

He tossed his bag to the ground. "I can't believe you went to Sal without talking to me first," Beck snarled. "That should have been my call."

"And you should have made it," Jackie snapped back, alerting the guys to the heated conversation. "Sal's a reasonable man, and he's on your side."

"You could have ruined everything," Beck growled back in response.

"You already have!"

The guys stared at them with surprise and silence. Beck seemed stunned by Jackie's hostile outburst as well. He was suddenly at a loss for words, but Jackie had little trouble finding her own.

"We're only here because you pissed off your girlfriend," she lashed out. "Will may be a creep and he may be stalking her, but she was never in any danger. Maybe if you were a little more committed to your relationship, we wouldn't be here and Zack wouldn't be missing." She shook her head with disgust. "I have half a mind to call Ross."

The guys seemingly fidgeted at the same time. Jackie had no qualms about going over Beck's head; displaying a newly found lack of respect the others wouldn't dare show. At a moment when Beck should have been yelling back, he had nothing to offer.

"Zack came to me last night a broken man," she continued with less hostility and more sorrow. "He needed help. He *asked* for help, and now he's gone. Missing or worse." She glared at the five men. "We let him down. This is our fault!"

All five fidgeted, displaying their discomfort for what they already seemed to know. They heard resort jeeps approaching and immediately snapped to attention. Their differences and concerns would have to wait.

"Do you want to leave?" Beck asked Jackie then eyed the others. "Anyone who wants to leave can do it now. I'm upset about Zack too, I truly am, but I need to see this through."

The others glanced at Jackie, almost as if waiting for her response to the question. She suddenly felt subconscious that the rest of the team was looking to her for leadership. Going against Beck would be bad for moral, and she needed to think of the team.

She groaned softly and shook her head. "I'm not going anywhere," she informed Beck. "If Zack is alive, he'll come here. If something did happen to him, someone here is in danger. You're right. We should see it through."

The others immediately agreed with her, leaving Beck slightly dismayed by their loyalty to Jackie. Had Beck lost the respect of the team? Or was Zack's disappearance too much for any of them to bear? The resort jeeps approached and stopped before them. Heavily armed men jumped out and aimed their weapons at them. The remaining team raised their hands defensively in the air.

"It's okay," Beck announced. "We're with security. Corbin and Mr. Banks should have notified you."

One man checked his portable tablet then eyed Beck. "Are you Beck Larue?"

Beck nodded and lowered his hands. "Yeah, I'm Beck Larue."

"We'll have to clear the rest of these people," the man announced. "Let's go."

They secured their bags and joined the men inside the jeeps. Within seconds, the guards whisked them away to the resort.

Chapter Twenty-seven

The resort, although smaller than most island resorts, was lavish and catered to a filthy rich clientele. The building itself was only four floors with less than two hundred rooms. There was exotic beauty everywhere. Colorful flowers covered every corner of the painstakingly landscaped resort. The pool was small and intimate with several hot tubs isolated in romantic coves throughout, giving guests a feeling of seclusion. The white, sandy beach with plush lounge chairs scattered about was clean and raked every morning. Wait staff were on hand to serve guests exotic, fruity drinks on the beach, tending to their every whim.

Jackie and Bogart walked along the soft white sand in colorful island shirts and white shorts they'd picked up in Columbia in an effort to fit in. Bogart wore exceptionally dark sunglasses, allowing him to watch people without them realizing he was spying on them. Despite their attempts to blend, they looked more like hotel workers than guests. The guests were mostly millionaires and dressed the part even in something as simple as beachwear. With good reason, both felt slightly out of place and uncomfortable. Jackie held her cell phone to her ear then disconnected the call with annoyance.

"Holden still not answering?"

"Cell phones don't seem to work on this island," Jackie replied with a soft groan.

"The resort has landlines," Bogart informed her. "I have to assume they're crappy, but you should be able to get a call through to him."

"I left him a message before we left Columbia," she replied then frowned. "I hate feeling isolated."

"People pay big bucks for isolation."

"Yeah? Well, obviously they were never in the witness protection program," she remarked.

Bogart hid his smile at the comment then casually glanced around the beach and focused his attention on Will, who stood near one of the small bars while talking with Luke.

"How exactly did that little shit get invited to this cartel soiree?" Bogart asked while indicating Will.

"Good question," Jackie replied. "What are the chances that some guy from the Colorado sticks just happens to know the same crime families as Pinto's father?"

"I'd say little to none," Bogart remarked then eyed her through his dark sunglasses. "Suppose he went to that little hick burg just to weasel his way into Pinto's life?"

"It's worth considering."

"Which means Beck's onto something," Bogart continued while raising a dark brow above his sunglasses.

"I hate to admit it, but it looks that way." She sighed softly. "After my little temper tantrum, I suppose I'll have to apologize to Beck."

"No," Bogart replied without hesitation. "You were in the right. He needed to hear that. His priorities are all over the place right now. If he can't commit to Pinto then he deserves to lose her."

Jackie eyed Bogart with some surprise then grinned. "Look at you," she boldly announced. "I never expected you to be pro-marriage."

"I'm all for marriage," he informed her. "Just not for me, at least for now. I haven't met the right woman." He frowned and looked around. "I sometimes think I never will. The only women I seem to attract are only interested in meaningless sex. I can't remember the last time I went on an actual date. Maybe I'm not meant for that lifestyle."

"Do you want that lifestyle?"

"I thought I did," he replied. "You know, hanging out with you and Holden for those few months. I liked that. Now that I've finally been accepted as one of the team, I don't think there's room for that sort of commitment to another person. Beck's sort of proven that."

"Ross is making it work," Jackie announced.

"Yeah, well, Ross's girlfriend needs her head examined," Bogart muttered. "He's gone more than he's home. She's left alone with his niece and brother-in-law a lot. Ross's brother-in-law is a good-looking guy and a widower to boot. That's a bad scene just waiting to play out."

"You're all doom and gloom lately," Jackie remarked with surprise.

"I'm bugged about Zack's disappearance," Bogart informed her then stopped and faced her. He removed his sunglasses and stared into her eyes. "He's been part of them forever. If they take his absence so lightly, what happens when someone like me goes missing? Just shrug and get on with their lives?" He frowned and returned his sunglasses to his face. "I've never much mattered to anyone. I never had a real family. Hanging with you guys is as close as I've ever come to having a family."

Jackie smiled and clung to Bogart's arm, surprising him. "Even if it turns out you're not my brother, you're still my family, Bogart."

He looked at her and smiled proudly. "You're an awesome sister."

"I can't believe you're still here," Pinto scoffed from behind them.

Jackie and Bogart turned and stared at the attractive woman in her colorful bikini and flowered sarong. Pinto folded her arms across her chest and glared at them.

"My father said you were staying until the reception as 'additional security'," Pinto huffed. "You can give Beck a message for me--"

Jackie placed her hands firmly on her hips and glared back at Pinto. "You can give Beck your own damned message," she snapped. "As far as I'm concerned, you two deserve each other. I don't know how two people who claim to love each other can do so without communicating. Your life may very well be in danger, but all you can do is whine about your boyfriend riding in on a white horse to save your ass." Jackie raised her brows with hostility. "Zack and two security guards are missing, and Gil dug a slug out of the ship's railing. Personally, at this point, I don't give a damn about your relationship with Beck. You both deserve to be alone and miserable. I only care about stopping whatever nightmare is about to unfold on this island. Go cry to someone else. I've no more fucks to give right now."

Jackie grabbed Bogart's arm and practically pulled him off his feet, forcing him to follow her. He was too stunned to protest, unable even to process what had just happened.

"Don't you think you were a little hard on her?" Bogart remarked as they walked away. "You're certainly doing a fine job at pissing people off today."

"Maybe if they're all mad at me they'll have less energy to be mad at each other," she remarked. "Someone has to open the line of communication between those two."

They heard a commotion further down the beach, alerting them to something having happened. As a crowd quickly gathered fifty yards away, they heard someone scream, "A body washed ashore!"

Bogart and Jackie ran after the crowd. Jackie couldn't deny the pang in her heart at the thought of who may have washed onto shore. They pushed their way through the crowd and joined security, having just arrived. Although less than twelve hours in the water, Allen's body was severely bloated and almost unrecognizable as one of the guards from the ship. He had a bullet hole in his back, but most of the blood washed away in the water. Jackie and Bogart held their breath but were relieved it wasn't Zack. Just because it wasn't Zack, that didn't alter the fact that Zack was still missing. Jackie pulled Bogart aside.

"That guard was shot in the back," Jackie said to him in a hushed tone. "I'm willing to bet we find the same slug in him as the one Gil found in the railing."

"I'm guessing it was a 9mm," a male voice behind them announced.

Jackie and Bogart turned to the familiar voice and saw Zack standing just behind them, straining to see the dead body on shore. He was dressed head to toe in white beachwear and a white straw fedora to complete the ensemble. Jackie cried out when she saw him. She threw her arms around his neck and clung to him while fighting her tears. He eagerly returned the embrace.

"Miss me already?" he teased.

She pulled away and looked at him while grinning. "You look like a Columbian drug lord," Jackie remarked. "Where'd you get the threads?"

"You don't want to know," Zack muttered then eyed Bogart, who just stared at him. Zack's look was demanding. "Who took my bag? I need to get out of these pretty boy clothes before anyone important sees me like this."

Bogart didn't say anything but instead just stared with his mouth hanging open.

Zack glared at him, quickly becoming annoyed. "What's with you?" he demanded. "Didn't you ever see anyone back from the dead before?"

Bogart threw his arms around Zack and hugged him, startling the man. "I'm so happy you're alive!"

Zack pulled away and put some distance between them. "Friendship aside," he announced firmly. "Do that again, and I'm stabbing your ass."

Bogart held his hands in the air and grinned boyishly. "Understood."

"What happened?" Jackie asked while moving further away from the crowd to speak more freely.

"Some fucker shot me twice in the chest," Zack remarked while gingerly rubbing his chest.

"Who?"

"If I knew, he'd be dead already," he informed her. "Thankfully my new combat jacket came equipped with a bulletproof lining. A lifesaver but a real bastard to swim in." He indicated the body. "Is that Allen?"

"It's one of the guards from the wedding party," Jackie informed him. "I don't know his name."

"Yeah, that's Allen," Zack replied while frowning. "We were having some coffee in the lounge. I found the lounge waiter dead in the bathroom. I went to warn Allen, but they'd already gotten to him. Whoever killed them was waiting on deck to ambush me. When I found myself floating in the water, I assumed it wasn't a hallucination for a change."

"No, I suppose it wasn't," Jackie replied.

"But Katya, your father, and the other dead crewmen--?" Zack asked with a curious look.

"Hallucinations," Jackie replied.

He considered the comment, appeared deep in thought, and then eyed her. "You ravaging me?"

Bogart stared at him with some surprise. Jackie felt her cheeks redden as she fidgeted, uncomfortable by the question. "*Definitely* a hallucination."

He sighed and casually waved her off. "It's probably for the best," Zack remarked with little emotion. "The last thing this world

135

needs is a bunch of little ass kicking, Jackie-Zack half-breeds running around."

"I couldn't even imagine," Jackie muttered and again fidgeted. She eyed Zack with a serious look. "If they were waiting on deck for you, but you hadn't seen them initially--"

"Yeah, I know," Zack reluctantly groaned. "I was a target. At least one of them. They may have thought I was one of the guards."

"And maybe someone just wanted to kill you," Jackie informed him.

"I considered that," Zack replied. "But I'd only met up with the guard a few minutes before that. No one followed me, which means they were following him."

"I know it may sound irrational--" Jackie began.

Zack cocked his head and smirked. "Whatever it is, I like it already."

"If you were the intended target or even if someone thinks you're dead," Jackie continued, "maybe you should stay dead a while longer."

"I'm good at playing dead," Zack replied then gently scratched his body through his excessively white outfit. "Seriously, where is my bag? I need to change. I wouldn't be caught dead in this outfit."

Jackie smirked and handed Zack her room key. "Your bag is in my room. Keep out of sight until we can sort this out."

He took the key then eyed her suspiciously. "We're sharing a room now? Are you sure we didn't have a little affair d'amour?"

She glared at him with limited patience. He grinned at the look he'd received then left.

Chapter Twenty-eight

Zack woke with a close-up view of bright, colorful carpet with a tacky design. He suddenly jerked and flipped onto his backside, uncertain where he was or how he'd even gotten there. He looked around the familiar casino from an assignment not so long ago. It was the casino in Sal's abandoned hotel. As he hesitantly stood, considering how he'd gotten there, he felt a tremendous pain in his side. Zack touched his side and looked down. There was blood covering his hand and shirt. He'd been wounded. Beyond the bloodied torn shirt, he could see the laceration where a bullet grazed him. He struggled to remember what had happened. Was this all another hallucination? Or was everything that had happened on the *Andrea Maria* actually the fake reality?

As he turned, he saw Ross clinging to a younger woman on the floor alongside one of the blackjack tables. Zack hurried toward them then suddenly stopped when he realized they were dead. By the way Ross held his girlfriend, Lee, against his chest, someone executed them without giving them a chance to fight back. Zack uncertainly backed away with horror on his face. As he turned, he saw Monroe lying face down on the floor with blood surrounding him. Kirk was propped against one of the slot machines, a gun in his bloodied hand and his eyes open as he stared up. Several bullet holes were visible over his heart, clearly precision kill shots by someone highly trained. Zack ran his fingers through his hair as his heart raced.

He scanned the casino and saw Bogart slumped in one of the chairs before a slot machine, blood pouring from his head across the machine and dripping down his arm. Gil and Beck sat back to back with guns limp in their hands and huge chunks of their skulls missing as they made their last stand. There was so much blood they were almost unrecognizable. Zack held his head and looked around with horror as something suddenly occurred to him.

"Jackie!"

There was no response. As he looked around, he saw a woman's hand sticking out beyond one of the blackjack tables. Zack ran for the woman then slowed as he neared the table. Jackie lay on the floor with her throat torn out as she stared at him with horror in her dead eyes. Zack fell to his knees alongside her and gathered her into his arms while sobbing. He held her to his chest while clinging to her despite her blood soaking into his clothes. He heard the sound of dripping blood then realized someone was standing over him. Zack held back his grief and lifted his head with a psychotic look in his eyes, prepared to meet the person who killed his friends. Holden stood over Zack with a gun clutched in his blood covered hand. Blood ran down his face from a large laceration on his temple. He'd been shot several times with blood seeping from wounds on his side and leg.

"You bastard," Holden gasped, barely able to speak. "You killed them! You killed Jackie!"

Holden raised the gun level to Zack's face. Zack stared at Holden with horror and shook his head as tears streaked his face.

"No," he protested. "I'd never do this. They're my friends. I'd never kill them--especially Jackie. You have to believe me."

Holden's finger tightened on the trigger. Although Zack could have escaped at that moment, he refused to release Jackie. He clung to her, buried his head into her blood-soaked neck, and shut his eyes while waiting for the gunshot. The sound of a gun firing echoed through the empty casino. Zack hesitantly opened his eyes and saw Holden standing motionless a moment. Blood seeped through the bullet wound in the center of his forehead. His eyes rolled back as he sank to his knees, collapsing to the floor. Zack looked down and saw he was holding a semiautomatic in his hand. He suddenly gasped and tossed it aside. He looked for Jackie, but she was gone. Zack sprang to his feet and looked around the casino. They were gone. He clutched his head and cried out in sorrow and rage.

"What are you doing--?" a woman's voice announced.

Zack lowered his hands from his face and stared across the unfamiliar casino at a face he hadn't seen in some time. Macbeth, frequently called Mac, was a dark-haired beauty in her mid-thirties. Although her fresh face and athletic frame suggested she was a high maintenance, classy woman, the truth was less flattering.

The moment she saw him, the hostility and hatred showed in her eyes as they widened. "You!" she gasped with surprise and a hint of anger. "What the hell are you doing here?" Her look became more hateful. "Did Sal send you to find me?"

"Mac?" Zack gasped with surprise then looked around the empty casino. He looked back at her then held his head and groaned softly. "Oh, this just keeps getting better and better."

"Yeah, well, I'm not exactly happy to see you either," she snarled.

He waved her off and walked past her. "You're just another hallucination," he informed her. "I could care less what you think." Zack looked at his watch. It was after three in the morning. "How the hell did I get here?" he demanded then considered. "Where the hell is here?"

"You're in the casino, idiot," Mac scoffed. "What's this about hallucinations?"

"What would be the point in explaining," he muttered and headed for the main doors. "I need to find the rest of the team."

Mac caught up to him and grabbed his arm, causing him to turn defensively. He was prepared to strike but held back. She immediately released his arm.

"What's this about the rest of the team?" she demanded with concern. "Are they here?"

"Of course they're here," he snapped. "You're not a very informed hallucination. At least Katya was helpful."

Mac stared at him with her mouth hanging open. She was about to ask but shook her head and dismissed it. "Why are you here?"

"Must I really rehash this with you?" He groaned with annoyance. "Beck thinks Pinto and Sal might be in danger, so he brought us on this trip from hell to fight imaginary bad guys." He considered the comment. "Even more imaginary for me."

Her eyes widened with horror. "Sal's here?" she gasped then looked around while running her fingers through her hair. "He can't know I'm here. He'll kill me."

"Oh relax," Zack scoffed while waving her off. "You're just a figment of my imagination anyway."

"What is wrong with you?" she demanded. "Have you lost what few marbles you had left?"

"No, it's the concussion," he replied without care then rolled his eyes. "Why am I bothering?"

Mac groaned with annoyance and grabbed his crotch, startling him. She raised her brows while smiling slyly. "Is this your imagination?"

He brushed her hand from his crotch and waved her off. "That's all you imaginary women want," he remarked. "Enough with the seduction scenes. I have bigger concerns." As he turned and walked away from her, he mildly adjusted himself and gave the incident a moment of consideration.

Mac stared at him with surprise. "You're kidding, right?"

As he left the casino, Mac hurried after him. They walked along the unusually quiet corridor. Everyone had gone to bed, leaving the hotel silent.

"You can't tell anyone I'm here," she informed him with desperation in her voice.

"They all think I'm nuts already," he remarked. "I'm certainly not going to mention another delusion. Your imaginary existence is safe with me."

"You really need your head examined," she insisted.

"It's on my to-do list," he muttered.

Chapter Twenty-nine

Nearly two hundred wedding guests enjoyed a lavish brunch set up on the veranda overlooking the beach. It was late morning Friday, the day before the wedding. Belle and Marco, the bride and groom, greeted their guests. They were a happy, attractive couple with their whole lives ahead of them. Both had the classic Italian look with dark, almost black hair. Belle was somewhat tiny in height and frame. She was possibly an inch or two over five feet while Marco was lean and athletic. His nearly six-foot frame allowed him to tower over his bride-to-be. Both were excessively tan, suggesting they'd spent some time on the island already.

The father of the groom and the island owner, Giovanni, remained close to the outside bar with two guards only arm's length from him. Giovanni looked like an older version of his son. He had a little more girth to him, yet he somehow looked more imposing. Perhaps it was just his reputation affecting his outward appearance. No one messed with Giovanni or his family. He talked with his son's future father-in-law, Matt. Luke stood near his father, but his attention was anywhere but on their conversation. Sealy remained a few feet from Matt and resembled a Secret Service agent on guard duty.

"Your daughter is well protected," Giovanni insisted. "I have dozens of trained men guarding the resort, and there are security cameras everywhere."

Matt didn't appear convinced, although he kept his voice down and attempted to keep his concerns from showing around the other guests. "What about the guard they found washed ashore?" he demanded. "You sent that man to protect us, and someone put a bullet in his back. I haven't seen my own bodyguard since our first night on the ship. What if he's dead too?"

"I'll talk to Corbin," Giovanni informed him. "He'll do whatever it is he does to keep things running smoothly. I assure you, whatever happened on the ship was unfortunate, but it can't happen here. Security is too tight."

"Then tell that one to stop following me around," Matt remarked while indicating Sealy. "Put him at my daughter's side. She's the important one."

"I'll pull our kids aside after brunch and go over security with them, if it'll make you happy," Giovanni announced. "Believe me, Matt; if this island wasn't safe, I'd be dead by now."

"I suppose you have a point," Matt muttered. He groaned softly and attempted to control his anxiety. "I'm going to have a drink and try to enjoy today. After the wedding tomorrow, I'll be able to relax."

"It'll all be fine," Giovanni insisted.

Matt walked away. Luke seemed to realize his father had left then hurried after him. Sealy approached Giovanni after receiving a glare.

"I want to know what's going on around here," Giovanni demanded in an angry whisper. "Find Corbin. Make sure he has everything under control. I want to know how Allen was killed onboard that ship."

"Yes, sir," Sealy announced then left.

Sealy passed Sal and Pinto where they sat at their table. Pinto watched the way her father stared after the large bodyguard. His look was troubling. She leaned across the table, having a difficult time hiding her concern.

"Something wrong, Dad?"

He was silent a moment then seemed to realize she was speaking. Sal forced a smile and attempted to look relaxed.

"No, dear," Sal replied. "Everything is fine. Nothing for you to worry about."

She stared at him and didn't appear convinced. "Why are you lying to me?"

Sal eyed her then sighed softly. "Giovanni has made plenty of enemies in his time," he informed her. "Something just doesn't feel right." He reached across the table, took her hands in his, and stared into her eyes, concerning her. "If anything happens, I want you to find Beck's team, no matter how you feel about him right now, and do whatever they tell you."

"What do you think's going to happen?" she nearly gasped, alarmed by the comment.

"I don't know," Sal remarked while drifting off into his own world. "They say a shark can smell blood in the water. I'm smelling blood."

"This has nothing to do with Will, does it?" Pinto asked with concern.

"Not anymore," Sal muttered.

Giovanni approached their table with a broad grin on his face. His son, Marco, and Marco's bride-to-be, Belle, were directly behind him. Sal immediately stood and gave his old friend an Italian hug then pulled away.

"Marco," Giovanni announced cheerfully. "You remember my good friend, Salvatore Romano."

Marco politely shook Sal's hand. "Yes, I remember very well."

"Do you also remember his daughter, Pinto?"

Marco eyed Pinto with some surprise then laughed while saying something in Italian. She stood and allowed Marco to hug her the same way Giovanni hugged her father. He pulled back and marveled at Pinto.

"It's been a long time, Pinto," Marco announced cheerfully. "We were just teenagers when I last saw you." He laughed softly. "You used to follow me around everywhere I went."

Pinto laughed at the memory. "It's wonderful to see you again, Marco."

"I'm so glad you could make it to the wedding," he announced then pulled Belle to his side. "You never met my bride-to-be. Belle, this is Pinto, a dear friend of the family."

The women politely shook hands. Belle was everything a well-bred woman should be. It was obvious she came from a wealthy family. Although her family was wealthier than Sal, she was gracious toward Pinto.

"I've heard many stories about Marco's childhood," Belle announced cheerfully. "It's nice to finally meet some of his friends from when he was a boy."

"I don't know that we were friends," Pinto teased while grinning at Marco. "Your future husband used to chase me around the mansion grounds with garter snakes."

Marco laughed and hid his smile. "I loved the way you screamed," he teased.

Belle attempted to frown but couldn't be upset with Marco. She shook her head then looked at Pinto. "All young boys are bad at that age," she remarked. "My brother, Luke, was the worst. Have you met Luke?"

Pinto shifted uncomfortably then smiled. "Yes, we spent some time together on the ship."

"I'll bet," Belle announced and gave her a quick once over. "He was probably stuck on you like glue. Honestly, he hasn't matured that much over the years. Don't be afraid to tell him where to go."

Pinto laughed knowingly.

✝

Sealy walked along a path in the garden, being the quickest way to the hotel entrance near the security office. Someone darted along the path near the generator shed. Sealy stopped and stared only a moment then hurried after the suspicious person. The generator building was responsible for maintaining power to the resort. If anyone tampered with it, the results would be devastating, particularly before the wedding tomorrow. Sealy touched his ear transmitter.

"Corbin, do you copy?" he announced.

"Yeah, Sealy, I copy," came Corbin's voice over his ear transmitter.

"I have suspicious activity near the generator building. I'm going to check it out," Sealy informed him. "Have maintenance give the generator a thorough inspection."

"I'll have someone there in five minutes," Corbin replied. "Do you need backup?"

"Nah, I'm fine," Sealy replied with little care. "It's probably nothing."

"Okay," he responded. "Corbin out."

Sealy removed a semiautomatic from his hidden shoulder holster and approached the nearby building in search of his mysterious intruder. He circled the building but didn't see anyone nearby. Sealy checked the door. The massive lock was broken. He cursed softly under his breath, again looked around, and then entered the generator building. Sealy wandered past the massive generator and looked around for any signs of trespassers, although it seemed as if the intruder had fled the scene already. As he glanced over the generator for signs of tampering, he noticed a smudge of something on the machine. Sealy touched the smear and looked at the blood on his fingertips. He immediately became alert and looked around. The door opened and a maintenance man in a navy blue jumpsuit, wearing a tool belt, approached while carrying his toolbox.

"Someone was in here," Sealy informed him and again looked around. "Who was supposed to be on duty here? We need a head count."

When the maintenance man didn't respond, Sealy turned to look at him. The man stood in the shadows. By the time Sealy saw the gun in his hand, it was too late. The maintenance man impersonator fired the weapon affixed with a silencer twice, shooting Sealy in the chest. Sealy fell back against the generator, dropping his gun. He slowly sank down the machine to the floor.

✝

The expensive fourth-floor suite remained dimly lit despite being only late afternoon. All the curtains and blinds were drawn, which wasn't typical for housekeeping to leave the room dark once they made their rounds. Another blind mysteriously closed, making the suite even darker. A small figure mostly in black slipped across the room and approached a decorative armoire. The cabinet door opened to reveal the television and a small safe just beneath it. A code was entered into the keypad, allowing the safe door to open. Black gloved hands scooped out the contents into an awaiting black bag. The gloved hand paused and held Emily's ruby and diamond tennis bracelet, admiring it. It went into the bag. The safe door closed. A chisel struck the edges of the safe near the latch, leaving enough damage to create the illusion that someone physically broke into the safe. The thief turned to leave. A blind suddenly opened casting bright light onto the thief.

Mac shielded her eyes from the light and looked at the balcony door. Zack leaned against the frame with his arms folded across his chest and shook his head in disapproval.

"Oh, Mac," he scolded softly. "You're like the bad little kitten putting pulls in the curtains."

"I resent that," she scoffed and became annoyed. "Why are you following me?"

"I'm bored," he announced simply. "Playing dead isn't as much fun as it used to be. I thought I'd play with my imaginary friends instead."

She rolled her eyes and headed for the door. "You've got no friends. Find another playmate."

The black bag suddenly flew from her hand, surprising her. She turned and narrowly avoided Zack's black, booted foot to her face. Mac became enraged and spun into a roundhouse kick, nearly clipping him. He dodged the kick and deflected the return kick, which immediately followed. He went low and swept her legs out from beneath her then watched her crash to the floor with satisfaction. As he sprang back up from his low spin, Mac kicked upward, catching him in the chest and sending him backward into the bed. As she attempted to grab her bag and leave, Zack sprang to his feet and spun into a high kick for her head. She ducked and punched for his crotch, missing and striking his inner thigh. It stung despite being off target. Zack blocked her next punch and held her immobile a moment.

"No cheap shots, Mac."

"You don't make the rules," she snarled and pulled free, again attempting to punch him in the crotch.

Zack kicked her in the inner thigh, purposely avoiding center. She cried out and glared at him.

"I can play that game too," he teased while smirking with satisfaction.

She cried out with frustration and threw fast punches and kicks, causing him to block several blows while backing up. He caught her around the neck and slammed her onto the bed, landing on top of her. He easily pinned her to the mattress. She fought against his body and hands holding her wrists to the bed. His look was serious as he stared into her eyes.

"What the hell do you do for fun on this boring island?" he casually asked.

Mac stopped struggling and stared at him with surprise. "What?"

"I'm bored," he again informed her. "I need something to do or I'll go out of my mind."

She stared at him almost at a loss for words as her mouth fell open. She hesitated only a moment then fumbled for an answer. "There's an archery range," Mac replied, uncertain whether he was serious or not. "I could find you a nice crossbow to play with."

He released her and sighed. "That'll do."

She slowly sat up while staring at him then shook her head. "You're one strange man."

"Well, we all can't be well-adjusted role models like you, Mac," he replied while heading for the bedroom door then cast a look at her discarded bag on the floor. "Don't forget your bag." He left the bedroom.

Mac sprang up from the bed, snatched her bag, and uncertainly followed Zack.

Chapter Thirty

The remaining six members of the team sat at one of the tables on the veranda overlooking the ocean. Gil fed Darth some leftovers from the elegant brunch while they discussed the new plan. The wedding guests had dispersed and most went back to their rooms to change for an afternoon on the beach or enjoying other activities, leaving the resort unusually silent.

Beck played with his dainty cup of coffee while eyeing Jackie. "You were right telling Zack to stay dead for now," he announced. "We need to figure out what's going on. Obviously, the dead guard stumbled upon something."

"The biggest target here is Giovanni," Gil added while feeding Darth leftovers.

"Banks is high on that list too," Monroe informed them. "He probably has more money than Giovanni and a pretty ugly resume."

"Maybe we should keep our butts on the sidelines and let them kill each other," Bogart suggested with disinterest. "Why should we put our asses on the line for a couple of murdering mob bosses anyway?"

Kirk leaned back in his chair and casually shrugged. "I'm with Bogart on this one. Let them kill each other."

"As much as I share your sediments regarding the head honchos," Jackie informed both men, "you have to remember there are innocent people staying here."

"Yeah, like my girlfriend," Beck snapped.

"If we stand aside and let this happen, there's no telling how many people could be killed," Jackie announced. "We don't even know what they're planning."

"We don't even know who *they* are," Bogart interjected.

"That's why we have to figure out what's going down before it happens," Beck replied. "I'd like to get a look at their security system."

Monroe suddenly cleared his throat and leaned back in his chair while playing with his napkin. He'd given the silent signal that someone was approaching, indicating they should change the subject.

Jackie leaned across the table and smiled cheerfully. "Remember the time he dropped his pants in front of that general to show him the scar on his ass?"

The guys laughed as Corbin approached their table.

Corbin eyed all six and attempted to join in with their cheerful enthusiasm. "Stories about Zack?" he asked while pulling up a chair from a nearby table. Corbin sat in the chair facing backward and leaned on the backrest.

"Actually, we were talking about my father," Jackie informed him.

Corbin considered the comment a moment then nodded and smiled with realization. "That's right," he announced and pointed at her. "You're Jackson's daughter."

"Guilty," Jackie replied.

"Jackson Remus," Corbin remarked while shaking his head. "He was legend." He eyed the men. "You all bailed after his death."

They nodded.

"Had no choice," Kirk boldly announced. "Zack stopped taking orders long before that. He knew he'd never survive another commander, so he already planned on retiring when Jackson announced his retirement."

"With the commander and Zack gone, there wasn't much of a team left," Monroe continued. "The trick to staying alive is trusting your team."

"New guys tend to get old guys killed," Kirk remarked then eyed Bogart.

Bogart groaned, taking the meaning, and looked away with disgust.

"You don't have to tell me. I've lived that nightmare too," Corbin announced then sat up straight. "Are you guys ready to get to work?"

"Sure," Beck replied and immediately straightened in his chair. "What's the ops?"

"We lost contact with Sealy this morning," Corbin informed them. "Something stinks around here, and I don't like it. We're doing a sweep of the resort and the entire area surrounding it. All hands on deck on this one. We have a lot of ground to cover, but I want every inch of the resort checked and double-checked."

"Count us in," Beck replied with enthusiasm. "Where would you like us to start?"

Corbin removed a copy of the resort map from his pocket and placed it on the table. "We have trails, beaches, waterfront, and the zip line area on top of the mountain. All this area needs to be covered." He indicated red marks. "I have enough guys scouring the resort and the immediate area surrounding it. The rough terrain is more your speed." He frowned and shook his head with disgust. "I hate to admit it, but the guards we've hired aren't exactly the outdoor type."

"Lucky for you, we are," Kirk teased.

"One soldier is worth ten Academy cadets," Corbin replied. "We have ATVs, horses, and jeeps for the wider trails. Take your pick and have at it. Grab some handheld radios and supplies from the security office."

"What do you have?" Kirk asked. "Rifles or shotguns?"

"Neither," Corbin replied without hesitation. "We're not in the habit of frightening our guests with armed men running around. This is a resort for the rich and spoiled." He then chuckled softly in his throat. "I'm sure you're all packing knives. That's all the weapons any of you need."

"He's got you there," Jackie teased.

The guys considered the comment then laughed in response. Bogart was the only one who didn't get the joke. Once Corbin left, their serious moods returned. Beck immediately leaned across the table.

"We'll need our own radio channel other than the one they assign," Beck informed them. "Trust no one."

"They have skeet shooting," Kirk announced while indicating the amenities listed on the map. "I could secure us some shotguns and a couple boxes of shells."

"No," Beck launched back. "He said no weapons." There was a brief silence. "That means anything visible to guests. We have our Bowie knives and stun guns." He then looked at Jackie. "Do you have your tactical batons?"

"Of course," she replied almost offended. "Never leave home without them."

"We can search Zack's bag and see what goodies he slipped past ship's security," Monroe announced. "There has to be something useful in there."

"We'll go in two-man teams and then separate as the terrain expands," Beck announced. "Jackie and I will take the jeep to this point." He pointed to a spot on the map. "We'll then hike north and south from this point." He indicated the beach. "Monroe and Gil will take this area and split up right around this rock formation. Gil and Darth can take the area by land, and Monroe can secure one of those water bikes." He then indicated another part of the woods. "Kirk and Bogart will take this area on ATVs and split up around this point."

"That's some rough terrain," Bogart announced, indicating the hiking symbol and horse. "I should probably take a horse instead."

"You're not getting me on one of those beasts," Kirk remarked. "I'll take the ATV."

Beck folded the map and stuck it in his pocket. "We'll grab more maps from the front desk," he announced. "While Monroe and Gil search Zack's bag of tricks, the rest of us will head to the security office. I can get a better look at their security system while we wait."

"Sounds like a plan," Monroe announced.

All six stood and headed inside.

Chapter Thirty-one

The ATV cruised along the moderately rocky path in the woods. Once Kirk reached flatter terrain, the four-wheeler picked up speed. The thrill of speed and power beneath him was one of the few things that made the hardened man smile. He decreased his speed as he entered another rocky area in a small canyon pass. Kirk stopped the ATV to take a better look at the rocky hillside surrounding the trail. His grip tightened on the handlebars as he considered continuing through the pass. He again hesitated. Kirk studied the terrain then eyed the tops of the ridges on either side. He felt his jacket for his shoulder holster then cursed softly under his breath. Being unarmed was worse than being naked.

"You're being paranoid, you idiot," he cursed softly to himself.

He finally gave in and proceeded through the pass. Without warning, he went faster and swerved to the right, riding part of the rocky incline, then came back down before swerving to the left. He reached the opposite end of the pass without incident. He was obviously suffering from paranoia after years of covert missions. It seemed silly to believe someone was always waiting to strike within some random kill box like the one he just successfully passed through. He gave the four-wheeler some gas, speeding up when he heard the distinct sound of rifle fire. He didn't have to look up, having felt the bullet whiz past his head and striking the rocks just on the other side. If he hadn't picked up speed at the precise moment he had, the bullet would have found its way into his head.

"I knew I wasn't being paranoid," he cried out as he drove faster over the last of the rocky terrain and onto the broad, flat path.

Several rifle blasts followed, hitting rocks behind him. He drove as fast as the ATV would allow for the conditions of the trail. Once he was sure he was clear of the attack, he slowed and whipped out his handheld radio.

"Yo, anyone copy?" he shouted into the radio above the engine of the ATV.

All he could hear was someone's voice and static. He drove faster and headed up a path to get away from the rocky ravine. Once he reached a clearing, he tried the radio again.

"Anyone copy?" he again announced.

Bogart responded through the static, but it was unclear what he was saying.

"Bogart, if you can hear me," he announced firm and loud. "Some fucker just took shots at me. Watch your twenty!"

He could no longer hear Bogart's voice only static. The sound of rocks crashing against one another as they fell down behind him caught Kirk's attention.

"You don't need a shotgun, Kirk," he snarled mimicking Corbin. "The precious, rich crybabies will piss in their pants if they see guns. Never mind my poor, hairy ass!"

He gave the ATV excessive gas, causing it to jet forward. He swerved to avoid a large rock in his path. The four-wheeler launched into the air, taking Kirk with it and crashing several feet away. Within minutes, a man dressed in camouflage appeared from the ravine with his rifle leveled and ready for action. The four-wheeler was on its side just beyond the large rock. Kirk's black boot stuck out from beneath the vehicle, indicating he'd been pinned beneath it when it hit the ground. The man hurried toward the overturned ATV, rounded it, and aimed his rifle. It was an empty boot! The man turned around to scan the area. Kirk stood behind him and grinned with a sinister look in his eyes.

"Momma's boys shouldn't play with guns," he announced as he punched the man in the face.

The man immediately dropped to the ground. Kirk snatched the rifle containing a hunting scope from him as he fell and looked it over. His eyes gleamed.

"Thanks, I needed one of these," he announced then kneeled alongside the barely moving man. The man groaned. Kirk punched him again. "What else did you bring me?" he asked and searched the man's pockets for weapons. He removed a semiautomatic and nodded his approval. "Needed one of these too." He continued his search then eyed the unconscious man. "No handcuffs, zip ties, or ropes, huh? I guess you didn't intend to take any prisoners." He sat back on his feet and sighed while shaking his head. "It's unfortunate for you I'm not Zack. Kill first; ask questions later. Me? I love a good, old-fashioned interrogation."

Moments later, the man in camouflage woke and stared at an upside version of Kirk where he crouched only a few feet away. He cleaned dirt out from under his fingernails with his Bowie knife then eyed the man who was hanging from a tree branch by his ankle with his belt and the rifle shoulder strap.

"Finally," Kirk announced and replaced his Bowie knife to his boot sheath. "Since I'm a little pressed for time, why don't you tell me what I want to know the first time I ask, and we'll all be around to celebrate another day."

"Fuck you," the man scoffed.

Kirk groaned softly then leaned forward and punched the man in the face just hard enough to get his attention. "That's not an appropriate answer, and I didn't even ask a question yet." He returned to a more comfortable position. "And for the record, I'm not considered a patient man, so keep that in mind in case I accidentally kill you."

†

Bogart rode a large, stocky black horse along the trail in the woods. He stopped the horse and listened to the faint sounds of rifle fire. The shots seemed to echo from every direction, so it was impossible to tell which way they came. He listened a moment longer, but there were no further sounds. Bogart patted the horse's muscular neck as it lightly pranced in place, ready to continue onward.

"I'm telling you, Buttons," he announced to the horse. "There was a time I'd hear gunshots and run away from them as fast as I could. I hate that I suddenly feel the urge to run toward them. You know what I mean?" He leaned down in the saddle and eyed the horse, who seemed to be looking back at him. "Who the hell names a horse Buttons?" He straightened in the saddle and nudged the horse to continue along the trail at a fast walk. The horse only had one walking speed. "I'm going to call you Othello," he announced proudly. "He's about your size. It's fitting. Othello it is."

They rode a few minutes in silence before his handheld radio crackled. Bogart snatched the radio and listened a moment.

"Someone calling? Over," he announced into the radio. The static continued although it sounded as if someone was speaking. He could almost make out his name. "Kirk? Is that you? Did you hear those shots?"

The crackling got worse. Bogart groaned and replaced the radio. "You'd think mobsters could afford better equipment," he informed the horse then looked around. "What a crazy ass place this is. We should just grab Pinto and run for home. Sort it all out later."

The horse snickered almost as if responding to the remark. Bogart again eyed the horse.

"No, you misunderstood," he informed the horse. "Pinto is a girl. She's not a horse. That's a completely different kind of pinto." He sank into his thoughts a moment. "She's quite a looker though. I'll never understand why she settled for Beck. He was probably cool at one time, but he can be a bit of a tight ass. Sometimes a whining little bitch too." The horse sneezed. "Yeah, he's okay, I suppose." He again leaned forward in the saddle and looked at the horse's face. "What about you? You have a nice little filly waiting in your paddock?"

The horse suddenly stopped and its head raised high in the air. His muscles tightened beneath the saddle. Bogart watched the horse's ears turn in several directions like radar. He followed the direction the horse's ears turned. Bogart appeared concerned as he gently leaned toward the horse's neck. He gently patted the horse and spoke softly while casting looks around the woods.

"Gunshots, radio static, and now you've got the willies?" Bogart announced softly to the horse. "Othello, I'd say we have a situation."

The horse suddenly snorted loudly, causing his entire body to rise and fall. Bogart sat deep in the saddle, preparing for any sudden reactions from the horse.

"You aren't just faking me out over a deer or some shit, are you?" he asked while scanning the area for any sign of movement.

The horse stared into the woods before them and seemed to lock on whatever it was that caused its nervous reaction.

"So spookesville is that way," Bogart announced gently although he still didn't see anything. "Then that means we go this way."

He sharply turned the horse around and headed along a different path. The horse seemed to be in more of a hurry than just a few minutes ago.

"Don't make me look bad," Bogart remarked to the horse. "I'm good at doing that on my own."

The sound of the horse's hooves snapping twigs and scraping rocks was almost deafening. Bogart groaned and rolled his eyes.

"Can you walk a little quieter?" he demanded. "I don't need you giving away our position. Bad guys carry guns and they ain't afraid to shoot horses." The horse snickered. "Yeah, even the pretty ones. Sorry, amigos."

After several minutes of riding in a large circle around the area of concern, the horse again stopped looking ahead and slightly to the right. Bogart scanned the area. A man in camouflage stood near a large tree while holding a rifle cradled in his arms. He spoke into his handheld radio.

"Now that's interesting," Bogart remarked softly to the horse. "Suppose he's looking for these two good-looking studs?"

Bogart removed his radio, turned the volume down, and began switching channels while watching the man in the distance. He finally found the proper channel and listened a moment.

"He didn't show," the man spoke into the handheld radio. "What do you want me to do? Over."

Another voice then came over the radio with some static. "Hold your position. Over."

"Roger. Over and out."

Bogart gently patted the horse while leaning on his neck. "You certainly pissed off someone, Othello," he informed the horse. "We can do this the old-fashioned way and turn back, or we can do this the brass balls way and take out the prick."

The horse snickered softly. Bogart eyed the horse with surprise. "That's mighty tough talk for a fella who ain't got any." He sighed softly and watched the man in the distance. "Fine, we'll do it your way."

A few minutes had passed as the man with the rifle waited impatiently by the tree, nearly invisible to anyone passing on the main trail. The crunching of branches and leaves announced someone approaching from behind. The man turned with his rifle aimed and hesitated to see the black horse trotting along the smaller path not far from him without its rider. The man frowned and raised his handheld radio.

"The idiot must've fallen off the horse," he reported and approached the horse as it trotted along the path.

The man reached the horse and attempted to grab its reins from the side to stop it. Bogart suddenly flipped over the horse's saddle from the opposite side, using the horse's body to hide his, and kicked the man in the face. The man hit the ground hard, losing his rifle. Bogart landed on his feet on the other side of the horse and lunged for the discarded weapon. He grabbed the rifle and aimed it at the fallen man. He waited a minute, but the man didn't get up. Bogart cast a look at the horse. The horse snorted and threw its head in the air.

"How the hell am I supposed to know?" he demanded. "I'm not the littlest ninja of this boyband. I'm sure you kick harder."

Bogart anxiously approached the man while keeping the rifle trained on him. He stared at the way the man laid on the ground with his eyes open and his head in an unnatural position. Bogart suddenly gasped and jumped back a step closer to the horse.

"Oh, hell," he cried out. "He's dead!"

The horse sneezed.

Bogart glared at the horse and waved his hand erratically. "You think I did it on purpose? That's just mean, Othello."

Chapter Thirty-two

Gil walked along the white sandy beach while Darth ran along the surf, playfully chasing the waves. Monroe whizzed by on his water bike further out in the ocean. He waved to Gil before disappearing. Gil frowned and shook his head.

"Why do I get the feeling he's enjoying his assignment?" he muttered to himself. He then watched Darth playing in the waves. "Oh, Darth. You too?"

Gil looked down at his moderately dressy shoes now filling with sand. He sighed then removed his shoes and socks. He scrunched his toes in the sand and considered the sensation. Gil frowned.

"I've got to learn to relax," he muttered. "Take a lesson from the dog."

"You could probably start by not talking to yourself," a woman remarked from a few feet behind him.

Gil turned and looked toward the woods, although not particularly startled by the woman's presence. Valerie walked onto the beach not far from him. She wore a light sundress, a moderately floppy hat, and carried her sandals. Gil watched the woman with little emotion as she approached. She observed his serious look and almost laughed.

"You really are wound tight," she remarked while grinning.

"Have we met?" Gil asked.

"Not officially," she replied, "but I'm sure you've heard about me."

"Oh?"

"I'm Valerie."

Gil raised his brow in question, indicating that he knew who she was.

"Yeah, that Valerie," she replied.

"Sal's former girlfriend."

"I don't know what he's told you about me," she announced with a moderately humored smile, "but I assure you, I'm not nearly that bad."

"Did you break all the windows in his Mercedes?" Gil asked with little reaction.

She fidgeted slightly. "I suppose that part is true," Valerie replied. "We had a bad break-up."

"Did you threaten to kill him after he had his security guards remove you from his house when you broke in?" Gil continued his interrogation.

Valerie again fidgeted from the line of questioning. "That was a long time ago."

"That was last year," Gil casually replied.

She groaned with defeat. "Haven't you ever made any mistakes?"

"I've made plenty of mistakes," Gil informed her. "I just don't expect anyone to forgive those mistakes as if they'd never happened."

"I'm not asking him to act like nothing ever happened," she interjected.

"I'm also not going to talk him on your behalf."

"I'm not asking you to," she huffed.

"Why are you here, Valerie?" Gil finally asked.

"For a wedding," she replied with some surprise then laughed. "Why else?"

"I don't know. You tell me," Gil remarked. "I heard you and the mother-of-the-groom had a falling-out."

"Everyone fights from time-to-time."

"I heard you had no intentions of attending the wedding until last month when you started dating Dr. Sherman," Gil announced. Despite the accusation, he didn't alter his tone. "Could it be you're only here in a desperate attempt to make Sal jealous? You're secretly hoping he'll want you back."

"No, that's not true," she scoffed and became angry. "If you'll excuse me, I'm sorry I bothered stopping when I saw you out here alone."

"Stopping?" he questioned then managed a soft laugh. "You followed me from the resort. If you were looking for a bleeding heart to plead your case, you should have gone after Bogart. He's a sucker for women, a romantic at heart, and Sal likes him for some odd reason."

"Good to know," she scoffed then walked away.

Gil watched her leave then shook his head. "There's another notch for your bedpost, Bogart," he muttered then chuckled softly in his throat. "You're welcome."

The faint echo of rifle fire caught Gil's attention. It sounded as if it came from deep within the woods. Gil listened and counted the shots. He listened after the last shot was fired then noted the time on his watch. He removed his hand radio.

"Anyone copy?"

There was no response, not even static. Gil switched frequencies and still didn't get any sound.

"Useless piece of shit," he muttered. He removed his cell phone, eyed the lack of signal, and then groaned with disgust. "I hate paradise."

Darth looked toward the woods and snarled. Gil looked from the dog to the woods. Sunlight glistened off something shiny. Gil's eyes widened slightly. As he threw himself to the sand, the ground exploded near him from the nearly silent gunshot. Gil rolled twice to avoid the two shots that followed. Darth ran across the beach for the woods, alarming Gil.

"Ah, hell," he gasped while swiftly removing his Bowie knife from his boot sheath.

Gil sprang to his feet when no other shots followed, uncertain if Darth became the new target for the nearly silent gunfire. He ran for the woods as Darth's snarls turned vicious. The dog had a man dressed in camouflage on the ground while tearing into his lower arm, keeping him from using the gun containing a silencer. As Gil ran for them, the man grabbed the gun from his right hand with his left and aimed it at Darth. Gil flipped his knife in his hand, catching it by the tip, and threw it. The knife embedded deep into the man's neck. He dropped the gun, gasped several times, and finally lay motionless. Darth released the man's arm, sniffed him, and then ran back to Gil. Gil patted the dog affectionately then approached the dead man with little emotion. He crouched alongside the unfamiliar man, studied him a moment, and then searched his pockets, removing weapons.

Gil was alerted to Monroe's water bike speeding past on the nearby beach.

"Darth," he announced and gave a nod. "Find Monroe."

The dog ran from the woods and onto the beach. Gil finished grabbing whatever weapons he could find and yanked his Bowie knife from the man's neck. He wiped the bloodied blade on the man's uniform and then headed for the beach.

✝

Monroe looked behind him with concern while speeding through the water. A speedboat chased after him as one man fired nearly silent shots from his semiautomatic. The water near Monroe exploded, alerting him to the shots fired. He swerved several times in a serpentine formation to avoid the gunfire. Had the man been holding an assault rifle, he'd be an easy target, but it was obvious they were attempting to keep the noise level to a minimum. The speedboat successfully kept him from reaching the resort beach, confirming the notion that they didn't want any of the guests alerted to the attack. They had weapons and a faster ride. It was only a matter of time before they'd get off a lucky shot or ram him with their speedboat.

Monroe saw Gil run onto the beach behind Darth. Despite his speed and sudden direction changes, Monroe was able to make out the gun Gil held in his hand. Gil aimed the gun, but he had no shot with their distance from the beach. Monroe had to get the bad guys closer to the beach in order for Gil to take his shot. As Monroe maneuvered the water bike in an effort to change direction, the speedboat circled and kept him from getting closer to his friend. Monroe's only advantage was a smaller craft with better banking abilities. He headed for some rocks, which the boat immediately passed him and cut off his path, as he anticipated. Monroe circled away from them as the speedboat now skirted the rock formation and started to circle back.

Monroe headed straight for their broadside at maximum speed. The man standing in the boat fired at him while Monroe counted.

"Two, one," Monroe said to himself then grinned. "And reload."

The man ejected his magazine and slammed in a new one. Monroe jumped down hard on the water bike, causing it to leap

161

through the air at the boat while he dove off the back. The driver and the shooter saw the water bike coming for them and instantly panicked. The driver attempted to speed forward but sideswiped a rock. The shooter cried out as the water bike landed on top of him within the boat and crushed him. Monroe surfaced, shook the water from his head, and looked around. The driver attempted to circle the speedboat despite the crashed water bike and a gaping hole on its starboard side. He drove the boat straight for Monroe where he bobbed in the water.

"Oh, shit!"

Monroe dove underwater. Gil ran along the rock formation taking him further into the ocean and bringing him closer to the action. He stopped on one of the larger rocks, took aim, and fired the entire magazine into the water bike sticking out of the boat. There was a tremendous explosion, tearing the speedboat apart. It only burned a moment before sinking into the water. Monroe again surfaced and watched the boat sink only a few yards from him. He looked at Gil standing on the rocks with the semiautomatic in his hand and gave him a thumbs-up. Gil ran along the rocks as Monroe swam to shore. Monroe stumbled onto the beach and half collapsed on the sand. Darth ran to him and licked his face. He scratched the dog's scruff then used him as a crutch to get his legs under him. Gil joined him, grabbed his arm through the wetsuit, and hurried him toward the woods.

"What's the hurry?" Monroe announced.

"Someone may have heard that explosion," Gil informed him as both took refuge in the wooded area just beyond the beach.

Monroe was about to comment when he saw the dead man in camouflage with blood on the ground surrounding him. "Well, this is one fucked up resort." He then eyed Gil. "Did we get too close to the head honcho's mansion?"

"I'd like to believe it was that simple," Gil replied while looking around as he reloaded the semiautomatic. "Right before I was ambushed, I heard rifle fire deep within the island."

Monroe stared at him with concern then cocked his head. "You mean in the direction our team had gone?"

"Possibly," he replied. "The radios don't work."

"The only person who knew where we were going was Corbin," Monroe remarked then turned angry. "That son-of-a-bitch sold us out."

"That's one possibility," Gil announced while remaining alert. "Corbin's a prick, but he's played on our side for years. He's also in charge of protecting public enemy number one and is down three men already."

"So those guys may not be after our team but security in general," Monroe replied with a groan. "We need to find the others and regroup. There's no telling how many of them are lurking around the woods."

"We're low on weapons," Gil reminded him.

"We could go back to the resort for the shotguns, but that's going to take time," Monroe announced.

"Then we'll just need to collect some weapons along the way," Gil casually replied. "According to the map, Beck and Jackie are closest to us. Jackie was heading toward the interior and the zip line course. Beck was heading toward the exterior on the nature walk along the cliffs."

"I saw a crude roadway from the water about one hundred yards that way," he announced while pointing. "We can hug the beach under the protection of the woods' edge and follow that road. The road leads straight to the zip line course. One of us can take the road to Jackie and the other can head up the path to intercept Beck on the nature hike."

Darth snarled softly while staring toward the beach. Both men looked at what caught the dog's attention. Two men in camouflage holding rifles ran along the sand and pointed to the remains of the boat smoldering in the water. Gil and Monroe stepped behind the trees to avoid giving their position away. Gil aimed the gun and fired two shots. Both men went down. He casually straightened and eyed Monroe.

"There are our weapons," Gil announced with little emotion. "We should get going."

Monroe gave him a quick once over. "Maybe you should put on some shoes, island Gil."

Gil looked down at his bare feet then glanced around the beach. He'd successfully lost his shoes somewhere. "Maybe I'll just borrow a pair of boots from these guys. Those shoes weren't good for hiking anyway."

Chapter Thirty-three

Beck walked along the path in the woods and came to a large clearing. He crossed the clearing and approached the cliff overlooking the ocean. It was a breathtaking view and a rather steep drop to the water below. He crouched near the edge and sank into his own thoughts. Beck ran his fingers through his hair then cursed softly. The sound of rifle fire in the near distance was enough to put him on alert. He straightened and listened. Despite the absence of further shots, Beck listened intently to the sounds all around him. He heard static on his handheld radio along with a voice that sounded like Kirk.

"Kirk?" he responded into the radio, but there was no response.

Another voice came over the radio, which he could almost identify as Bogart, but there was too much static to be sure. Beck tapped his thumb to the radio and stared into the woods a moment. Nothing moved, and he didn't see anything. Several yards within the woods, a man in camouflage pressed his back against a large tree and held his rifle. He peered around the tree and leveled the rifle for the nearby cliff. The man lifted his eyes from the scope and looked at the empty clearing. Beck was gone. He straightened while removing his hand radio.

"I lost the target," the man announced into the radio while turning.

Beck stood directly behind him and smiled almost charmingly. "Hey," he announced cheerfully then punched the man square in the face.

The man fell back against the tree but didn't drop his rifle. Beck grabbed the rifle and twisted it in the man's hand while delivering a throat punch. The man gasped, clutched his throat, and sank to his knees. Beck examined the rifle with little concern for the man writing in agony by his feet.

"Is it just me, or does this stink of a setup?" Beck remarked then finally eyed the man gasping and wheezing. He rolled his eyes and groaned. "Big baby," Beck scoffed. "Consider yourself lucky; I'm the nice one."

Despite writhing and gasping, the man reached behind his back. Beck casually grabbed his thumb and bent it back until it snapped. The man cried out. Beck removed the semiautomatic from the holster on the man's belt and eyed it. He then glared at the screaming man.

"It's just dislocated," Beck scoffed then twisted his thumb the other way. It again snapped causing the man to scream more. "You'll live." He then considered. "Maybe. That remains to be seen." Beck assessed the situation, carefully considering his options. "Take your boots off. We're going for a little walk back to the resort."

"Take my boots off," the man gasped, barely able to speak from the throat punch.

"Yeah," Beck casually replied. "You won't be able to run far or fast in this terrain without your boots." He offered an innocent look. "Hey, I'm taking you alive. You should be overwhelmed with relief."

The man reluctantly removed his combat boots, tossed them aside, and then stood.

Beck grabbed one of the boots and removed the shoelace. "Okay, turn around. Wrists together."

The man eyed Beck then did as he commanded. He easily tied the man's wrists together behind his back then placed the pistol down the back of his pants and carried the rifle.

"Let's go. Start walking," Beck announced then pointed with the rifle. "It's only three or four miles that way."

They walked along the path for a few minutes with Beck bringing up the rear. He fiddled with his prisoner's handheld radio, which mysteriously contained no static.

"Jackie, do you copy?" There was no response. "These things have lousy range." Beck cradled the rifle in his arms and removed his own handheld radio. He compared the two and appeared curious. "They look the same, but mine is a cheaper model." He eyed his prisoner, who walked ahead of him while carefully stepping around stones. "Who were you out to screw? My team or security in general?"

The man didn't comment, which wasn't surprising.

He again tried the hand radio. "Jackie, you copy?"

"She's probably already dead," the man remarked with little care.

Beck took a quick step toward the man from behind and kicked him in the back of the knee, driving him to the ground. The man flipped onto his back and looked up at Beck only to see the barrel of the rifle aimed at his face.

"For your sake, she better not be dead," he snarled with anger. "I'm not above blowing your head off on principle alone. Now get up!"

The man attempted to stand. With his hands tied behind his back, it took several attempts.

Beck collected his emotions and resumed his calm demeanor. "Change of plans," he lightly snarled. "We're heading uphill to find Jackie. If she has one hair out of place, you'll be begging me to kill you."

✝

Jackie hiked up the hillside on the worn path typically used by four-wheelers to reach the zip line course. Others could take the jeep trail to arrive at the same destination. Although she was covering ground slower than by vehicle, she was getting a better lay of the land. The zip line tower was only a few yards ahead of her. Naturally, there was no one there, whether workers or guests. Since the hotel remained closed to non-wedding guests, the zip line was open by appointment only. Sal's rich friends weren't exactly the outdoor, thrill-seeking type.

The sound of rifle fire in the near distance caught her attention. It was just far enough away that it would be impossible to investigate. She wasn't sure, but it sounded as if it came from the section of woods Kirk and Bogart had traveled. She paused and listened, but after the initial rifle fire, there was no sound. Her radio suddenly crackled. She could make out Kirk's voice, but she didn't know what he was saying. Bogart's voice followed, but the static was even worse. Jackie suspiciously eyed the hand radio then turned it off and looked around the woods. Without knowing what either man said, she wasn't sure if it was just idle radio chatter or if one of them needed assistance. From her current position, she was too far away to reach either.

She continued toward the zip line tower, which looked more like a shed with open doorways containing platforms on three sides. Something suddenly didn't feel right. The rifle fire followed by radio chatter from the team had her on edge for some reason. If her father taught her anything, it was to trust her instincts. Sometimes, though, she worried her instincts were just paranoia. Perhaps they were the same thing. She removed her tactical batons from her rear belt holster and gave both a flick, extending them to two feet each. She twirled them in her hands and continued along the trail, stepping as silently as possible to hear all sounds around her. She reached the small shed and relaxed when she discovered it was empty. Jackie looked over the neatly organized harnesses and various sized helmets. A map tacked to the wall revealed three separate zip line courses heading in different directions. She consulted the map and took note where each line eventually ended.

The openings in the shed on three sides contained small perches of sorts where the rider would step out, have their harnesses hooked up, and then take a leap of faith. Jackie had done it many times as well as other rugged outdoorsy type things with her father and his team over the years. She wasn't a fan of zip lines, but parachuting was number one on her most loathed list. As she studied the zip line map, she realized the first course would deposit her somewhere near where Bogart and Kirk had headed. Still, that didn't mean she'd ever find them in the vast wooded area. She thought better of it and stepped out the back of the enclosure to resume her hike.

She heard a twig snap and spun toward the sound with her tactical batons in attack position. A man in camouflage stood several feet away with a rifle aimed at her. Jackie considered her options, which she had several. As she cast a look around to plot her next move, she saw three more men also in camouflage appear from the woods with rifles aimed at her. Four men seemed like overkill to her. They couldn't possibly know she could handle two armed men yet it did reek of setup.

"Good afternoon, boys," she announced while eying the four men strategically positioned around her. She didn't lower her weapons but remained completely still. "I believe there's some misunderstanding. I'm working for Corbin."

"No," the one man replied. "There's no misunderstanding. We're the ones they sent you to find. Fortunately for you, the boss wants you taken alive." He gave her a quick once over and grinned. "Can't say I blame him. The others sent to find us weren't nearly as lucky."

Jackie stared at the first man and showed little emotion, although her body twitched. By his words, the rest of her team had been ambushed the same as she had. She had to have faith that they were clever enough to survive or risk letting her emotions get in the way of what she needed to do.

"Now drop your sticks like a good a little girl," he continued.

Did he just tell her to be a 'good little girl'? She felt her hostility rising. She hated when men spoke to her like a child, especially from men she could easily take down. She lowered her tactical batons while contemplating which man she'd need to take out first and in what order they needed to fall. The man directly in front of her had the best shot of taking her down, so he needed to go first. The number one man on her hit list suddenly cried out while clutching a Bowie knife sticking out of his neck. It wasn't as if she didn't know whose knife that was. By the direction the knife had come, she knew to attack the man on the opposite side. Jackie fought both men to her left, striking their rifles in an attempt to knock them from their hands. Zack seemed to appear out of nowhere behind the man to her right before he could get off a shot and kicked him in the head with a high, roundhouse kick. As the man fell, Zack threw himself into a forward roll and snatched the rifle before the attacker fell to the ground.

Jackie aggressively struck both men with her tactical batons and added a few kicks in for added effect. Once the last man hit the ground, she looked at Zack, who was already searching the fallen men for weapons.

"You've been here less than a day," Zack remarked without looking at her. "How did you piss off so many people in such a short time?"

"Taking lessons from you," she replied.

"If you were taking lessons from me, you'd have traded in those wuss sticks for a pair of samurai swords by now."

"Stop trying to turn me into your fantasy assassin, Zack," she scoffed and collected weapons from the two men she took down. "No swords and no gymnastics."

"All the best female superheroes--"

"I'm not learning gymnastics, so I can do high-flying flips with swords for your perverse pleasure," she bluntly informed him. "Get your rocks off elsewhere."

"You're really no fun," he scoffed. He continued his search of the man's pockets and removed something of interest. His grin told a grim story. "What have we here?"

Jackie glanced at Zack and saw him slip a grenade into his leg pocket. She rolled her eyes and shook her head. The last thing she needed was Zack with anything that went boom. He got into enough trouble with his bare hands. Zack heard something Jackie didn't. As he tackled her to the ground, a rifle fired and struck the man she'd been searching. Zack rolled off her and both immediately fired blindly into the wood while scrambling to their feet. They darted inside the zip line shed. The rifle bullets splintered the wood inside near them.

"This isn't going to offer much cover for long," Jackie informed him.

"I know," he replied. "Suit up."

She eyed the zip line harness and groaned. "No, I'd rather not."

"Why are you such a big baby about jumping from heights?" he demanded. "Damn it, suit up."

Jackie secured her tactical batons to her waist holster. She reluctantly grabbed a harness and slipped into it while Zack fired randomly into the woods out the back. Jackie secured the harness, slung her rifle over her shoulder, and then apprehensively stepped onto the first platform. As she looked down the steep drop, she felt a dull pang in her stomach. Taking on the armed men seemed the lesser of two evils. She attached the line to her harness and looked back at Zack.

"Are you coming?"

"Go," he announced. "I'm right behind you."

Jackie stood on the edge of the platform and again looked down. She shut her eyes while working up the courage to take that first step.

Zack eyed her and groaned. "This is like that summer at Fort Brag all over again."

She glared back at him. Before Jackie could make a snide comment, Zack fired several shots out the door while running across the shed for her. She shut her eyes and found herself reliving every jump from a plane the guys had forced her to do all for their adrenaline rush. Zack slung the rifle over his shoulder mid-stride, grabbed the bars above her head, and propelled them from the platform. Jackie screamed the moment her feet left the platform. The line bounced more than she'd remembered from any of the other times she'd been forced to slide down the rope of death. Jackie clung to her harness cables and screamed while watching the countryside whiz by as Zack dangled behind her, hooting and hollering with enthusiasm. They continued to bounce wildly on the cable, increasing Jackie's heart rate and level of nausea. She was convinced she'd throw up once they reached the bottom but feared it'd come sooner.

"Can this thing hold two people?" she screamed while panic filled her body.

"Do you really want me to answer that?" Zack replied close to her ear.

She again screamed and clung to her harness cable. As they zipped high above the trees on their rapid descent, they could see the guys on assorted paths beneath them, looking up and watching them pass overhead.

Chapter Thirty-four

Jackie and Zack reached the end of the course at the bottom of the hill. A slight upward incline allowed for a gentle, gradual stop, but that didn't fit into Zack's plans. Once they slowed, he removed one hand from the grip above Jackie and skillfully released her harness from the line. She plummeted three feet to the ground, partially landing on her feet then falling to her buttocks. Zack landed gracefully on his feet like a pouncing cat, grinned boyishly, and extended his hand to her. She glared at him where she sat on the ground, her buttocks throbbing from the harsh landing. She slapped her hand hard into his, showing her disapproval, and allowed him to help her to her feet.

Despite anticipating Zack's enthusiastic reaction to plummeting toward near death, Jackie was still unable to prevent him from pulling her against him and kissing her quickly on the lips. She cursed at him while pushing him away, but he'd already gotten his celebratory kiss. Adrenaline rushes, near death experiences, and mortal combat seemed to turn on Zack. For some reason, Jackie was always in his line of fire at those moments. She knew it was coming, but she could never manage to prevent it. They heard movement coming from the woods. Both pulled their rifles they had slung over their shoulders on their wild ride and aimed them at the sound. Darth appeared from the woods, barked excitedly, and greeted them. Beck and Monroe were only a moment behind. The sound of hoof beats alerted them toward one of the trails. Bogart rode his horse at a gallop toward them then came to a sliding stop.

"I'm glad I ran into you guys," he announced. "You won't believe what happened."

"Try us," Jackie muttered while brushing dirt from her backside.

Kirk approached on his four-wheeler with his prisoner securely strapped across the back of the vehicle. The man in camouflage looked like a prized hunting trophy Kirk had shot on safari. He received several looks.

"Is he alive?" Jackie asked.

Kirk shrugged with little care and walked past them. "Alive enough."

Beck was the last to arrive with his barefoot prisoner and glanced at his team. He didn't seem surprised they'd all survived. "Now that we've assembled, we should move someplace safe," he announced. "Half the woods either heard or saw the two of you. They'll be coming this way."

"I've got prisoner detail," Zack announced and cut the man free from Kirk's ATV, allowing him to fall to the ground with a thud.

Beck pointed a warning finger at him. "Play nice," he snarled.

Zack flipped his Bowie knife in his hand and grinned. "I always do."

There was a round of groans. Leaving Zack in charge of prisoners was almost as bad as leaving a cat alone with mice. Despite their reservations, the rest of the team left without further comment. Jackie eyed Zack's moderately evil grin as he collected the two prisoners then shook her head and hurried after Beck. The prisoners caught her disapproving look then eyed Zack and showed concern for the first time.

†

The black horse was tied to the four-wheeler just within the woods, keeping both out of sight. An old ship, its rotting remains partially buried in the sand, had run aground decades ago on the remote beach far from the resort. Within the ship's decayed skeleton, the team minus Zack had regrouped and made themselves comfortable while remaining out of sight.

"Until we have proof either way," Beck announced while sitting on the rotted, wooden floor, "Corbin is on our short list of suspects. Just because we trusted him when we served together, that doesn't mean he hasn't sold us out."

"We have to consider this has nothing to do with us personally," Monroe informed them while looking at the others. "Two of Giovanni's guards are either dead or missing. Maybe more that we don't even know about. It's possible we were just on the same list as the other guards."

"I disagree," Jackie announced surprising them. All eyes were suddenly on her. "The guys after each of you tried to kill you. The ones I encountered said they were to take me alive. They sent four men after me, yet only one after each of you."

"Those bastards," Bogart scoffed with anger. "They thought they could take you as a sex slave? I'll kill them."

All eyes were suddenly on Bogart with looks of shared confusion.

"Curb your imagination, Bogart," Beck snarled.

"Not exactly where I was going with that," she remarked while staring at Bogart. "If they were randomly attacking guards, why send four after the only woman? They knew something about me."

"And we're back to Corbin," Kirk remarked as he leaned against the rotted wall of the old ship. "He may never have met you, but he's certainly heard of you. That would also explain why Zack was taken out first on the ship."

"Look," Beck announced. "This was set up long before we arrived on the scene. No one even knew we were going to be on that ship. Hell, even we didn't know that until the day before. It can't be about us."

"The only way it's about us is if someone assumed we'd show up," Gil remarked and received several looks from the rest of the team.

"Impossible," Beck retorted.

"I'm just going to state the obvious," Gil announced while looking at the others. "There are two people on this island who'd have reasonable suspicions that we might show up."

There was an odd silence as they exchanged concerned looks while considering the comment.

Beck's mouth fell open as he stared at his friend. It was hard to tell if he was surprised or enraged. "What?" he suddenly gasped then turned almost hostile. "Are you suggesting Sal or even Pinto set us up?"

"All it requires is a beautiful woman and a jealous man," Gil replied then held his hands up in the air defensively. "I'm just pointing out another possibility."

"That's the stupidest thing to ever come from your mouth," Beck launched.

There was an odd silence from the others, causing Beck to look around at the team.

"Let's just save that debate for another day," Monroe remarked, attempting to end the feud before it launched into something worse.

"We should discuss it now," Gil remarked not giving up on his theory.

"It's more important that we know where Zack will stow the rifles," Kirk informed them. "I'm not going back out there without equal firepower."

"Zack's going to stow the rifles in the generator building," Beck informed Kirk. "There's a small ledge beneath the bench just inside the door. They'll be inside a duffle bag along with extra magazines. In the meantime, we have enough handguns that we can each have one on us at all times. Emergency use only. We need to stay below radar on this, especially if Corbin and any other guards are involved." Beck's stolen hand radio crackled twice, alerting the group. "That's Zack's signal."

Beck changed the radio to a different channel, allowing them to hear clear voices over the stolen handheld radio.

†

The two prisoners hung by their ankles from the zip line while attempting to scream through the gags in their mouths. Six men with rifles approached the clearing and searched the area. Two more men cut them down.

"Where the hell are they?" the one man demanded while looking around.

"Several men aren't responding," another man replied. "They must have gotten the slip on them. No one's reporting any kills or captures."

"Damn it," the first man cursed and eyed his team. "So they all got away?"

"Seems that way."

Not far from the zip line, the handheld radio hung from one of the trees with the talk button taped to the on position, capturing their entire conversation for the hidden team. A little farther away, Zack relaxed comfortably reclined in a tree and watched the entire scene as it unfolded. He looked through the scope of the rifle at each man and frowned each time he knew he shouldn't pull the trigger. He lowered the rifle with disgust then leaned his head back against the tree within his perch.

Chapter Thirty-five

Corbin walked the grassy area near the beach where the caterers were setting up chairs for the wedding, which would take place tomorrow morning. He ordered his men to check certain areas in preparation for the wedding and its high-profile guests. Beck and Kirk approached Corbin, although Kirk lagged behind by several feet as if keeping guard. Corbin saw the men approaching and hurried toward them looking relieved.

"Beck," he gasped and extended his hand.

Beck hesitantly accepted his hand and gave the informal handshake chest bump.

"I'm so glad to see you," Corbin announced. "Four of my men never reported in after their sweep. We couldn't contact you or your team. I was worried something had happened to you as well."

"Oh, something happened," Beck informed him. "We were ambushed by a bunch of Boy Scouts."

"Is everyone okay?"

"Yeah, we're all fine," he replied. "I can't say the same for our attackers. You're going to need a few body bags."

"Who were they?"

"Hard to say," Beck remarked. "I just hope you don't know either. I wouldn't want us to have a problem."

"What?" he gasped. "How long have we known each other? I'd need to send a militia after you and your men. Let's be honest.

If I had wanted to kill you and failed, do you really think I'd still be here?"

"Not if you were smart," he announced with little emotion. "I'm just trying to figure out how smart you are, Corbin."

"I'm here to protect Giovanni and his guests," Corbin insisted, taking offense to the line of questioning. "I have no reason to kill my old comrades. Trust me, Beck. Whoever attacked you in the woods had no idea who they were dealing with. It wasn't personal against you or your team. It had to do with our high profile guests."

"If you still want our help, we'll do our own security sweeps in teams and on our terms," Beck informed him. "We work outside your authority."

"I don't think that's a good--"

"Then we're out of here," Beck informed him. "We have our own ride, and there's nothing keeping us here."

"What about your girlfriend and her father?"

"They're going with us," Beck insisted. "It won't be pretty, but that's how it's going down."

"No, we need you now more than ever," Corbin insisted. "I've lost too many men already. Whatever you need, you've got it. If you insist on being stubborn, you can spend the rest of the day figuring out what happened to my men and who's behind it."

"Already on it, Corbin," Beck casually remarked without taking his eyes off the intimidating man.

†

The garden was in full bloom with tropical flowers and plants taking up every inch of the area. Decorative paths led through the garden filled with many gazebos for the guests to have private, romantic moments. Sal stormed along the path with a scowl on his moderately reddened face. He was obviously fuming over something. Valerie followed him, attempting to keep up.

"I just want to talk," Valerie announced. "Why won't you just talk to me?"

He waved her off without bothering to look back. "I'm not interested in anything you have to say," he snapped hotly. "I don't care if you intended to get down on your knees and beg for forgiveness, I still don't want to talk to you."

"I'm trying to make amends here, Sal," she informed him. "I'm not trying to trick you into taking me back. I have someone, remember?"

He cast a glance back at her, refusing to make eye contact, and almost laughed. He didn't stop or even slow his pace. "Yes, that was very convenient, you finding a date at the last minute for a wedding you had no intention of attending."

"Wade and I have been dating a few months," she insisted. "There's nothing convenient about it. He asked me out. Just ask him if you don't believe me."

"I don't really care," Sal informed her. "I may be stuck on this island with you, but that doesn't mean I have to talk to you. Go away!"

As he stormed off with Valerie in hot pursuit, Mac stepped around a nearby gazebo and watched them pass. She appeared lost in her own thoughts.

"Stalking your former boss?" Zack asked, startling her.

Mac quickly turned to see Zack standing behind her just far enough away that she couldn't strike him without proper warning. "I just happened to be working out here. I *am* the gardener," she remarked while glaring at him. "You seem to be the one doing the stalking. If you're looking for a repeat of our last encounter, I'm not interested." She subconsciously pulled her shirtsleeve down to cover the ruby and diamond tennis bracelet she wore. Although her intention was to hide it, she actually drew his attention to it.

"Which encounter?" he questioned while raising a suggestive brow. "The one where you had your way with me? Or the one where you tried to kill me?"

"Either or both," she scoffed. "I'm trying to get on with my life, and I don't need you or Sal complicating things for me. I have a good thing going here."

Zack nodded then smirked. "I see," he announced. "You're regretting your less than noble double-cross and wishing you had a second chance to make things right."

"What does it matter?" Mac demanded while folding her arms across her chest. "Sal's never going to forgive me."

"I don't see why not," Zack replied. "I never told him what happened *after* you ravished me."

She stared at him with some surprise, allowing her arms to fall to her sides. "You didn't?" she practically gasped then resumed her moderately serious tone. "Why not?"

He shrugged without care. "It would've served no purpose," Zack replied. "We all do stupid things. No point having him gunning to kill you over yours."

Mac continued to stare at him. "I can't believe you did that," she remarked in a softer voice. "You went out of your way to protect me after what I did to you?"

"Wouldn't be the first time I've encountered your kind," he remarked and leaned against the gazebo.

"My kind?" she demanded defensively.

"Yeah, the black widow type," he replied. "Mate and then devour your partner."

"Are you hunting for an apology?"

"Nope," he replied without care. "I don't hold grudges. I either kill you or I don't." Zack eyed her suspiciously then straightened. "Besides, if it turns out you're just another hallucination, what good would an apology do?"

She groaned softly and shook her head. "What did they do? Scramble your brains?" Mac demanded and turned defensive. "Of course I'm real."

"Well, real or not, I could use your special talent," he informed her.

She suddenly raised her brow and eyed him suspiciously. "Which special talent? I already told you I'm not interested--"

He groaned with annoyance and ran his fingers through his short hair. "Not sex," Zack scoffed, becoming impatient. "What is it with you imaginary women? You're all horny as hell." He collected himself and straightened proudly. "I'm talking about a little recon here."

She suddenly became interested. It would seem old habits were hard to break. "Who's under surveillance?"

"That's the question," Zack replied. "Something is going down either at the wedding or the reception, but it's unclear who's the target or the perp."

"This place has been a little strange lately," she informed him. "A lot of security, yet it doesn't feel safe. I feel like I'm being watched and not in a good way."

"That may have something to do with your night hobby," he remarked while glancing at the barely visible bracelet.

Mac frowned and vigorously pulled her sleeve over the remainder of the bracelet.

"Have you heard anything suspicious?" he asked.

"No," she replied. "I'm a glorified gardener. I don't socialize with the guests or security. I mostly work alone. The way I like it."

"Corbin may be behind what's going on or his men are plotting a mutiny," Zack informed her.

"I see security hanging out in the pool house a lot," she informed him. "I just assumed they were sneaking off for a cigarette break."

"Have they seen you?"

"No, I don't think so," she replied. "Do you think there's something going on in that pool house?"

"I'm not sure, but I'm going to check it out," he informed her.

"I'm coming with you."

He shrugged. "Suit yourself."

✝

Mac followed Zack into the large pool house, which the resort mostly used for pool parties and special occasions. Both looked around at the stacks of beach and pool furniture being stored, possibly removed to accommodate the nearly two hundred folding chairs needed for the wedding. They walked around the cluttered building and looked for anything suspicious.

"I guess the guys were just sneaking in here for a smoke," she informed Zack. "There's nothing here."

Zack approached the corner where round, wicker lounge beds were stacked on top of one another. He crouched close to the floor and rubbed the concrete. Mac looked over his shoulder.

"What is it?"

"Bloodstain."

"That doesn't mean anything," she announced. "People cut themselves. It's barely even a smear."

Zack removed his Bowie knife and cut through the lining of the lounge bed partially sticking out on the bottom. He pulled the material up. Mac removed a small penlight from her pocket and shined it into the six-inch opening he'd made. They saw a man's hand beneath some sort of clear plastic bag or plastic lining. Mac looked at Zack with surprise.

"It's a dead guy!"

"I can see that," Zack remarked then straightened and carefully lifted each of the hollow lounge beds with some effort. "Quite weighty."

"You mean--?"

"I think we found the missing guards," Zack announced while studying the stacked lounge beds. "I have to wonder. Are they the ones Corbin claimed vanished? Or are they the guys who were hunting us in the woods?"

"Or are they one in the same?" Mac remarked then looked at him while cleverly raising her brow.

"All good questions."

"So do we alert Corbin?"

"No," Zack replied. "If he already knows they're here, he won't be happy that we found them. We need to concentrate on what's going down at the wedding tomorrow."

She patted him on the back and smirked. "Good luck to you," Mac announced. "I have a boat to steal in the morning, and then I'm skipping town."

"You don't want to stick around and see if I get myself killed?" he asked with a curious look. He turned and leaned against the stacked lounge beds. "You need to stop running, Mac. Even if you are just a hallucination, you have to own up to your mistakes eventually."

"Have you?" she demanded.

"I'm going to hell no matter what, so that's irrelevant," he replied then eyed her. "You still have a sporting chance to save your soul."

"Thanks, but I think I'd rather stay alive," she replied. "If you don't get yourself killed, look me up sometime. We'll have drinks." Mac turned and left the pool house.

Chapter Thirty-six

It was the perfect morning for a beach wedding. Workers continued to scurry about making last minute adjustments to the area being set up for the wedding. The resort was moderately quiet after an early breakfast buffet for its guests. Everyone took time dressing for the lavish wedding, which would begin in a little under two hours. Beck reviewed security plans for the wedding with Gil and Bogart. Gil securely adjusted Darth's bulletproof vest then inserted a spare semiautomatic in one slot and a Bowie knife in the built-in sheath on the other side. He grinned and affectionately scratched the dog's ears.

"Who's the dangerous puppy?" Gil announced in a babyish tone. "You're the dangerous puppy."

"Would you two like a moment alone?" Beck demanded, becoming impatient.

Gil frowned then glared at Beck while straightening. Gil and Bogart looked past Beck, fidgeted, and excused themselves with little warning. Beck turned around and saw Pinto standing a few feet behind him. She was already dressed for the wedding, wearing a flattering ivory and pink dress. Beck couldn't help taking in an eyeful of the gorgeous woman but knew she wasn't there to seduce him.

"You, uh, look beautiful," he told her gently while fidgeting, uncertain what to do with his hands.

"We should talk," she informed him without acknowledging the compliment.

Beck stared at her as if she'd given him the kiss of death. He turned into an awkward teenage boy before her eyes and nodded as if anticipating a stern scolding from his mother.

"There's nothing between Will and me," she informed him. "We're just friends."

"I know," he replied timidly.

"Then why are you acting like you don't trust me?" she practically demanded.

"It's not you I don't trust," he informed her a little too quickly then drew a deep breath, straightened proudly, and stared back at her. "It's Will I don't trust." He raised his brows sharply. "Did you know he'd be here?"

Pinto hesitated then shook her head. "I didn't know he knew either the bride or groom's family," she replied. "He never mentioned it, but I never said anything about the wedding either, since I had no plans on going. I'm sure you didn't know your doctor friend was going to be here either and with Valerie no less. Coincidences do happen, Beck."

"And sometimes coincidences happen because they're designed to happen," he informed her. "Will just happens to be invited to the same wedding you were invited to, but he failed to mention that he was attending? You didn't know you were going until the last minute. Did he mention anything to you that he'd be out of town nearly two weeks?"

Pinto considered the question. Her expression revealed the answer. She stared at Beck with some surprise. "Actually, he said he'd bought tickets to some concert in Boulder for this weekend," she remarked.

"And he asked you to go along?"

She stared at him and seemed prepared to snap a witty comeback but hesitated. "I suppose he could have forgotten about the wedding."

"Yes, he conveniently forgot until he found out you were going," Beck informed her.

"I never told him I was going," she remarked with some arrogance. "My father showed up and basically whisked me away with little warning. I never even told him I was leaving."

"Yet on the day your father shows up, he buys plane tickets to Florida, and he just happens to be booked on the same cruise ship," Beck remarked.

"He wasn't on the cruise ship," she insisted without hesitation. "He flew in from the mainland the day we arrived on the island."

"I saw him leaving your stateroom on the ship," Beck informed her.

She stared at him with some surprise, allowing her mouth to fall open. She quickly gathered her emotions and stood proudly. "That's impossible."

He laughed in a mildly unsettling manner. "It's not impossible, Pinto," he practically cried out then gestured wildly with his hands. "The guy's been trying to put a wedge between us from the beginning, and it worked." He shook his head in disbelief. "I'm trained to read people, and I had Will pegged from the moment I met him. I warned you about him not out of jealousy but from experience." He stared into her eyes with a slightly demanding expression. "You refused to believe me about him. You chose faith in him as a friend over my established instincts. You made *me* the bad guy."

She fidgeted slightly and avoided eye contact with him. "If it makes you feel any better, I told Will to back off for a while until I sorted all this out."

"For your sake, I'm happy about that," Beck informed her, "but our relationship issues are the least of my worries at the moment." He eyed the area surrounding them. "Something big is going down, and I have no doubt it's happening at the wedding or during the reception. Half a dozen armed men attempted to take down my team yesterday. We've recently learned that whatever is happening has nothing to do with you. Now I have my team and two hundred civilians to think about." He folded his arms across his chest and stared at her. "It's time for you to pick a side," he informed her firmly. "I can't protect the people at this wedding if I'm busy begging you to trust me."

She stared at him a moment, inhaled deeply, and stood straight. "Of course I trust you," she insisted.

"Then you and Sal need to stay in your suite with the door locked until after the wedding and reception," he informed her. "It's the only way I'll know you're safe. It's the only way I can protect you while keeping the others safe. Maybe I'm overreacting, but if I'm not, it's going to get bad out here."

Pinto stared at him a moment then gently nodded without hesitation. "My father is in his room," she informed him. "I'll meet him there, and we won't leave the room until you're convinced it's safe."

"Thank you," Beck replied softly. "I can't do what I have to if I'm worrying about your safety."

"I understand," she replied then kissed him quickly on the lips and stared into his eyes. "Be careful."

𝓉

Pinto hurried across the lobby as fast as her high heels would carry her. Sal would soon be ready, and she needed to keep him from leaving the room. Despite being in a hurry, Luke caught up with her and attempted to hold her back.

"Hey, Pinto," he announced cheerfully and swept a look over her. "You look stunning."

She didn't ease her pace on her way to the elevator. "Thanks, Luke," she replied with little acknowledgment.

"I was wondering if you'd save me a dance at the reception," he announced without slowing his pace then seemed to notice she was in a hurry. "Something wrong?"

"No," she replied while casting a quick glance at him then paused before the elevator. "I just wanted to catch my father before he left the room."

"Oh, for a minute there, I thought you were attempting to avoid me," he remarked.

She hit the elevator button several times with growing anxiety then glanced at Luke. "No, I'm not avoiding you. I just have a lot to do before the wedding." Pinto then eyed him. "Don't you have things you should be doing as well? Considering you're one of the groomsmen."

"Yeah, but I have time," he informed her. "What did your ex-boyfriend want?"

Pinto gave him a strange look. "Ex-boyfriend? Who said he was my ex-boyfriend?"

"It's a fair assumption," Luke remarked. "You came with your father and not him. I thought that maybe he was harassing you. I could have him removed if he's bothering you."

"No," she informed him with little interest. "He wasn't harassing me."

When the elevator doors opened, Pinto stepped inside. Luke followed her, which seemed to annoy her. She pressed the button for her floor and he pressed the button for the floor above hers, where the wedding party suites were located.

Pinto sank into thought then glanced at Luke. "How did you know he was my boyfriend?" she suddenly asked.

Luke glanced at her then laughed softly. "Well, he's certainly not one of the family," he informed her, humored by the comment.

"The only people being dressed by department stores at this resort are the hired help."

"Yes, but you referred to him as my boyfriend," she remarked. "Why wouldn't you assume he was just another security guard? I mean, he looks like a security guard. Why would you automatically assume he was my boyfriend?"

"Your father must've have pointed him out," Luke insisted with little interest.

Pinto now stared at Luke. "Doubtful."

She fidgeted slightly. When the elevator doors opened on Pinto's floor, she attempted to bolt away from him. Luke caught her around the waist and placed his hand over her mouth to keep her from screaming. She fought against him but was unable to break free from his grip. The door closed and continued to the top floor. Once the doors opened, he pulled her from the elevator as she struggled against him. A security guard immediately ran to him and subdued Pinto. They forced her into the nearby bridal suite. Belle and Matt were surprised to see the guard and Luke forcing Pinto into the room.

"What's going on?" Belle demanded.

"She knows something," Luke proclaimed while looking concerned. "We have to do something with her."

"Are you insane?" Matt cried out. "Why'd you bring her here?"

"I didn't know what else to do," Luke snapped back. "We were in the elevator. She was going to tell her father something. I had to do something fast."

"Idiot," Matt scoffed, turning hostile toward his son. "As soon as Sal realizes she's missing, he's going to have his SEAL team buddies tear this place apart looking for her. We don't need that kind of heat."

"I'll stall him," Luke snarled, annoyed by the lecture. "By the time he realizes she's missing, it'll be too late."

"No, I'll stall him," Matt snapped back. "You just see that she's kept hidden and quiet until this is over."

Belle folded her arms across her chest over top her satin robe. "You two are pathetic," she lashed out. "You're going to ruin my wedding. The reception is going to suck as it is. The least you could do is let me have my wedding."

"No one's ruining your wedding," Matt informed his daughter with a mixture of compassion and irritation. "You just finish getting ready. Your bridesmaids will be here any minute." He then glared at the guard and Luke with disapproval. "Get her out of here and someplace where she won't be seen. Make sure she keeps quiet. Use the connecting door to my suite."

The guard and Luke forced Pinto across the honeymoon suite, despite her struggling, and through the connecting door into Matt's adjoining suite.

Chapter Thirty-seven

Sal mingled with the other guests on the lawn before the beach, a glass of champagne in his hand. The wedding was about to start in a few minutes, and the guests were getting ready to take their seats. A live band played, indicating the ceremony was about to begin. Will joined Sal and admired the romantic and expensive wedding laid out before them.

"Have you seen Pinto?" Will asked while looking around. "She's been a little cool to me ever since her ex-boyfriend showed up." He eyed Sal with a concerned look. "I don't trust that guy. I think he's trying to pressure her into taking him back. I'm worried for her safety."

Sal eyed the young man and raised an arrogant brow. "Son," Sal announced while offering a tiny smile. "I think you had better stay away from my daughter and find another woman to lust after. Make no mistake, if you so much as smile at my daughter, I'm going to send some friends to your house. They'll have you fitted with a nice pair of cement boots, and we'll see how long you can hold your breath." Sal smiled pleasantly. "Are we clear?"

Will stared at Sal with horror on his face and took a step back from him. "Uh, yeah. Perfectly clear, Mr. Romano." He quickly turned and ran back to the hotel.

"That felt good." Sal smiled smugly, satisfied with himself and sipped his champagne.

Beck hurried to join Sal and gave him a bewildered look. "What are you doing down here?" he almost demanded.

Sal eyed him with a strange look then grinned. "Attending my friend's son's wedding," he cheerfully reported. "Great news.

Will stopped by and said he was leaving right after the wedding. He was sorry for all the trouble he caused between you and Pinto and won't be hanging around anymore. Isn't that wonderful news?"

Beck gave him a strange look. "Just like that?"

"Yeah, kids today don't know what they want," Sal replied and casually waved him off. "I wouldn't be surprised if he leaves Colorado."

Beck maintained his stare at Sal with some distrust.

Sal seemed to enjoy the baffled look he received, although he didn't bother to elaborate further. "I thought you were securing this place from a distance."

Beck stared at him a moment almost unable to speak then snapped out of his daze and shook his head, giving up trying to figure out Sal. "You're not supposed to be down here. Pinto promised she'd keep you with her upstairs where it's safe."

He appeared surprised and stared at Beck. "When did you talk to her?"

"About an hour ago," Beck replied. "Didn't she meet you in your room?"

Sal's look turned concerned. "No, I haven't seen her since she headed out after she changed for the wedding nearly two hours ago." He set his champagne glass down and stared at Beck with a shattered expression. "Is she okay?"

Beck uncertainly shook his head then removed his hand radio. "Guys, I need a twenty on Pinto. Anyone have eyes on her?"

There was a round of negative responses.

"I haven't seen her since she got into the elevator over an hour ago," Bogart announced over the radio. "I believe she was heading to her room. She went up."

"Was she alone?" Beck demanded.

"Uh, negative," Bogart replied. "She was with the brother of the bride. What's his name?"

Beck's mind appeared to be reeling with the new information. "Jackie," Beck practically yelled into the radio.

"I'm heading there now," came Jackie's response.

"I'm meeting Jackie on the third floor," Beck announced over the hand radio. "Everyone else stay in position."

"She's not in our room," Sal informed Beck. "I would have seen her."

Beck again raised his radio. "Jackie, meet me on the fourth floor. You start in the north corridor. I'll take the south."

"I should come along," Sal announced, eager to join the search party.

Holly Copella

"No, you stay here and keep your eyes open," Beck informed him. "Anything happens, hit the ground then make your way to the poolside bar."

"Why the poolside bar?"

"Because that's where Zack's going to be," Beck replied then took off.

✝

Belle paced within the lobby while her father watched, looking slightly nervous himself. The bridesmaids collected in a group and giggled while checking out the groomsmen on the patio.

Belle turned toward her father with an annoyed look. "Where is he?" she demanded.

"He'll be here," Matt announced. "You know your brother. He's always fashionably late."

"He's still hounding that girl, isn't he?" she demanded while staring at him with hostility in her eyes. "I told you not to leave him alone with her."

"Whether he's here or not is irrelevant," Matt gently informed her. "Once the wedding is official, none of this matters." Matt then frowned and muttered under his breath. "If that bastard doesn't double-cross us."

"I don't care," she snarled. "I still want my wedding to be perfect, and Luke is ruining it."

"Honey, trust me," he announced boldly. "Your wedding is going to be the most talked about, remembered wedding ever. It'll even make the history books."

She eyed her father while maintaining her frown. "You promise?"

"Absolutely," he announced while gently rubbing her bare shoulders. "You're going to be famous."

Belle grinned at the comment.

✝

Pinto sat on the plush chair within Matt's suite with her wrists duct taped together in front of her. A piece of duct tape covered her mouth to keep her quiet as well. Luke said something to the guard, who grinned then left the room. Pinto watched Luke approach her where she sat in the plush chair. He sat on the edge of the glass coffee table before her and smiled his intentions.

"No one's going to hurt you," he informed her. "I won't let them; as long as you play your cards right."

Luke placed his hand on her bare knee just below her dress. Pinto kicked him in the knee with her high heel. He bellowed and leaped off the coffee table while clutching his leg. Luke straightened while glaring at her with rage. He punched her in the face. Pinto struck the back of the large, plush chair, cushioning the blow, but she was obviously dazed from the hit. Luke flexed his hand while glaring at her.

"I don't have to be nice," he informed her. "Nothing I do to you matters. Once my sister marries that pushover, Marco, she's part of Giovanni's family. When Giovanni dies, she'll be giving the orders." He glared hatefully at her. "You'll be just another victim among the massacre."

Pinto stared at him with concern, although she was unable to respond.

Luke chuckled in an evil manner. "Yes, that's right," he informed her. "Once the happy bride and groom walk back down the aisle, it's open season on Giovanni and his guests. It'll be a massacre they'll talk about for decades, and Nelson Banks will take the fall for it. Of course, he'll be dead too, but it's easier to frame a dead guy." His evil grin turned angry as he grabbed her arm. "I haven't got all day, so we'll just speed our courtship along, if you don't mind."

Pinto fought against him as he pulled her from the chair and attempted to drag her toward the bedroom. She drove her high heel into his foot just above his expensive shoes. He cried out and again punched her. He knocked her off her feet and into the glass coffee table. It shattered beneath her weight. For a moment, she lay on the floor battered and bleeding. Luke toppled the coffee table, tossing her onto the floor with the broken glass. He grabbed her arm and attempted to pull her to her feet. The guard entered the room and looked around. Luke pointed a warning finger at him.

"This doesn't concern you!"

The guard flew across the room, surprising Luke. Jackie leaped over the plush chair and kicked Luke in the chest with both feet. He hit the floor with tremendous force, rolled across the room, and struck the entertainment cabinet. Pinto was now able to free her hands from the duct tape and weakly pulled herself onto her hands and knees. She stared at Jackie while covered with glass and blood. The guard was already jumping to his feet.

Jackie held her hand up near Pinto while keeping her eyes on the guard. "Just stay down," she ordered.

Pinto managed to pull the duct tape from her mouth and barely had enough strength to nod. As the guard lunged for Jackie, she went into a series of forward and backward kicks, striking him with speed and force. The guard attempted to pull his weapon on her. Jackie twisted his arm and knocked the gun from his hand. Pinto watched the semiautomatic hit the floor near her. Jackie kicked the man without releasing his arm then flipped him over her, using his arm as leverage. The guard struck what remained of the coffee table, shattering the wood frame. Luke grabbed a decorative candlestick and attempted to strike Jackie. She caught his arm and kicked him in the face, dazing him.

Pinto stared at the unfolding assault with hateful eyes as blood seeped from the corner of her mouth and other cuts along her body. "Balls," she growled softly with anger.

Jackie barely looked back at Pinto before punching Luke in the groin. He gasped and doubled over. She then punched him in the face, causing him to straighten, and kicked him in the groin with enough force to elevate him from the floor before allowing him to drop. He didn't move from the moment he hit the floor.

"Thanks," Pinto whispered, barely able to hold herself up.

The guard grabbed his discarded gun while springing to his feet and aimed it at the back of Pinto's head. Beck entered the room, took only a moment to see his girlfriend's condition, and then fired the semiautomatic, unloading the entire magazine into the guard before he had a chance to hit the ground. Pinto again watched the gun fall to the floor near her. Beck replaced his empty gun to his pants and ran for Pinto, dropping to his knees alongside her. He assessed her injuries with horror.

"Are you okay?" he gasped.

She sobbed while painfully throwing her arms around his neck and clinging to him. Beck held her against him in his arms.

"It's okay," he whispered. "We'll call for a medivac for you. You're going to be okay."

"I'm fine," she gently replied then pulled away to look into his eyes. "You have to stop Matt. They intend to kill Giovanni and use the massacre of his guests to cover it up. It's going down right after the bride and groom are out of the way."

"We need to stop that wedding," Jackie gasped.

"It's already started," Beck informed her. "I heard the wedding march as I was crossing the lobby. We have to find the shooters." He gently took Pinto's battered, bleeding face in his hands and stared into her eyes. "Are you sure you're okay? I don't want to leave you."

"Go," she gasped softly while breathing heavily. "I'll be fine. Stop them from killing the guests. Save my father."

Beck fought his tears while caressing her bleeding face then nodded. "I'll save him. Stay here. You're safe now."

Jackie and Beck ran from the room. Pinto slowly pulled herself to her knees while grasping the discarded semiautomatic laying on the floor. She clutched it in her bloody hands and stared at it while sinking into her own thoughts.

Chapter Thirty-eight

The wedding was straight from the pages of a fairytale. Belle looked like a princess bride in her excessively elegant, white wedding dress with a lengthy train, while Marco was her dashing Prince Charming in his hand-tailored, designer tuxedo. The beach and ocean provided the perfect backdrop behind the bride and groom at the makeshift altar covered entirely in tropical flowers. The nearly two hundred guests sat in white folding chairs lined up along the entire grassy area between the hotel and the sand. They watched the young, wealthy couple with envy. No one even noticed that the groomsmen were one man short. Their attention remained happily focused on the beauty of the bride and her amazing dress. Beck and Jackie ran onto the second-floor balcony overlooking the wedding just before the beach. Both scanned the area for possible snipers while Beck frantically alerted the men through their handheld radios to the danger.

"We need to stop the wedding," Beck announced. "I need options."

"We can lure Giovanni away from the wedding," Gil suggested through his radio. "It won't be easy."

"Anyone gets near Giovanni and they may start firing," Beck replied. "Anyone see any snipers?"

"We have over twenty armed guards," Zack reported from his perch above the poolside bar. "They're all potential snipers. None with itchy trigger fingers yet."

"We need a diversion," Jackie told Beck then offered a concerned look. "But almost anything that interrupts this wedding will almost certainly provoke the snipers."

"Who's closest to Giovanni?" Beck asked through the radio. It was apparent he was starting to feel the pressure with each passing minute.

"I am," came a soft, familiar voice yet definitely not one of their team.

Beck stared at his radio with surprise. "Sal?"

Jackie and Beck scanned the guests and saw Sal sitting in the second row behind Giovanni with several people between them. He wasn't quite close enough to pass a secret warning without alerting the snipers.

"You shouldn't be anywhere near Giovanni," Beck snarled into the radio.

"Do you have my daughter?" he casually responded back, keeping his hand radio neatly tucked into his jacket near his shoulder, so he could speak softly into it without being noticed by those around him. He had somehow secured an earbud to keep sound from his radio leaking out for others to hear.

"She's safe," Beck informed him. "Damn it, Sal. You're in the combat zone. Get out of there."

"You let me worry about my own safety," came his muttered response. "Do what you do best."

The bride and groom exchanged rings and 'I dos'. Any minute, they would be leaving the guests and the massacre would begin.

"We're running out of time," Jackie muttered to Beck. "Let me go down there and stop this."

"And do what?"

"I'll think of something."

"Oh, fuck," came Kirk's voice over their radios. "We have a situation!"

Jackie and Beck looked back at the wedding venue. What they saw was beyond shocking. Pinto walked barefoot down the aisle in her torn dress and her moderately battered body covered in blood. She carried a bouquet of fresh flowers strewn with blood as well. As she passed the rows of guests on either side of the aisle, all eyes were suddenly upon her. She approached the makeshift altar and caught the attention of the wedding party as well. When the minister fell silent just short of making the nuptials official, the bride and groom simultaneously turned and looked at Pinto. Loud murmurs came from the crowd of guests as they stared with horror at the battered, bleeding woman.

Sal stared at his daughter with horror as his mouth hung open. "Pinto," he gasped.

"Someone stop her," Matt cried out with anger covering his fear.

"She's going to ruin the wedding," Belle pouted, practically pleading for someone to take Pinto down quietly.

"She's been injured," Marco announced to his soon-to-be bride and hurried toward Pinto as she got closer.

Pinto looked into Marco's eyes as he stopped before her. "She intends to kill your father," she whispered to the groom.

Marco hesitated a moment and stared at her with a bewildered look while clinging to her elbows despite the blood. Belle ran for them, looking more angry than concerned.

"Get away from her, Marco," Belle cried out demandingly as she approached them. "You don't know what she's up to."

"Up to?" Marco bellowed with surprise and barely glanced at his future wife. "She's a close family friend. Why would she be up to anything?"

Belle stopped before her future husband and Pinto, glaring at the injured woman. "I don't trust her!"

Pinto suddenly sneered while dropping the bouquet of flowers and aimed the semiautomatic at Belle's face. She whirled around the bride-to-be, caught her around the neck, and held the gun to her temple while standing behind her.

"Call them off," Pinto cried out while glaring at Matt. "Call off the hit on Giovanni or I'll kill your daughter!"

There were several gasps followed by frightening silence. Sal leaped over the chairs and tackled Giovanni to the ground. Marco looked from Belle to Matt with horror.

"Did you order a hit on my father?" Marco suddenly demanded and took a step toward Matt.

Kirk and Monroe moved along the crowd from opposite ends while keeping their rifles aimed in the direction of the guards surrounding the venue in an attempt to keep the guests safe.

"Everyone inside," Monroe ordered. "Now!"

The crowd panicked by his words and started running for the safety of the hotel. Bogart moved in and stood in front of Sal, who was covering Giovanni on the ground.

"Go! Keep low," Bogart ordered.

Sal helped Giovanni to his feet. Giovanni ran for his son, collected him despite his protests, and attempted to follow the others with Sal running interference. Bogart backed up behind them at a fast clip and kept his rifle trained on the hidden guards, waiting for any of them to move.

Matt sneered and tapped his ear transmitter. "Take the shot," he ordered.

Several men started firing, causing the remaining guests to scream and scramble for cover, creating chaos everywhere. Sal, Giovanni, and Marco joined Banks, Valerie, and Wade now under the protection of Corbin. Corbin fired back at the guards shooting at them along with Beck's team. It was now obvious that all the guards were on Matt's payroll. One of the guards shot Pinto, grazing her shoulder, forcing her to release Belle. The plan backfired when Pinto clutched Belle's wedding dress and took her to the ground with her. Belle immediately elbowed Pinto in the chest then scrambled to her feet. The guard who'd shot Pinto now had a clean shot to finish her. He was about to fire the fatal shot when his head suddenly snapped back from a precision shot to his temple, exploding out the other side, taking most of his skull with it. Zack lowered his rifle from where he now stood on the roof of the poolside bar.

Pinto pulled herself to her hands and knees as Belle leaped for the discarded gun. Pinto grabbed the excessively long train of her dress, yanked back with all her strength, and knocked her to the ground. Pinto leaped for the gun as Belle recovered and lunged for her. Pinto barely had time to aim and squeezed the trigger several times. All three shots found their way into the evil bride, although not dropping her to the ground. She took two shots to her abdomen and one to the chest just above the neckline of the elegant dress. Blood saturated the front of her once white dress. Belle stood still a moment and stared at Pinto with horror in her eyes. Blood seeped from her mouth as she gasped her last breath. Pinto held the gun firmly in her hands and, without flinching, watched the bride fall to the ground. A rifle shot exploded the ground alongside Pinto, causing her to scream and shield her head.

Beck was suddenly crouched alongside Pinto and fired at the men attempting to kill her. The others gave them some cover, allowing Beck to pull Pinto to her feet and take her to the safety of the poolside bar. When they looked around, Corbin had already led Sal, Giovanni, and the others to safety, but they were gone, causing Beck to panic. Beck held up his hand radio while his team continued to fire at the guards.

"Sal, do you copy?"

"Beck," came Sal's unusually calm voice over the radio. There was an unnerving pause of silence from Sal. "It's too late for me, Beck. Tell Pinto I love her."

They heard a gunshot over the hand radio followed by silence. The faint gunshot echoed from somewhere beyond the resort, possibly from the jeep parking area.

"Dad, no," Pinto cried out with horror.

✝

Corbin's men herded the others away from the resort, taking them as prisoners. One guard held a gun on Sal where he partially lay on the ground clutching his bleeding arm. The hand radio lay several feet away from him. Sal stared at the man standing over him and showed no fear despite his obvious pain.

"They'll find you," Sal informed the man and offered an unsettling smile despite his situation. "And when they do, they'll kill you."

"We'll deal with them when and if that time comes," the man replied and tightened his finger on the trigger while aiming the gun at Sal's head.

Sal closed his eyes and held his head up proudly, waiting for the sound of the shot and the sting of the bullet. The guard suddenly groaned. Sal opened his eyes to see Mac kick the guard several times before tossing him to the ground and disarming him. She aimed the pistol at the guard and, without hesitation, shot him in the head. She looked back at Sal and tossed the gun before him.

"We're even," she announced then hurried for the dock.

Sal stared after her with a look of surprise. "Mac?" he gasped in disbelief.

Chapter Thirty-nine

The once elegant wedding venue was scattered with nearly two hundred toppled chairs, a dozen dead guards, and covered with crushed flowers. The bride lay dead in what was left of the aisle, her expensive white wedding dress soaked with blood. The long, elegant train of the wedding dress cascaded alongside her dead body in picturesque beauty. Pinto sat on the ground and fought her tears near the poolside bar while Emily Banks tended to her injured shoulder. The bullet had only grazed her shoulder, but the wound was deep enough to require stitches. Emily did her best to clean and dress the wound with a first aid kit from the resort. Both women watched Beck and Jackie patrol the area with their rifles cradled in their arms. The rest of the team, minus Zack, hurried across the resort grounds and joined them. Darth ran to Pinto, licked her bloodstained hand, and then lay alongside her while placing his head on her lap.

"No sign of Corbin or his hostages," Monroe announced while allowing his rifle to fall against his shoulder.

"The resort is secure. The remaining guards fled the area," Gil informed Beck. "They could be planning an escape."

"What about my father?" Pinto gasped softly while staring at the guys with tears and mascara streaking her battered and bleeding face.

"We haven't found him either," Bogart replied gently then forced a tiny, reassuring smile. "We'll find him though. I'm sure he's just fine."

The rest of the team glared at Bogart. He fidgeted from the looks he'd received. Lying to Pinto wasn't helping anyone. They were almost certain of Sal's fate after what they'd heard over the radio.

"My husband," Emily announced from where she kneeled alongside Pinto with concern on her face. "They have my husband, don't they?"

Beck stared at the concerned woman and nodded. "Yeah, Mrs. Banks, they have your husband. We're going to get them back," he insisted.

Zack jogged across the resort toward them. "Several jeeps are missing," he informed them as he approached. "There are fresh burn marks where they were parked. They headed into the island's interior."

"We'll have to split up and search the island for them," Beck announced. "They'll be heading for a dock of some sort. There weren't any landing fields for a hidden a plane, so they must intend to leave by boat."

"When we did the fly-by, there were several isolated docks," Jackie replied, "but I didn't see any boats. They could be heading for the mansion."

"That's not the way the tire tracks went," Zack insisted in a stern tone.

"Maybe they circled back to the mansion," Beck remarked, almost disregarding Zack's report.

"No, they went into the island's interior," Zack reconfirmed with frustration. "I'm not some delusional mental patient. You need to trust my intel if we're going to save those hostages."

Beck fidgeted and eyed the rest of the team, uncertain if he could take Zack at face value, especially after all his false alarms onboard the ship.

Jackie stared at Zack's expression then looked at Beck. "There was a dock on the far end of the island," she announced in Zack's defense. "If they went through the island's interior, they could be heading there. I could take the helicopter and beat them to it."

"I'm with Jackie," Zack insisted with little room for objection.

Beck reluctantly nodded not that Zack would have listened to him anyway. Jackie and Zack ran from the ransacked wedding area and through the hotel, being the quicker route.

"If the plan was to kill Giovanni, what are they waiting for?" Pinto asked while sniffing. "Why take prisoners? Why kill my father when they already had the man they wanted?"

"They've been caught," Beck replied gently. "They need a few bargaining chips. They'll undoubtedly keep Giovanni alive until they know they're safe." He then looked at his team. "Gil and I will take a jeep north toward the mansion. Kirk can head through the island's interior with a four-wheeler on the off chance Zack is right. Monroe and Bogart can take a jeep and head south." Beck crouched alongside Pinto and gently took her hand in his. "You stay here with the others. Go inside and lock yourself in your room. I'll be back for you, I promise." He kissed her gently on the forehead then looked into her frightened eyes.

"Be careful," she whispered.

He smiled and nodded then placed a semiautomatic pistol in her hand. "You too."

As the five men and Darth ran from the destroyed wedding venue, Emily helped Pinto to her feet. She leaned heavily on the woman as they headed toward the resort.

"Honey!"

Both women stopped and looked around for the voice. Sal ran toward them while clutching his bleeding arm. Pinto gasped with surprise and limped for her father. They hugged happily while Pinto sobbed.

She pulled away and looked at him with concern. "You're bleeding," she cried out.

He eyed her knowingly. "Yeah, so are you." Sal looked around. "Where are the guys?"

"They went to find Corbin and his men," Pinto informed him. "They took hostages."

"They're heading into the island's interior," Sal informed them and scanned the disastrous area. "I need to warn them. I need another hand radio." He ran to one of the dead guards and picked up the blood-covered radio. He attempted to reach the guys, but the hand radio didn't work. He tossed it aside with disgust and continued to scan the area for another.

"How did you get away?" Pinto asked.

Sal snorted a soft laugh. "You'd never believe me if I told you." He sank into thought then looked around. "I need to help the guys."

"They're chasing after trained killers," Emily informed him. "What can you do to help?"

Sal eyed Emily and shook his head while revealing a tiny smile. "My dear lady," he announced. "Have you forgotten *what* you married into?"

†

The helicopter flew above the tall trees, barely leaving enough room to pass over them while following one of the jeep trails. With the thick woods, it was impossible to check every inch of road, but Jackie and Zack could cover more ground from the air and would likely see a fleeing jeep. While Jackie piloted the older helicopter, Zack sat in the aft-sliding side opening with his rifle in hand looking as if he were about to jump from the moving helicopter. Jackie tried to focus her attention on the road through the thick woods, but it was difficult not to keep an eye on the man half hanging out the side opening, especially without a cable tethered to a harness. She saw dirt kicking up from one of the trails then caught a glimpse of the jeep's rear bumper.

"Found them," Jackie announced, alerting Zack.

She used the helicopter radio to contact Beck, although there was a lot of static.

"Beck, Zack was right. They're heading for the opposite shore. I count three jeeps," she announced then looked around. "I'm going to veer south and sweep the shore for their escape route. I'm sure they hear me in the sky, but I don't want them to think I've seen them. I don't want to give them any reason to start killing hostages."

"Copy," Beck replied through the static. "We're regrouping and heading your way."

Jackie veered south and headed for the far shore. They made the far beach nearly fifteen minutes before those in the jeep would arrive. A decent sized yacht sat anchored just off shore with a motorized raft pulled onto the beach. Matt must have alerted someone; since the yacht hadn't been there the day she did the fly-by. Jackie lowered the helicopter and watched Zack leap from the side, barely waiting until they were low enough. Jackie shook her head then flew away from the extraction boat. She landed in a clearing a safe distance away. If they made it to the boat, she'd still have plenty of time to fly after them before they'd get very far. She secured her tactical batons in her holster, placed a gun down the back of her pants, and then grabbed her rifle. She hurried from the helicopter and made her way to the location where Zack had dropped.

†

The four-wheeler flew along the jeep trail in the center of the island. Jeeps from both sides filed in behind Kirk on his ATV as they raced for the opposite end of the island. The hostage jeep bringing up the rear appeared just ahead of them. They had separated the hostages among the three jeeps, purposely making each vehicle a fragile target. The last jeep veered to the left and the middle jeep to the right. Kirk chased the one to the left, while Monroe and Bogart followed the jeep to the right. Gil and Beck with Darth in the back stayed on the lead jeep containing only one hostage...Giovanni.

Chapter Forty

The jeep raced along the wider path heading toward the south side of the island with Marco sitting in the front passenger seat and Nelson Banks between two guards in the backseat. Nelson glanced over his shoulder several times as Kirk gained on them despite the guard shooting at him. Marco kept an eye on the ATV through the side view mirror as well. The jeep jumped the woods' edge and landed on the beach, tearing up the sand. Nelson looked at Marco in the passenger seat in front of him.

"Marco," Nelson suddenly yelled, alerting him. Nelson thrust his body into the guard sitting forward. "Jump!"

As he threw the guard off balance, Marco instantly reacted and dove from the speeding jeep, landing in the sand and rolling several times. The guard who had been firing at Kirk struck Nelson with his gun, nearly knocking him unconscious with the violent hit. Kirk eyed the fallen man in the sand. Marco moved to his knees and motioned him to go after Nelson. Kirk raced along the sand, picking up speed and keeping low on the ATV to avoid stray rounds of rifle fire. Both men in the backseat on either side of Nelson now fired at Kirk.

Bullets ricocheting off the ATV were a little close for comfort. Kirk kept his rifle snug against his body and propped on the handlebars to maintain control over the vehicle and still take his shot. Nelson again glanced behind him, despite his bleeding head. Without warning, Nelson leaped into the man on his left and knocked him from the jeep. Both men struck the sand with Nelson landing on top. Nelson punched the man in the face, but the guard still managed to aim his firearm. Nelson held his breath. The guard suddenly took a shot to the chest, sending him backward onto the sand.

Nelson looked up as Kirk flew past while skillfully cocking the rifle with one hand while steering the ATV with the other. Nelson grinned and saluted him. Marco ran across the sand to join his father's friend. He grabbed his arm and hurried him back into the woods to get them out of the fire zone in case Kirk lost the battle. Kirk suddenly skidded to a stop, partially spinning the four-wheeler in a semicircle and sending sand flying. He took careful aim through the riflescope and fired. The bullet struck the gas tank causing the jeep to explode and flip, propelling both burning guards through the air. Nelson and Marco stopped just short of the woods and looked back. Kirk motioned them back to the resort then raced along the beach to the rendezvous.

†

The jeep on the north trail flew over large rocks, jolting its two hostages, Wade in the front passenger seat and Valerie in the back center between Matt and another guard. Matt and the guard in the back attempted to shoot at the jeep in hot pursuit, but they found it nearly impossible with the rough terrain. Bogart jetted the jeep over the rocks while Monroe attempted to hold onto the roll cage where he stood in the back with his rifle.

"How about keeping this rig steady?" Monroe cried out to the driver.

Bogart concentrated on his driving, looking much like a racecar driver tackling a road course. "Driving here," he snarled back.

"Damn it," Monroe shouted in a mild temper tantrum. "Next time, I'm driving!"

"I've got this!"

"Get a little closer, Mario," Monroe yelled at him while motioning at the jeep ahead of them.

"You want closer?" Bogart demanded then grinned while cocking his head. "I'll get you closer!"

Bogart stepped on the gas despite the rough terrain and nearly launched the jeep into the air. Monroe clung to the roll cage and screamed as his eyes widened with horror. The jeep caught up to the one in front of it and rammed its back bumper, jolting the jeep and nearly sending it off what barely qualified as a road. Bogart rammed the jeep again.

"I said get closer," Monroe cried out. "I didn't say kill the hostages!"

"Quit your whining and shoot the bastards," Bogart shouted back while concentrating on his driving.

Monroe again raised his rifle. As Matt and the guard attempted to fire at them, Bogart again rammed them. Both men were thrown off balance, interrupting their ability to shoot. Monroe stood straight in the bouncing jeep, maintained his balance in spite of Bogart's driving, and fired. The shell pierced the guard through the chest, exploded through his back, and struck the driver in the head.

"Yeah," Monroe shouted. "A twofer--!"

As the driver fell against the steering wheel, the driverless jeep veered sharply out of control. Bogart slammed on the brakes. The jeep sideswiped a tree then rammed a second with its left front fender, jolting it to a stop. Matt was moderately dazed, realized what had happened, and attempted to jump out the side of the jeep. Bogart's jeep slammed into the back of the totaled vehicle, sending Matt flying out the side and to the ground. Monroe leaped out the side of the jeep, ran for the fallen man, and aimed the rifle at his face. Matt stared up the barrel of the rifle to the devilishly grinning Monroe. His finger tightened on the trigger.

"Any last words, wabbit?"

Matt nervously put his hands in the air while trembling. Monroe stared down the barrel of the rifle.

"Pow!" he cried out.

Matt screamed and cowered, believing Monroe shot him. Once he realized he'd been duped, he looked at Monroe. Monroe struck him in the face with the butt of the rifle then grinned deviously. Valerie and Wade stumbled from the jeep and looked from Matt to Monroe.

"Is it over?" Valerie asked.

"I think you've done your part," Monroe informed them. "We have a few loose ends yet." He tossed Wade two zip ties. "Remember how to use these, Doc?"

Wade caught the zip ties, eyed Monroe, and then nodded. "Yeah, sure."

"Take care of that one for us," Monroe announced. "We'll swing by to collect the trash on the way back."

Monroe jumped into the jeep with Bogart. The battered jeep grinded slightly, but Bogart was able to get it to run. He turned the jeep on the narrow path then headed for the interior road to meet the others on the far beach. Valerie leaned against the wrecked jeep and groaned softly while eying Wade.

"And you thought weddings were boring," she announced while breathing heavily and holding her chest.

He smiled and chuckled softly while picking up Matt's discarded gun. "I stand corrected."

Chapter Forty-one

Gil drove the jeep behind Corbin's jeep, keeping a safe distance on the rocky trail. He allowed enough space to swerve to avoid the rifle fire from both men in back surrounding Giovanni, who mostly kept his head down. Giovanni knew enough to keep low while the hired professionals killed one another. Beck fired a shot then ducked in the passenger seat while grabbing the hand radio. Darth sat up several times to enjoy the open jeep experience, but Gil kept giving him the 'down' signal. He'd resume his position on the floor in the back to avoid stray shots. The beach was just ahead of Corbin's jeep.

"Jackie," Beck shouted into the radio. "Tell me you and Zack are in place. We're coming in hot!"

"Bring the party to us," Jackie announced over the radio. "We're ready to rock."

Beck looked at Gil, who now watched him. He nodded. Gil's look turned a frightening shade of serious as he stepped on the gas and jetted after Corbin's jeep. By the time Corbin's jeep hit the sand, Gil was practically on their bumper. He rammed the jeep in front of him, knocking both men back into their seats on either side of Giovanni. A rifle fired, striking the man in the rear passenger side. He flew out the back of the jeep and hit the sand. Gil didn't even attempt to swerve, running over the man in his path. Beck stood up straight and fired his rifle in time with two unseen shooters. Gil raced alongside Corbin's jeep and immediately rammed into their side.

Corbin attempted to get a shot at Gil from the front passenger seat but was unable to make the shot from the sudden impact. Beck tossed his rifle aside and leaped into the back of Corbin's jeep. In one fluid motion, he punched the man with the rifle and tackled Giovanni out the opposite side of the jeep. Once they were clear of Beck and Giovanni, Gil rammed the jeep again then veered off. Darth sat up in the back and barked his threatening warning. Corbin flew from the jeep just before it rolled. Several rifle shots from hidden locations fired at the rolling jeep. It suddenly exploded mid-roll. Corbin attempted to flee the scene, but a rifle fired and the sand exploded in front of him. He stopped and raised his hands in the air. Jackie and Zack approached from their hidden positions behind some large rocks while keeping their guns trained on Corbin. Beck helped Giovanni to his feet.

"My son?" Giovanni cried out.

"Safely on the south beach," Beck informed him.

Bogart's jeep appeared from the path in the woods and drove along the sand toward them. Kirk on his four-wheeler approached from the south beach.

"Are we clear?" Beck asked the men.

"All bad guys accounted for," Kirk announced. "Dead, but accounted for."

"Matt's a little shaken, but he's contained," Monroe informed them. "Doc's taking care of him. We just need to collect the trash on the way back."

"You leave that trash to me," Giovanni growled.

The guys exchanged looks but didn't comment either way. Although not their usual practice, none wanted to piss off one of the most notorious mob bosses.

Zack allowed his rifle to rest on his shoulder and grinned. "I'm good with that solution."

The severely damaged jeep appeared on the beach from the trail in the woods. Valerie drove the jeep with Wade in the passenger seat and Matt tied in the back. Monroe groaned lowly, shook his head, and made his way toward them as they approached in the battered jeep.

"I told you to wait for us, Doc," Monroe informed him with annoyance in his tone.

"It's a trap!" Valerie screamed.

Matt suddenly revealed a gun and shot Valerie in the head. She fell from the jeep. Before anyone could react, Wade aimed his semiautomatic and shot Monroe, throwing him to the sand. Darth snarled and barked viciously. Wade and Matt aimed their weapons at the team. Before anyone could react, Corbin pulled a concealed gun from his pants and aimed it at Giovanni.

"Let's not do anything stupid," Corbin snarled, catching everyone's attention.

Wade and Matt climbed out of the jeep while keeping their weapons on the guys. Corbin switched directions and aimed his gun at Jackie then looked around the group.

"Everyone drop your weapons, or I'll shoot the Commander's daughter," he announced boldly.

Bogart twitched while grinding his teeth. Beck cast looks at the guys, indicating for them to drop their weapons. All reluctantly tossed their weapons to the sand, although seemingly in calculated positions as if coordinating an attack. Darth continued to snarl at Corbin. Gil snapped his fingers to silence the dog. Once their weapons were down, Corbin moved his gun away from Jackie. Without warning, he fired three shots into Zack, catching him in the chest with at least one, and knocking him to the sand. Jackie cried out. The guys stared with horror at their fallen man. Darth again snarled and barked viciously but awaited the command to attack.

"You bastard," Bogart cried out and was about to lunge for Corbin.

Corbin turned the gun back on Jackie while grinning at Bogart. "Try it," he snarled.

Bogart stopped himself and looked at the others for some secret signal that didn't seem to come. Gil again snapped his fingers at Darth, silencing him. He then gave the dog another signal. Darth lay on the sand and awaited further orders.

"It was nothing personal," Corbin announced while grinning. "I just wanted to make sure the wild card was out of play, that's all."

"I told you he wasn't dead," Wade scoffed while approaching and collecting rifles from the captured team. "The bastard just refuses to die."

"Maybe if you'd done your job," Corbin snarled back at Wade.

"I did enough," Wade lashed back. He looked at Beck and smirked. "The first week of Zack's pills did help his concussion, but the second bottle was a special concoction of mine. I can only imagine the hallucinations he must've been having while tripping.

Honestly, I figured he'd completely lose his mind and eat a bullet, but he somehow held it together." The doc casually shrugged it off. "It all worked out though. We got what we needed. He was destabilized just enough to throw him off his game while chasing shadows and keep him out of our way."

Darth crawled on his belly a few inches at a time getting closer to Gil's jeep until he finally disappeared behind it.

"Out of the way for what?" Beck demanded. "When we came to see you, you had no idea we'd end up on this island protecting Giovanni."

Darth trotted behind the jeep, waited at the rear bumper, and then kept low while slipping behind Kirk's ATV. He again remained hidden then darted behind the totaled jeep just past Valerie's lifeless body. He disappeared beneath the jeep.

"No, I never suspected you'd put your lives on the line for a lowlife mob boss like Giovanni, but Giovanni was Matt's hit," Wade informed them. "You and your team were ours. It was the perfect opportunity. Corbin and I lured your team here to isolate and kill you. Your girlfriend and her creepy stalker gave us the perfect scenario. After I heard what you said in my office waiting room, I knew I could use that little pervert to lure you here. Especially after I arranged the break-in at Sal's mansion. I left just enough clues for you to chase after your girlfriend, fearing for her safety. Naturally, your team would follow you with little resistance."

"How'd that work for you?" Beck snapped while raising his brows.

"You're too stupid to figure out you're already dead," Corbin remarked.

"Not dead yet," Beck informed him then looked back at Wade. "What was the price to betray us, Doc?"

"Don't flatter yourself," Wade replied. "Not nearly as much as Matt was willing to pay for the hit on Giovanni, but it was enough to make it worth my while."

"Who was footing the bill?" Gil demanded.

"You'd be surprised," Corbin replied while chuckling.

"Story time over," Matt snarled, becoming irritated by his accomplices. "I know the two of you have your own agenda, but we need to get out of here. We need to kill Giovanni and cover our tracks."

"Killing Giovanni is of little consequence now," Corbin remarked. "Beck's little bitch killed that sniveling brat of yours. You've got nothing to gain from killing him. His men will just hunt you down for nothing."

"How dare you speak of my daughter--?"

Corbin aimed his gun at Matt and stared him down. "Don't try me, old man. I'm not stupid. I highly doubt you'd pay me for the hit now that you have nothing to gain. You mean very little to me at this moment."

"Enough," Wade lashed out, becoming angry with his partners. "First things first. We need to make sure Zack is really dead this time."

"You probably should have thought about that five minutes ago before you started monologuing," Beck announced while folding his arms across his chest as he grinned. "Zack's not the only one who knows how to play dead."

All three men looked back at the totaled jeep. Monroe was gone, leaving only a small amount of blood in the sand.

"Son-of-a-bitch!" Corbin glared at Wade and waved his gun around. "Find that bastard!"

"Oops, lost another," Beck casually announced with a look of humor on his face.

They looked to the sand where Zack had fallen. He was also gone. Wade lunged for Jackie, positioned himself behind her at a safe distance to prevent her from striking, and aimed his gun at her.

"I'm aware of your talents," Wade snarled at her. "One sudden move and I'll shoot you." He looked around, although he didn't see any sign of Zack. "You hear me, Zack? I'll kill her if you try anything!" No one moved. "Jackie and I are taking a little walk to that helicopter she has hidden around here. Anyone follows and I'll kill her."

"Then who'll fly you?" Gil asked with little reaction. "You can't fly a helicopter. Only Jackie and I can. Let her go, and I'll take you wherever you want to go."

Wade laughed with apparent humor. "Nice try, hero," he announced. "Something tells me she values her life more than you value yours. She foolishly thinks she has something to live for. I'll take my chances with her."

"Zack's less likely to tear you apart over me," Gil informed him. "You may want to consider that before you point a gun at her."

"Thanks, but I'm good," Wade remarked.

Corbin stared at him with surprise and attempted to walk toward him. Wade aimed a second gun at Corbin.

"You're double-crossing me?" Corbin snarled with anger.

"Don't be so surprised," Wade remarked. "You'd do the same in my position."

Wade forced Jackie away from the guys on the beach. They watched her gradually disappear with little reaction, almost as if they assumed she'd figure it out on her own. Bogart was the only one itching to react.

Beck casually turned and eyed Corbin. "Your friends are dropping like flies," he remarked. "Don't worry about your friend, the doc. He'll be dead before they reach the helicopter. Zack may be crazy, but Jackie's a conniving rattlesnake. My money's on the girl."

Matt nervously clutched his gun and looked around for signs of Zack or Monroe. He seemed spooked by every sound. Corbin felt compelled to stare down Beck while keeping his gun trained on him.

"That game doesn't work on me, Beck," Corbin remarked. "We're cut from the same cloth. We're the same."

Beck shook his head. "No, Corbin," he replied. "We're nothing alike. My friends can't be bought. Yours turn on you the moment things go sideways."

"I still have Matt," Corbin informed him then looked where Matt had stood. He was gone. Corbin appeared surprised and looked around. "Matt?"

When Corbin looked back toward the demolished jeep, he saw Monroe casually leaning against it with a semiautomatic aimed at him. Darth sat by his side and panted happily. Monroe threw a blood-covered Bowie knife into the sand. He looked at Corbin with little emotion.

"Someone forgot to frisk the dog for weapons," Monroe announced then sneered with annoyance. "Can we get on with this little gunfight? I'm having a really bad day." He managed an unsettling smirk. "I mean, not nearly as bad of a day as your friend, Matt." Monroe casually flicked his foot behind him and kicked Matt's head across the sand. He stared at Corbin without blinking. "Not worth losing your head over though, right bro?"

Corbin barely flinched. Without warning, he fired a shot at Beck, nearly clipping him, and jumped over the smoldering jeep. The guys took cover and prepared for a gunfight. The sound of several approaching jeeps caught their attention. Corbin laughed from the other side of his overturned jeep.

"Looks like my men regrouped," Corbin announced, humored by the change of events. "I don't think this is going to end the way you were thinking it would."

Several jeeps flew onto the beach and skidded to a stop. A dozen men jumped out of them armed with shotguns. Sal and the other wedding guests approached while cocking their pump action shotguns. The men with shotguns surrounded the jeep and aimed their weapons at Corbin. He tossed his gun aside and frowned while raising his hands in the air. Beck saw Sal and laughed softly as he approached.

Sal grinned at Beck while resting the shotgun against his shoulder. "Thought you could use some additional backup."

"Thanks, Sal," Beck announced then looked at Bogart and Kirk. "Go fetch Jackie." He raised a brow, smirked, and casually shrugged. "If Zack's in a mood, let him have the doc. It's good therapy for him."

Bogart and Kirk ran after Jackie and Wade.

Chapter Forty-two

Jackie walked along the path and veered left, luring Wade away from the helicopter. She wasn't about to make it easy on him. Wade eyed the area then laughed softly.

"Nice try, Jackie," he announced, "but I'm not your average idiot. The only clearing around here is to the right, heading back toward the beach." He motioned her right with his gun, keeping just out of kicking distance.

"Why are you doing this?" she asked while heading right. "You were friends with my father and his team. They trusted you. How could you betray them?"

"I thought we already covered this," Wade remarked. "Simple greed, Jackie. While other doctors were getting specialist degrees, I was serving our country. By the time my tour ended, becoming a general practitioner was all I was qualified to do, despite all the surgeries I'd performed."

"I thought your surgeon's license was revoked," she remarked without looking back at him. She saw blood on some plants as they passed. Her heart suddenly skipped a beat. Blood? She assumed Zack had been wearing his vest. Was it possible his injury was serious? "I heard you'd screwed up a few simple surgeries because you couldn't handle the stress."

"Seems we both did our research," he remarked. "When Corbin came to me with this golden opportunity, I couldn't pass it up. I needed the money. I had to get out of nowhere Colorado. I had to get away from gout, migraines, and warts."

The helicopter came into view. Jackie scanned the area, searching for signs of Zack without giving his position away. It took a long time to learn his invisibility technique. She didn't see any sign

215

of him. Wade was a little less confident now as they approached the helicopter. He kept a watchful eye out for Zack, expecting him to appear from under some rock. Jackie saw blood on the open aft-side door and held back her concern. It was possible she was waiting for a secret signal that wouldn't come. Wade noticed the blood as well and scanned the area. He leaped alongside the opening with his gun aimed inside just far enough away to avoid having it removed. The helicopter was empty. Jackie suddenly realized she was on her own and yet she was more frightened for Zack than her own safety. When Wade was convinced Zack wasn't hiding in or around the helicopter, he motioned her into the pilot's seat.

"Time to go," he announced firmly.

Jackie was hesitant, but she climbed into the passenger seat before sliding into the pilot's seat, allowing Wade to slip in next to her. She flipped a few switches and prepped the helicopter. Her heart pounded with each passing second Zack didn't appear.

"So not only don't you get your payday," Jackie announced, stalling for time, "but now you're on Giovanni's hit list." She then considered the comment. "Providing Matt and Corbin survive, they won't be exactly happy with you either."

"That's where you're wrong," Wade informed her. "Corbin's yacht was just a failsafe in the event something went wrong. Matt has a luxury yacht at his private dock in Columbia. What Corbin didn't realize is that's where Matt stashed our fee. I just need to reach that yacht before anyone knows the job went sideways, and I can disappear a very wealthy man. No one will ever find me."

"Zack will find you," she replied with little emotion. "He'll find you, and he *will* kill you."

"Zack's dead," he replied simply. "He would have been here to rescue you by now. Don't think I didn't notice the blood as well. Eventually, death finds us all. Zack was living on borrowed time for years." He indicated the windshield. "Now, if you don't mind, I'd like to go."

Jackie frowned and eased the helicopter off the ground. Her mind was working in overtime now. She needed to plot her escape. Wade knew to keep the gun just far enough away that he could still pull the trigger before she could take him down. Now that she was piloting the helicopter, she had less opportunity to react and tighter quarters. That left her two options. She could risk waiting until they landed in Columbia to make her move, which is probably when he intended to shoot her, or crash the helicopter and kill them both. Her thoughts strayed to Holden. He'd be brokenhearted to lose her.

She then came up with a third, secret option. It was risky, but it had to work. As she lifted off the ground, Bogart and Kirk ran into the clearing and watched the helicopter pass overhead with horror. Zack's wet jacket fell to the ground only a few feet from them. Kirk picked up the jacket and sniffed it, making a face. It was soaked with gasoline.

Bogart stared at the jacket then looked back at the helicopter. "Oh, hell no," he muttered. "What are we going to do?"

"She's heading straight through the center of the island," Kirk announced. "If we break a few speeding laws, we can meet her at the cliff."

"The cliff?" Bogart asked and suspiciously eyed Kirk. "What makes you think she's heading for the cliff?"

"Because that's the only chance she has to bail," Kirk replied. "She's going to need backup. Let's go!"

They turned and ran back down the path.

✝

Jackie flew the helicopter over the center of the island in no particular hurry. Wade glared at her several times while keeping his gun aimed at her from the far side of the helicopter.

"No one's going to rescue you," he informed her. "Mind picking up the pace?"

"You may think you know my guys," she informed him. "You may even think you know me, but you know shit about helicopters. This piece of shit is older than Satan." She eyed the gauges and appeared slightly surprised then hesitated. "And we're low on fuel. If you want to make it to Columbia, we need to conserve fuel or we'll end up in the ocean." She cast a look at him. "I don't know about you, but I don't feel like dying today." She then muttered, "These things go down like a lead balloon."

Jackie again eyed the fuel gauge. It continued to drop, which she knew wasn't right. The craft pulled slightly to the right. She allowed her eyes to shift without turning her head to attract attention. That sort of pull wasn't wind drag. She'd had guys jumping from helicopters and riding the skids during enough flights to know when someone was climbing around outside the moving helicopter. It was Zack! It had to be! He'd undoubtedly been well hidden beneath the helicopter and cut her fuel line. That he didn't make any sort of

move before takeoff told her he was without a gun and possibly
sustained enough of an injury that he couldn't take on an armed man
holding a hostage. The thought scared her, but she knew now she
had to continue with her original plan. She'd fly low enough to the
cliff so she could bail just before the edge and risk Wade shooting
her. The clearing and the cliff were coming into view. She felt
another slight pull on the right, indicating Zack was again moving.
The fuel light came on along with the warning alarm. The sound
alerted Wade.

"What's that?" he demanded.

"That's the fuel indicator," Jackie informed him. "We need
to set her down and refuel in the next ten minutes or she's going
down whether you like it or not."

"You said the fuel was low, not--"

Wade stopped mid-sentence and turned around with his gun
aimed. Zack punched him in the face. Jackie struggled to control
the helicopter as the two men fought for control of the gun. She
caught a glimpse of blood soaking through Zack's shirt low and off to
the side. She thought he'd taken the shots to his chest, but she must
have been mistaken. He'd been shot once beneath his special vest
jacket. Judging by the blood running down his hand, he also took a
shot to his upper arm as well, leaving him with less strength than
usual. As they struggled for the gun in Wade's hand, both men
punched each other, attempting to win the struggle.

Jackie tried to ignore the gun close to her face and circled the
area just before the cliff, hovering over it. She needed to set her
down. Wade pulled Zack into the front with him. Zack nearly
struck Jackie with his booted feet as he landed on top of her
passenger. Jackie again struggled with the controls, his actions causing
her to spin the helicopter slightly, bouncing it off the ground. The
fuel light continued to flash and the alarm wailed its dire warning.
The gun fired, striking the control panel. Sparks flew and the
helicopter controls jerked in Jackie's hands. She no longer had
control.

She fought to keep the craft from leaving the safety of the
clearing before the cliff. She saw flashes of the ocean below as the
craft spun in a circle. It bucked and jerked in her hands while the
two men continued to punch one another while wrestling in the seat
alongside her. One or both men kicked her several times while
struggling. The helicopter continued to pull against her while
spinning nearly out of control. The best she could do was keep it
from pulling down to the right. Jackie attempted to set it down, but
it pulled sharply, insisting on going down on an angle. The rotors

nearly hit the ground. The moment she kept it straight, it again spun in circles.

"I can't land," she cried out. "I can't hold on much longer. I'm losing control of her!"

"Bail!" Zack shouted now pinned between Wade and the door. He punched the doctor several times, but Wade refused to release the gun.

"No," Jackie yelled back above the loud roaring of the smoldering engine. "If I let go, she's going to go down to the right. *Your* right! You'll be killed!"

Zack eyed Jackie from his position beneath Wade. Their eyes met briefly. "I think that's inevitable now," he informed her.

Jackie saw the grenade in his free hand, causing her to gasp. He punched Wade twice in the face with the grenade and kept the gun from pointing at his face.

"I'm sorry, Jackie," he announced then kicked her with both feet in the shoulder.

Jackie flew against the helicopter door, her hands slipping from the controls. Zack kicked her again, throwing her through the door. Jackie fell several feet to the ground, landed harshly, and rolled several feet. She saw the helicopter rotors striking the ground near the cliff. The rotors tore from the craft and flew across the clearing, slicing trees. Jackie screamed and shielded herself. When she lowered her arms, she watched the helicopter hit the edge of the cliff. Several gunshots fired within the helicopter as blood spattered against the inner windshield. Jackie cried out and scrambled to her hands and knees. The helicopter tumbled over the cliff. Jackie made it to her feet and ran for the cliff while clinging to her aching leg. She stopped at the edge of the cliff just in time to see the helicopter hit the water below. A second later, it exploded.

"No," she cried out and ran from the cliff.

Despite the pain from her right thigh, Jackie ran along the steep trail. She stumbled and rolled several feet, striking a few rocks as she tumbled. She was momentarily dazed but managed to pull herself to her feet and again ran down the path. She reached a clear stretch and picked up the pace. Jackie half slid down another steep path that wasn't even a path, crashed at the bottom, and again picked herself up. She ran while limping and finally hit the sand. She ran along the beach nearly half a mile before coming to a stop.

The remains of the helicopter floated in the surf. Some debris had already found its way to shore. She saw a moderately burnt man's hand sticking out of water not far from shore. Jackie ran into the surf and clutched the hand, pulling it from the water.

She stared at the severed, burnt hand and immediately released it while screaming. She looked around at the smoldering debris and objects floating within the surf. Jackie grabbed a shirt floating in the water that she recognized as Zack's. She stared at the bloodstains and the bullet hole in the torn shirt then looked into the water.

"Zack!"

There was no response. Jackie began to sob while clinging to the shirt.

"Zack!"

Jackie fell to her knees within the surf and sobbed softly while clutching the shirt to her chest.

"No, don't do this to me," she sobbed softly.

She didn't know how long she'd been kneeling in the surf as debris floated past her to shore. She never even heard the jeep pull up on the beach. Bogart ran into the water after her while screaming her name, but she didn't hear him. He pulled her from the water, swept her into his arms, and carried her onto the beach while Kirk stood in the surf and stared in silence with his mouth hanging open. He placed his hand to his eyes a moment then screamed with rage. Bogart set Jackie down on the beach and nearly collapsed with her. She clung to him and the blood-soaked shirt while continuing to sob uncontrollably. Bogart held her against him as he trembled, fighting his own tears.

Chapter Forty-three

A little more than an hour later, the five men and Jackie stood on the beach with their rifles in their hands while Pinto and Sal remained behind them and watched. All six fired their rifles simultaneously and repeatedly in the air giving Zack his final, twenty-one gun salute. Sal held Pinto while she sobbed softly. Darth lay on the beach with his head on his paws and watched in silence. By the final round of the twenty-one gun salute, Jackie was nearly on her knees while sobbing. Monroe pulled Jackie into his arms and held her while the others watched the helicopter debris continuing to wash ashore.

"I thought he'd be back," she whispered to Monroe while clinging to him allowing the tears to streak her face. "He always comes home."

"I know," Monroe announced softly while caressing her almost as much for his own comfort.

The rest of the team exchanged sorrowful hugs and fought their own tears. Gil put on a tough act, but the glossed look in his eyes told a different story. Darth leaned against his leg and whimpered softly, feeling his pain.

"Did you call Ross?" Gil finally asked Beck once he was able to pull himself together.

"No," Beck replied softly while shaking his head and dabbing the corner of his eyes. "Let him have his vacation. We'll tell him when he gets back in a few days."

Gil nodded in agreement then looked back at the ocean and debris that continued to float around. "Do we wait for the authorities to come out and investigate?"

"From afar," Beck replied. "We should probably lay low with the others and let Giovanni handle the authorities. Giovanni's having his men bring the yacht Corbin left to the dock. He offered it to us for our passage home so we can avoid any misunderstandings. We can leave whenever--" Beck hesitated and looked across the beach to where Monroe held Jackie. He inhaled deeply. "--whenever Jackie's ready."

While Monroe held Jackie, Bogart put his arms around her from behind and hugged both her and Monroe while resting his head on Jackie's back. Monroe managed a smile and patted Bogart's arm. Jackie finally pulled free from both men and wiped her eyes while sniffing. She again stared out to the floating debris and rubbed her chilled arms.

"We should probably go," she announced gently. "I need to call Holden, and I don't want to do it from their unsecured resort lines."

"You won't get a cell phone signal until we reach Columbia," Monroe informed her. "Giovanni has a secured satellite phone you can use."

"I'll wait until we get to Columbia," she replied gently.

"Come on," Monroe announced and pulled her to his side. "I'll help you pack up Zack's things."

"Could you do that?" she asked then indicated the beach. "I'd like to stay here a little while longer. You know--" She shrugged. "Just in case."

"Want me to stay with you?" Bogart asked.

"No, I'd like to be alone," she gently replied.

"We'll leave you an ATV," Monroe informed her than lightly smacked Bogart on the shoulder and nodded to the jeep.

Once the guys were gone, Jackie sat on the beach and stared at the debris in the ocean and the helicopter pieces that gently washed to shore. She wasn't sure how long she sat there, and she didn't particularly care. Something glistening in the surf caught her attention. She stared at the object as the water washed past it a second time. She finally stood and approached the surf before the water could take away the object. Jackie picked up the ruby and diamond tennis bracelet and stared at it a moment with surprise. It was a rare and valuable find. Its presence seemed almost odd. She placed it in her pocket and stared back at the ocean. Zack wasn't coming back. It was time to go home.

†

Beck and Pinto walked along the beach past the devastation of the wedding. The staff had been working tirelessly to clean it up, but it was still a grim reminder of what had happened only a few hours earlier. Pinto limped alongside Beck with scrapes and cuts over nearly every part of her body. Beck eyed her several times and seemed to feel worse each time he saw her injuries.

"Are you sure you don't want to be checked out by the resort doctor?"

She laughed nervously and squeezed his hand. "Thanks, but I saw how he took care of Monroe's shoulder wound. Monroe had better get a tetanus shot and a double round of antibiotics after that meatball surgery."

"Ah, he's used to third world doctors," Beck teased and again eyed her. He stopped and forced her to face him, taking both her hands in his. "I'm so sorry this happened to you. It just feels like it's somehow my fault."

She smiled and gently touched his face. "You're not to blame for any of this," Pinto informed him. "I'm alive because of you."

"Wade *involved* you because of me," he corrected. "It is my fault." Beck groaned and looked away while fighting his tears. "We're all cursed. We'll never live like normal people." He looked back at Pinto. "Everyone we love will eventually be used against us. I don't want you dying because of me."

"You seem to forget who I have for a father," she remarked simply.

"Your father's involvement with the mob has never been proven," Beck reminded her.

She made a face and casually indicated the disaster left behind from the earlier attack. "I present exhibit 'A'."

"Which is exactly why I sometimes wonder if you should stay far away from me and my screwed up life," he remarked then groaned softly. "Even if I walked away from the team tomorrow, my past will always come back to haunt me. As long as you're in my life, you'll always be a target."

Pinto offered a warm smile. "Then you'll just have to teach me how to handle those situations," she replied. "I may look like death warmed over, but I'm still alive." She sank into thought with an odd smile on her face. "You know, earlier in Matt's suite, I witnessed Jackie take on two men. One was twice her size, and she literally kicked the shit out of them." Her smile brightened. "At that moment, I never felt so empowered. If I could defend myself like that, you wouldn't have to worry about me so much. If you didn't worry about me so much, maybe you'd stop feeling so guilty about involving me in your life."

Beck stared at her a long moment. "I've been pushing you away, haven't I?"

"Not so much pushing as avoiding," she replied gently. "I never know where our relationship is going from one day to the next. You seem to leave me hanging a lot."

He gently caressed her hand while staring into her eyes with the black and blue marks beneath them. "Pinto, I love you, and I always want you in my life no matter what. If I've failed to show you or tell you how I feel, I'm sorry." Beck drew a deep breath while clinging to her hands. "Let me go on record so there's never any doubt about how I feel for you." He lowered to his knee before her and stared into her eyes. "Pinto Romano, will you marry me?"

She stared at him with a moderately stunned look as her mouth hung open. Pinto held back her sobs and wiped her tears while nodding.

"Yes, Beck," she announced while slightly choked up. "Yes, I'll marry you."

Beck sprang to his feet, gathered her in his arms, and held her. He pulled away just long enough to kiss her warmly but passionately on the mouth. She returned the kiss while clinging to him.

Chapter Forty-four

Most of the team assembled at the dock just beyond the resort beach. Bogart was mysteriously missing the last hour and the guys were becoming restless. They had seen him riding the black horse bareback across the beach, which was against hotel policy, but with the condition of the beach after the wedding attack, it didn't seem to matter. He finally showed up slightly out of breath and without his duffel bag.

"Where's your gear?" Kirk demanded, growing impatient.

"Oh, I, uh, I'm catching a ride back to the states with Nelson Banks and his wife," Bogart informed them. "I'll be at the lodge in time for the funeral."

He received several strange looks.

"You're catching a ride home with Nelson and Emily Banks?" Gil remarked. "Is that wise? If he finds out you'd slept with his wife--"

"I don't get it," Beck remarked. "What am I missing? What are you up to?"

"Nothing," Bogart announced innocently.

"For the clever types," Jackie informed the guys, "you don't pay attention to much. Isn't it obvious?" They stared back at her still not understanding. "Bogart's stealing Giovanni's horse and Banks is shipping it to the states on his cruiser."

The guys looked from Jackie to Bogart with surprise. "A horse?" Kirk suddenly demanded.

Bogart urged him to keep his voice down with hand gestures. "Just a little souvenir."

"Souvenir?" Beck cried out. "It's a thousand pound animal. A resort bathrobe is a souvenir. What the hell are you going to do with that thing?"

"Ross has that big ranch with his horses," Bogart announced. "I thought I'd drop it off there."

There were several groans. The guys waved him off and headed for the dock with Darth leading the way.

"We'll see you in a few days," Beck muttered.

Once the guys were gone, Jackie and Bogart hugged briefly. She then looked into his eyes and gave him a stern glare.

"Stay away from Nelson's wife," she warned.

He playfully saluted her then grinned and ran across the beach.

"Yeah," she muttered softly. "He's my brother all right."

✝

The yacht sailed toward the port in Columbia where the team would disembark and catch a flight home. Jackie stood along the railing with Monroe, who stiffly flexed his injured shoulder. She tried her cell phone again and finally got a signal. She pressed the number for Holden's cell phone, gave Monroe a strange look, and then disconnected the call.

"That's strange," she informed him. "The voicemail isn't picking up. It just keeps ringing."

"Did you try the office?"

"No, not yet."

Her cell phone rang before she had a chance to try a different number. She looked at Monroe and smiled. "It's the Bureau number." Jackie accepted the call with enthusiasm. "Holden?" She hesitated and eyed Monroe. "Mr. Harris, I'm sorry. I thought you were Holden. I've been out of town." She fell silent then suddenly gasped, alerting Monroe. "What?" she cried out. "What happened? Is he okay?"

Monroe gave her his full attention. Beck approached while carrying his duffel bag and computer backpack. He seemed to sense the conversation and immediately listened.

Jackie shut her eyes a moment while holding her breath. She briefly choked up. Her voice crackled as she spoke. "Thanks for calling, Mr. Harris."

She disconnected the call and looked at Monroe and Beck. Both stared at her with indescribable horror on their faces. She exhaled softly. "There was an incident during a raid," she informed them while trembling. "Holden's been shot, but he's going to be okay."

Beck and Monroe both exhaled and clung to the railing. "Thank God," Monroe muttered. "I can't go through *that* again."

"Think you can find us a plane in Columbia?" Jackie asked while trembling. "I don't want to wait hours for a commercial flight home."

"Yeah, sure," Monroe announced. "I know half the country by name. I'll set it up."

"I'm going to call the hospital where they took Holden," she informed them. "His boss said they should let me talk to him."

Jackie hurried away while punching numbers into her phone. Monroe and Beck again exchanged looks and groaned softly. Both leaned on the railing.

"We can't lose anyone else," Beck muttered softly while shaking his head. "I don't think I can handle any more bad news."

"Yeah, they say cruises and island resorts are supposed to be so relaxing," Monroe remarked. "Honestly, I don't agree."

Monroe's cell phone vibrated in his pocket. He removed his phone and eyed the caller ID. He didn't recognize the number and replaced the phone in his pocket. It again vibrated but only once then stopped. The phone buzzed again in his pocket, vibrating three times, and then stopped again. Monroe eyed Beck and groaned.

"That's never good."

He pulled the phone from his pocket and stared at it as if anticipating another alert. The phone vibrated again. Monroe immediately answered the call.

"Yeah," he announced into the phone then listened to the voice on the other end. He groaned softly while rolling his eyes. "Hey, you old cocksucker. How's it hanging?" Monroe held the phone away from his ear, waited a moment, and then returned it. "You kiss your momma with that mouth?"

Beck stared at him, interested in his conversation. It wasn't Ross, since there was little to no respect coming from Monroe.

"Yeah, yeah, take it easy," Monroe scoffed and grabbed Beck's bag from his shoulder.

Beck gave him a 'what for' signal then placed his hands on his hips while glaring at Monroe. Monroe ignored him and unzipped the bag. He swiftly removed Beck's laptop and began working his magic on the computer. He frowned and shook his head.

"I've got nothing," Monroe informed him. There was a moment of silence. "It wouldn't be the first time someone wanted to cut off your pecker, man." There was more cursing from the other end. "Okay, just chill." Monroe continued to tap into the computer, hesitated, and then grinned. "Oh, I think I have just the ticket for you." He continued to type onto the laptop. "I can get you a backdoor entry on a cruise ship." He glanced at his watch. "But it's about to leave port any minute, so you'll have to hurry." He listened a moment then laughed. "Don't worry. It's a boring cruise ship. I'm sending you the information as we speak. The ship is called the *Andrea Maria* and it's leaving Costa Rico in less than an hour." Monroe listened to the caller on the other end. "That's the one. Bon voyage, dickhead."

Monroe disconnected the call and returned Beck's laptop to his bag. Beck stared at him and waited but Monroe didn't offer any information.

"Who was that?" Beck finally demanded.

"An old friend asking for a favor," Monroe informed him then laughed while grinning. "More recently known as Emry Hill."

Beck rolled his eyes and cursed softly under his breath. "Oh, man. I thought we had the worst luck. Bad news follows that guy wherever he goes."

"The *Andrea Maria* is the perfect cruise ship for him," Monroe remarked. "Seriously? What's the worst that could happen?"

The End

Coming Soon!

"Witness Protection 5"
Outside the Wire

After suffering several casualties on their last assignment, a retired Navy SEAL team discovers their misery is just beginning.

When Whiskey Tango Foxtrot returns home after suffering a devastating loss, they're hit with even more bad news regarding the rest of their team. Their grief is cut short when they discover their names are all on the same hit list. Hunted by relentless assassins, the scattered team must decide whether to remain safely hidden or find the man who put the price on their heads. Against the wishes of her teammates, Jackie strikes out on her own in order to save a friend who wants her dead. In a kill or be killed situation, will Jackie's emotions finally betray her?

Other books by Holly Copella!
Reviews left on Amazon are appreciated!

"The Battle for Andrea Maria"

A cruise ship attack turns six survivors into overnight celebrities after they take credit for the heroic act of a stowaway who died saving them.

The cruise is just what Jess needed--a bit of harmless fun far from her daily grind. But what begins as a relaxing vacation turns into a desperate fight for her life when terrorists take over the ship and start piling up bodies. Teaming up with a mysterious stowaway, Jess attempts to send out a distress call but knows they cannot wait for help to come. If she or the few remaining passengers have any hope for survival, Jess must act now. The papers dub it "The Battle for *Andrea Maria*," but to Jess it is the moment she fought side-by-side with her enigmatic Romeo, saving the ship--and losing him. She thinks the story ends there, but really, the nightmare is just beginning...

"Insanely Deadly"

When the dead return to life, it's up to an admiral's daughter and a mildly insane, former war hero to save their small town.

Jetta Cross, a Navy Admiral's daughter, is tasked with keeping her father's comrade, a former war hero turned town crazy, grounded in the real world. Capt. John Hunter is still fighting the war in his head, where imaginary dead people are part of his world. When a viral outbreak brings about a zombie uprising, Hunter is left to his own devices. He must resume his role as a one-man commando unit in order to destroy the ravenous undead. With Hunter still fighting his own inner demons as well as the undead, the townspeople fear their zombie neighbors may not be the only threat. Stranded at the island's luxurious resort with a handful of workers, Jetta is forced to live up to her father's reputation and take charge of the deteriorating situation at the hotel. She must wage her own war against the infected before the government declares her hometown a total loss.

"Deadly Institution"

A town recluse suspected of killing his wife teams up with a young woman in order to stop a killer.

After being accused of murdering his wife, Konrad Asher turns his back on the town that once adored him. Ten years later, he still holds his grudge and the title of the most feared man in town. With the reopening of the burned mental institution, where his wife had died, former employees are now murdered one-by-one, throwing suspicion back on Asher. A young local reporter, Jacey, is forced to reveal her long-time friendship with the infamous recluse in order to clear his name not only in the recent murders but to exonerate him in the death of his wife as well. Will Jacey's relationship with Asher invite the killer closer to her? Or is the killer already in her life?

"Screenplays: The Island Collection"
"Jungle Princess", "A.L.F. Resort", "Brighton Island"

Discover how romance and fun in the sun can be downright *chilling*!

"Jungle Princess" is a romantic/thriller that leaves a teenage girl stranded on an island with two male shipmates and a creature of "unknown" origin. She soon discovers the island is home to an abandoned prison with several prisoners roaming free. What really killed over one hundred prisoners? And is it still out there--?

"A.L.F. Resort" is a romantic/thriller set on an island resort with Artificial Life Forms as the main draw. At this resort, all your fantasies come true...until a malfunction removes safety inhibitors on the A.L.F.'s. Zombies, biker gangs, and mobsters run amuck, turning fantasies into nightmares. A young reporter gets more of a story than she anticipates, but will she survive long enough to write the story?

"Brighton Island" is a romantic/thriller set on a private island. When the owner's niece brings her psychic friend to the mansion, his presence awakens the spirits' tortured souls. As the psychic attempts to solve the old murders, the niece is confronted with the possibility that she's next to join the mansion ghosts. Stranded on the island with a crazed killer, her uncle wages his own war to save them. Will his "shock and awe" tactics actually save them or get them killed?

"Death Displacement"

A grief-stricken man travels back in time to seek revenge on the woman who murdered his girlfriend but inadvertently falls in love with her.

Kane is about to marry the woman he loves. His life is perfect. A few weeks before the wedding, a vindictive woman from his girlfriend's past mysteriously arrives and kills her. He learns of a traumatic accident that happened five years earlier, which triggers Riley's hatred for his girlfriend. Distraught over his girlfriend's death, Kane uses an antique time machine to travel into the past in order to find and destroy the woman responsible. When he runs into Riley's younger self, he realizes she's not the monster she later becomes, and he can't bring himself to destroy her. With a little help from his oddball friend from the past, they formulate a plan to prevent the accident that sends Riley down her destructive path. Kane's plan backfires when he falls for the younger Riley. His new tortured existence is further complicated when future Riley, his girlfriend's killer, shows up with her own devious agenda that doesn't include him. Will he be able to stop the time ripple, which ultimately ends with his girlfriend's death? Or will future Riley take him out of the timeline forever--

"Dead Village"

After strange happenings isolate a small resort town from the rest of the world, nearly one hundred residents seek refuge at the closed hotel. Only eight survive the night. And that's just the beginning...

One day after the entire population of Fox Ridge Village disappears, a car wreck forces several unsuspecting crash victims to seek help at the closed summer hotel. Within the hotel, they discover the grisly aftermath of a brutal slaughter. Crash victims Vander and Devon, a reluctant clairvoyant, team up to solve the riddle of the "haunted hotel" and the mass hysteria plaguing the remaining survivors. By the time they discover the hotel's secret, they're already drawn into the hysteria. As the body count continues to climb, it's a race to isolate the source and bring everyone back to reality before they kill one another. Will Devon be able to communicate with the traumatized spirits before their fate becomes her own?

"Misfits, Inc."

A seemingly ordinary, young woman meets four misfits who claim she has given them supernatural powers.

While on a business trip to a remote island paradise, a bored secretary, Hailey, has her world turned upside down when her path collides with a psychic freak, Skyler. He attempts to convince her that they had met in his dreams, and she had chosen him as one of her four mystic warriors. After Skyler foresees a woman's death, they discover an unidentified creature has killed one of the guests. They are joined by a lounge pianist and a rich playboy, who also claim they had met her in their dreams. If Skyler's prophecies are genuine, the evil entity controlling the ravenous creatures needs to destroy Hailey to ensure its survival. Reluctantly accepting her fate, Hailey has to locate the last and most powerful of her chosen warriors, The Guardian. Their fate is in doubt when The Guardian turns out to be a self-absorbed, former cat burglar with a bad attitude. Can Hailey turn her company of misfits into an elite team of mystic warriors? Or will The Guardian's secret agenda destroy them all?

"Basement Dwellers"

A viral outbreak at a hospital leaves a mortician, sheriff, and coroner fighting for their lives against a horde of undead and the CDC.

After a massive car wreck leaves several survivors in critical condition at the local hospital, a surgeon uses experimental drugs on his critical patients and accidentally causes a zombie outbreak. When local mortician, Lexx, receives an infected corpse as her client, she becomes stranded in the hospital basement during CDC quarantine along with the local sheriff and the coroner. The infamous surgeon struggles to find a cure for his infectious blunder by using the other survivors as test subjects. Meanwhile, Lexx and the sheriff attempt to locate his missing sister, who's stranded somewhere in the battle zone that once was the emergency room. It's a race against time and the ravenous undead. Can they survive the undead before CDC sanitizes the hospital of all infection?

"Witness Protection"
Also available in audiobook!

After witnessing an execution, a resourceful young woman attempts to disappear while being pursued by a hitman and a handsome federal agent.

A helicopter pilot, Jackie Remus, reluctantly agrees to go on a date with one of her clients, but her date is unexpectedly cut short when she witnesses a man being murdered. After narrowly escaping with her life, she is placed into protective custody. When the safe house is breached, Jackie makes a daring escape from both the hired killers and the handsome FBI agent, who wants to return her to protective custody. With a little help from her sly and crafty friend, Monroe, Jackie is convinced she can disappear until the trial. While on her journey to meet with her friend, she solicits help from a few shady but lovable characters along the way. Although she manages to stay one-step ahead of the hired killers, the federal agent remains in hot pursuit. Will Jackie reach Monroe before she's captured by the FBI and returned to protective custody? Or will the hired killers silence her first?

"Town Darling"

After surviving a brutal attack that claims the lives of those she loves, a young woman seeks revenge on a corrupt town.

Going back home is never easy, but for Casey, it means returning to her corrupt hometown where she barely survived a brutal attack. Accompanied by two family friends, she seeks justice for the night that destroyed her life. Her physical scars are nothing compared to her emotional ones, forcing the local sheriff to believe that the town darling is back for revenge. As the conspiracy for her revenge appears to be leading up to the coveted town fair, the sheriff is determined to stop her from fulfilling her vengeful scheme...but guilt over his role on that fateful night continues to haunt him. Will his desperate need for Casey's forgiveness be his undoing? Or will Casey's desire for revenge destroy them both?

"Unconditional"

A young woman puts her life on hold to care for an unstable, highly skilled combat soldier, who believes someone is trying to kill him.

A botched military coup leaves a team of elite fighters injured with one clinging to life in a coma. When Harlan wakes from his coma, he's left with no memory of his past life. His commander's daughter, Indy, takes it upon herself to care for the fallen war hero. She's challenged with more than just his physical care as she combats with not only his memory loss but also his newly found desire for her. His infatuation with her becomes the least of her worries when he sinks back into his role of a combat soldier. Believing his life is in danger, his fighting skills surface, turning him into an unpredictable and dangerous man. Will his memory return to him before Indy is forced to commit him? Or will he finally find his nemesis, "the coyote", and possibly claim the life of an innocent person?

"Witness Protection 2"
The Return of Whiskey Tango Foxtrot

Believing she holds the clue to millions in missing laundered money, a young woman is placed into the protective care of a former Navy SEAL team.

Feeling sorry for her recently separated co-worker, Leeann invites Wiley to join her and her friends on their night out. Little does she know that finding her co-worker murdered is just the beginning of her nightmare. Leeann unknowingly holds the key to fifty million dollars in potentially laundered mob money. With hired killers pursuing her, the FBI places her into a different kind of protective custody. Former Navy SEAL team Whiskey Tango Foxtrot reunites to keep Leeann alive at their secret hideaway. What should be an easy assignment takes an unscheduled turn when secrets, lies, and betrayal threaten to derail their mission. Is the team prepared for a war on their own doorstep? Will Leeann's misguided trust endanger the lives of those sent to protect her?

"Deadly Institution 2"

When blackmail turns into murder, a young woman finds herself caught in the killer's crosshairs.

The small town of Stony Ridge is no stranger to scandal and persecution of the innocent. When a brutal killing shakes the town's prestigious country club, Jacey McMurray seeks help from a self-proclaimed vigilante, Konrad Asher. As her professional and personal worlds collide, Jacey fears the stress of the country club killings have finally taken their toll on Asher. Can a stressed out vigilante stop the killer before he strikes again?

"Witness Protection 3"
Alpha Mike Foxtrot

A helicopter pilot risks her life to help a team of retired Navy SEALs rescue two girls from a killer.

When former Navy SEAL team Whiskey Tango Foxtrot asks for a simple favor, Jackie reluctantly offers her air-taxi services. What could go wrong? What begins as a search and rescue for two girls turns into a fight for survival against a heavily armed drug cartel. Wanted by the law with the cartel in hot pursuit and their home base breached, the team is forced to call in a favor from a questionable ally. Unfortunately, their new safe house isn't what it seems. Without knowing who the real enemy is, can Jackie and the team save their young witnesses from the hands of a killer?

"The Pen Pal"

In order to save her friend, she must enter the mind of a serial killer.

When her best friend is abducted, no one believes Jolynn saw it in a psychic vision. With nowhere to turn, Jolynn reluctantly joins Agent Harris Slade and his team on their hunt for a sadistic serial killer known only as "The Pen Pal". Finally confronted with the killer, Jolynn realizes she must enter the mind of the psychopath in order to stop the brutal killings. But when her vision reveals a particularly disturbing death, can Jolynn sacrifice her lover for her friend?

"Awaken the Dead"

A grieving innkeeper struggles to keep her haunted hotel out of foreclosure.

After losing her parents in a suspicious boating accident, Harley Brandon is determined to keep the family hotel out of foreclosure. Unfortunately, the hotel ghosts have other plans. Built with tainted money, the century old Horizon Hotel thrives on a tradition of murder, scandal, and suicide. As the paranormal activity increases to alarming levels, Harley discovers the truth about the hotel and its residents. Can Harley save her friends from the hotel's frightening hidden secrets?

"Already Dead"
Supernatural Collection

From the already dead to the undead. Three supernatural tales of "things that go bump in the night".

"Bloodletting" - A vampire themed resort allows guests to *participate* in their Bloodletting Ritual to celebrate the island's legendary vampires.

"Reaper of Souls" - A young woman must outwit an evil sorcerer in order to save her brother or become one of his minions forever.

"Already Dead" - When Flight 220 crashes, ten passengers make it to an isolated island, but only one man lives to tell the lie.

Coming Soon!
"Once Upon a Disaster"

ABOUT THE AUTHOR

Holly Copella has been writing since the age of twelve when her frustration at a book's poor plot drove her to author her own story. Over the last decade, she's written a number of screenplays, some of which she's now adapting into novels. Her fascination with zombies and other darker material lends an edge to her writing, which tends to lean toward horror. As a fan of Agatha Christie, she appreciates the craft of a good plot and the importance of creating significant characters.

Hailing from Pennsylvania, Copella lives in the Endless Mountains on a farm with her rescue horses and other animals. In addition to writing and reading fiction, she enjoys riding horses and traveling to Las Vegas and Disney World.

www.ingramcontent.com/pod-product-compliance
Lightning Source LLC
Chambersburg PA
CBHW060346180626
46813CB00011B/1101